SH
THI

A dreaming man, lost in a fugue, leads them down dark passages, through the streets of London - and underneath them.

An old friend is lost and found again, an old enemy resurfaces and Holmes must walk perilous paths for a second time.

A fall is coming, a fall that has haunted Holmes' dreams, and now must be faced again, in the place where past and present become one, and two old foes meet for a final battle.

PRAISE FOR WILLIAM MEIKLE AND THE DREAMING MAN

"William Meikle's ability to portray Holmes and Watson in a perfectly authentic fashion is nothing short of remarkable… he's able to paint vivid, visceral imagery on the canvas of his reader's mind, making you feel as if you've seen and experienced rather than read about the events of the story. And he can build a scene as well as anyone in the business… Whether you're a fan of Sherlock Holmes or not, The Dreaming Man is damn good fiction!" **HELLNOTES**

"For anyone who loves great storytelling and well-crafted stories this book is for you. For Sherlock Holmes fans this book is an absolute must and I highly recommend it!" **FAMOUS MONSTERS OF FILMLAND**

"Readers looking for superb supernatural spins with Holmes need look no further." **Rick Kleffel's AGONY COLUMN**

"Sir Arthur Conan Doyle would be proud. The feel of each story brings me back to those old tales of Sherlock Holmes, and one can easily believe that Meikle has unearthed some forgotten tome that contains all of the supernatural, extraterrestrial and just plain old unnatural adventures of Holmes and his trusty companion, Dr. Watson." **THE DEEPENING**

"Meikle writes Holmes and Watson with a warm friendship. Their interaction is reminiscent of the radio series featuring Rathbone as Holmes and Nigel Bruce as the story-telling Watson. The collection is a quick read, with plenty of twists and turns in each of the cases. Fans of Holmes in any medium will enjoy this anthology." **HORRORVIEW**

SHERLOCK HOLMES:

THE DREAMING MAN

WILLIAM MEIKLE

GRYPHONWOOD

Sherlock Holmes- The Dreaming Man

Copyright © 2017 by William Meikle

Published by Gryphonwood Press
www.gryphonwoodpress.com

ISBN-10: 1-940095-66-2
ISBN-13: 978-1-940095-66-0

This is a work of fiction. Names, characters, places, and incidents either are the product of the author's imagination or are used fictitiously. Any resemblance to actual events or locales or persons, living or dead, is entirely coincidental.

Cover Art by Wayne Miller

Gryphonwood Books by William Meikle

The Midnight Eye Files
The Amulet
The Sirens
The Skin Game

The Watchers
The Coming of the King
The Battle for the Throne
Culloden

Stand-Alone Works
Berserker
Island Life
The Invasion
The Valley
Concordances of the Red Serpent
Sherlock Holmes- The Dreaming Man

PART 1:
REVENANT

CHAPTER 1

Holmes has often berated me for a perceived habit of sensationalizing his cases in the writing down of the details. But in this particular matter there is so much that is already sensational that I fear I may under-report the import of them.

It began in September. I was late. The lecture in the Royal Hospital overran by some thirty minutes… thirty minutes of the driest of exposition on potential cures for tropical diseases. Things did not improve when I emerged into a rainstorm that meant all carriages were already taken. I had a choice to either stay in shelter or brave the elements. I did not have my heavy overcoat with me so I decided to wait the rain out. It proved a bad decision as it continued for almost an hour in a steady downpour.

It was already mid-morning by the time I arrived back in Baker Street and, knowing that Holmes would be getting impatient, I was in no mood for any further delay.

I say this in mitigation of my next actions. If I had paid more heed for those next few seconds much grief may have been averted later. But at the time I was more than a little annoyed to have a derelict stand in my path as I got down out of the carriage.

I took him for one of the itinerant beggars who have so recently plagued the area. In my heart I knew that many of them were in the situation of having to beg to eat through no fault of their own, but the man with the twisted lip had put me permanently on guard against blaggards and con men. I might have given him a penny just to get rid of him but I was already making excuses to Holmes in my mind. The vagrant stood directly in my path, and when I made to dodge around him he moved to block me.

"Move aside please," I said, trying to control a rising irritation. He did not give way. He was small, with a stoop that bent his head into deep shadow under a wide-brimmed hat. Wisps of straggly red hair showed under the brim. His clothes were of heavy cheap cotton, threadbare and muddy from head to toe, and his feet were bare showing cracked and split nails also caked in fresh mud.

"Can I help you?" I said, expecting him to put out a begging hand. Instead he seemed to ignore me. He muttered to himself, rapidly, a repeating pattern as if reciting his multiplication tables. It also sounded like something was *broken* inside his chest -- a rumble that spoke of deep-seated bronchitis or some similar ailment.

And that is as much as I remembered of him later, beyond the fact that when he finally spoke to me he had a broad Scots accent. And the words he spoke took me aback so much that I completely forgot to reply.

"Mr. Holmes will have need of this before the week is out," he said, and passed me a sheet of paper. I took it, and looked up to see him walking rapidly away in the kind of skipping gait you sometimes see in men who have suffered a badly set break in one leg. I might have followed him were I not already acutely aware of just how late I was for my appointment with Holmes.

I was, however, just curious enough to check what I had been given. The sheet of paper did not enlighten me any. It had been torn roughly from a book, and was an illuminated diagram titled *MALAGMA*. It showed a fiery red serpent eating the world, depicted as a shining golden disc hanging above an ocean. The page was also getting rather wet as more rain started to fall, heavy spatters of it threatening to turn the paper to a soggy mush. I folded it in half and put it in my inner pocket as I entered 221B Baker Street.

Holmes stood in the hallway waiting for me. I don't know how long he'd been there, but it had been more than long enough to make him irritable -- that was immediately obvious. I have seen Sherlock Holmes in many moods over the years of our acquaintance, but I do believe that this was also the only time he appeared to be flustered.

"You have been tardy Watson," he said, turning me around in the hall before I could even remove my hat. He passed me my heavy overcoat and almost marched me back outside while I struggled with the garment. "I would have gone without you had they not specifically requested that you join me."

"They?"

I did not get an answer. Instead I was shepherded onto the pavement. As we approached the kerb Holmes hailed a carriage and one stopped for him immediately. I did not hear his instructions to the driver as I was bundled quickly inside, but they must have been insistent for we set off at a rapid trot across the cobbles.

Holmes would not be drawn as to our destination; indeed he sat quiet for the whole journey, lost either in concentration or irritation, I knew not which. Given the manner in which I had been greeted, I more than expected it to be irritation.

I gathered we were about to embark on a new case. That thought gave me some satisfaction, for my friend had been moody of late due to a lack of activity to fuel his ever-busy mind. I had recently suffered several nights of his black gloom, attempting conversation only to be met with a taciturn sullen silence. If there was work ahead, I hoped it would be enough to lift him out of it, for a time at least.

The carriage took us south to Piccadilly Circus and then towards the river, which annoyed me somewhat for if Holmes had intimated our destination to me in advance I could have met him much earlier without having to return to Baker Street. But when I mentioned this fact all I got in reply was an irritated grunt. In truth I was glad when the journey came to an end, for Holmes in a temper is a most disagreeable travelling companion.

Much to my surprise we were deposited outside the Houses of Parliament. Flanked by two sullen policemen we were led at a march to the Member's Lounge for the Lords. Whatever matter had aroused Holmes into his present state of irritation, it seemed it was an important one.

The police left us at the door. Three people waited inside for us in an otherwise empty Member's Lounge -- two standing in animated discussion and the other slumped unmoving in an armchair. The taller of the two standing men turned and I recognized his bulky figure immediately. It was only then that Holmes spoke.

"I do hope this is not another of your cast-off cases Mycroft? You know that my preferred choice of adversary is always the criminal rather than the politician, despite the fact that there is often little to tell them apart."

For my part I now knew exactly what had irritated my friend so. To be *summoned* by his elder brother must have vexed Holmes severely, but he had been so lacking in work for that great brain of his that he would endure it for the chance of a fresh case. That did not, however, mean that he had to like it, nor that he had to hide his irritability.

Mycroft paid his brother no heed. He dismissed the man he had been speaking to with a curt wave of the hand. It was only when the three of us were alone with the man in the chair that Mycroft turned to me.

"I need your medical opinion Doctor Watson," he said. "As you can see, Lord Menzies here is somewhat indisposed."

I did not for one minute believe that I had been brought to the Lords for my *medical opinion*. There was a perfectly good infirmary in the building itself, staffed by a reliable man I knew well from my army days. No, this was part of the game that was always playing between the brothers; I just happened to be caught in the middle, and not for the first time. There was however an obviously sick man who needed attention, so I decided I would attend to him and leave the brothers to their own devices.

"Watson?" Mycroft said, and I was surprised to hear some irritability there, a rare thing from a man with a normally languid disposition. He motioned with a tilt of his head toward the slumped figure and I gave in to the inevitable.

My patient was an elderly gentleman, well dressed but somewhat rumpled, with what looked like an egg stain on the left lapel of his waistcoat and several streaks of ash on the other side that had been rubbed in rather than brushed away. His hair had that oily sheen you see in vain men of a certain age, and was so thin as to show liver spots on his scalp.

When I bent to examine him I spotted several other things almost immediately. He was most definitely alive. He breathed deeply and regularly and had the calm pulse of someone who was fast asleep. He was completely unconscious despite having his eyes wide open. His pupils did not respond to direct light, nor was there any reaction when I snapped my fingers by his ears. I folded one of his legs over the other, with some difficulty as there seemed to be no *give* there, almost as if rigor was setting in. He did however show a reflex when I struck just below his knee. He also seemed to be attempting to speak in so far as his lips moved, but no sounds were forthcoming. His hands felt somewhat cold and clammy to the touch, but there was no obvious sign of any kind of violence having been done on his person. I checked his head, searching under the hair for bumps or bruising but there was no sign of trauma.

I must admit I was completely stumped. I could only surmise a condition of the brain, although it was one I had never previously encountered.

"Well Watson, what is your diagnosis?" Mycroft said. He still had not acknowledged Holmes but I was now far too concerned for the stricken man to bother myself with fraternal politics.

"He has taken some kind of seizure by the looks of things," I said as I stood back. "This man needs to be removed to a hospital as soon as can be. There may be a build up of fluid in the brain causing these symptoms. Any delay in getting him the proper treatment could prove fatal."

I looked around in search of some support. None was forthcoming. Mycroft shook his head and did not seem in the least bit perturbed.

"I'm afraid that will not be possible Doctor. Let us sit a while," he said. "We shall wait and see what occurs next."

"Why ask that I bring Watson at all if you are merely going to ignore his counsel?" Holmes said, giving voice to the same question I was asking myself.

Mycroft however was most insistent.

"I did not bring you here merely to see a sick man," he said. "There is more to this than meets the eye, and I can assure you that your trip has not been in vain. Now please, sit. This should not take long."

I could see that Holmes was on the point of becoming agitated, and I too was loath to remain quiet while a sick man suffered in front of me. However Mycroft seemed to be taking it most calmly, so much so that he went to the door at the far end of the room and called for drinks to be brought from the bar. Holmes finally relented and, following his lead, I sat opposite the stricken man and lit a pipe. I did however watch the man most carefully, determined to act at any change in his condition.

There followed a strained ten minutes where we all tried not to stare at the slumped figure in the chair. Mycroft seemed completely unconcerned about the poor man's predicament and indeed launched into a lengthy anecdote about some drunken shenanigans that had taken place in this very room some three nights previously. I feigned attention but Holmes' mind was elsewhere. He spent several minutes in closely studying the Lord's mouth as it opened and closed but if he was able to make any sense from the lip-reading he said nothing.

After a time I could take it no more.

"Dash it all Mycroft, I may be a bally bad doctor, but I took an oath, and that oath will not allow me to remain quiet a minute longer. The poor chap's mind may be leaving him even while we sit here. I will not tolerate it."

Still Mycroft did not flinch. And much to my surprise Holmes took his brother's side in the matter.

"I know it vexes you Watson but please, just a few minutes longer? Mycroft, for all his faults, never does anything without good reason."

By this time Holmes himself had risen from his seat and had started pacing the floor. I could see that he would not nay-say Mycroft's wishes in his older brother's domain. I was about to make my case in a more forcible manner when the most remarkable thing happened.

Lord Menzies sat up straight, shook himself like a dog shedding water and inquired whether he might not 'Have a little port and brandy if that would be all right?'

I was up and at his side in a flash, pushing him back in his chair when he showed signs of wanting to rise.

"Please, sit still," I said. "I'm a doctor."

"A doctor?" he said, his voice full of outrage. "Why in blazes would I need a bally doctor? I am as fit as a butcher's dog."

And much to my astonishment it seemed he was. His breathing and pulse were as measured as before, but now he was in complete possession of all his faculties.

"I say old chap," the Lord said as I snapped my fingers at his ears. "Steady on there. You could do me a mischief."

There was no sign that only seconds before this man had been unconscious and unresponsive. I did not know what to make of it and the Lord himself was of no help. He became agitated at being the focus of so much attention.

"I say lads, play the game. Tell me what's going on here."

"We were rather hoping you could tell us?" Mycroft said.

"Fell asleep in the bally armchair is what happened. Too much kedgeree for breakfast I should think."

Holmes had still not spoken up but I could see he was less agitated now and clearly interested in the proceedings. My admiration for Mycroft went up a notch. He knew exactly how to ensnare Holmes' interest; not by telling him what was going on, but by letting him see for himself.

At that moment Lord Menzies stood without a hint of unsteadiness and bade us a good day.

"You should take it easy for the rest of the day my Lord," I said. "You have had a bit of a turn."

He looked at me as if he suspected I was making fun of him.

"A turn? I don't know what they teach doctors these

days, but I have never felt better."

And with that he left us for the comforts of the bar. Holmes and I allowed Mycroft to take us to a quiet corner of the room and, over a smoke and a drink, he finally explained to us why we had been brought here.

"It will be obvious to you by now that I did not ask you here on a whim. This is the fifth such occurrence in the past month," he said. "And all have ended the same way, with the Lord in question having no knowledge of anything untoward having happened." He went on to give us more details of each case, but really there was little more to tell. We had a genuine mystery on our hands, and Holmes had a new case.

Holmes did not speak to me until we were in a carriage.

"Well Watson, what do you make of it?"

I mentally reviewed what Mycroft had told us before replying.

"It does seem that there is too much of a pattern to it for it to be coincidence," I replied. "Five prominent politicians, all struck with the same malady in such close succession, and all recovered with no memory of anything untoward. It is dashed peculiar, and I can see why Mycroft would be worried. Such a thing could easily become a matter of national security in short order."

Holmes nodded in agreement.

"Dashed peculiar indeed. But I fear there is someone at work here with a deeper purpose in mind. Mark my words Watson, this case will have depths as yet unplumbed. Mycroft smells a rat; that is why he has asked for my involvement. He may well be the most lazy man in the Empire, but his instincts in matters such as this are sound."

This second carriage trip proved much more congenial than the first, and Holmes even managed a smile at several points. The mere fact of having work for his mind seemed somehow to energize him, bringing forward the part of him that was most vibrant, the part of him that actually enjoyed life. I called him my friend in whatever mood he chose to show the world, but *this* was the way I preferred to see him.

We started work on the case immediately. Before we left Parliament Mycroft had arranged for us to have access to the London residence of Lord Menzies. The carriage dropped us off in Belgravia outside a tall mid-terraced block of the most handsome dwellings and we were shown inside by a butler who insisted on following us around as if fearful we might abscond with the family silver.

He need not have worried. Lord Menzies obviously preferred a Spartan life-style and there was little in his lodgings to show for his presence beyond an obvious pride in his homeland; there were large portraits of his ancestors in full regalia, and a family crest done in the finest needlework on a large hanging tapestry.

"Tell me," Holmes asked the butler as we stood over a desk in what was clearly a study. "Was there anything strange in his Lordship's manner in recent days?"

The butler, clearly staunchly loyal to his charge, was slow to reply. I thought Holmes might offer a bribe, then realized that would be the wrong move with this man. All that an offer of money would get us would be hurt pride and outrage. Holmes as usual was ahead of me, using honey instead of vinegar.

"Anything you tell us will of course be kept in the strictest of confidence," he said. "My friend here is a doctor and he is most concerned about his Lordship's welfare."

The butler visibly softened at that, and took me into his confidence in the way that people often will with a medical man when they will talk to no one else.

"It was last Saturday," he began. "A cold night if you remember? I was downstairs stoking the fire when I heard a *thud*, as if a body had fallen to the floor upstairs. I immediately went to investigate for, as you know, his Lordship is not a young man. But just as I got to the door a voice called out, saying that everything was all right. It sounded a bit odd, like his Lordship, but then again, not really like him at all. But he called out my name and bid me enter. I stood, by this desk here, while he wrote two letters.

After that, despite the lateness of the hour, he had me deliver them, saying they were *most urgent matters of state.*

"He still sounded strange to me, more English than Scottish. I know I am not explaining this very well, for it was obviously my Lord sitting in the chair at the desk. But it did not *feel* like him.

"I did as I was asked and delivered the letters. But the funny thing is, in the morning he did not mention them again and did not ask whether they had been successfully dispatched. That again was most unlike the man, although by then he was at least back to speaking in his normal accent."

The butler suddenly seemed to realize that he was giving away perhaps *too* much of his Lordship's confidences and went quiet. He would only answer one last question from Holmes.

"Did you perchance see to whom these letters were addressed?"

"Only the top one of the two," the butler said. "And I remember it because it obviously *was* a matter of some import, for it was addressed to no less than the Home Secretary."

After that encounter Holmes had little more than a perfunctory stroll round the rest of the house, then led me back out onto the pavement.

"We will find nothing more here Watson," he said. "The key to this case lies in the positions of the men themselves. That, and their shared background."

"Shared?"

"Why yes," Holmes said. "Mycroft did not explicitly mention it, but I know enough of the peerage to say with some certainty that the afflicted men can all claim Scots heritage. I am sure we will find when we check that all five of them have a family history in that land going back for many centuries."

Holmes hailed a carriage to take us back to Baker Street. When one pulled up and we entered I reached for my cheroot case and my fingers touched the piece of paper the vagrant had forced on me. I had completely forgotten my earlier encounter.

"Speaking of Scotsmen," I said, taking out the page and handing it to Holmes. "What do you make of this?"

I told Holmes the details of my meeting in the street earlier that morning. He listened attentively, not unfolding the page until after I was finished.

"My dear Watson," he said. "I do not believe in coincidences. You must endeavor to pay more attention in future. You never know when something might have a bearing on a case."

He spent some time studying the page. He rubbed the sheet between his fingers.

"Late Elizabethan text," he said. "Possibly in itself Scottish. The ink has that peculiar red tint often seen in manuscripts of this age from north of the border. The paper seems authentic for the same period; late Sixteenth or early Seventeenth century at a guess, and probably from Spielman's mill in Dartford judging by the texture and flocking."

He paused as if in thought then started to quote.

In open show, then Sundry secret toys
Make rotten rags to yield a thickened froth
There it is stamped and washed as white as snow
Then flung on frame and hanged to dry, I trow
Thus paper straight it is to write upon
As it were rubbed and smoothed with slicking stone

Holmes smiled. "A piece of doggerel from the time… by Thomas Churchyard I believe."

To me it was just another astonishing example of Holmes' capacity to memorize even the most obscure of things, laying them away against a later time when they might prove useful.

"And of course the symbol in the drawing is alchemical in nature," he continued.

"What do you mean, alchemical?"

"If you ask a lay person, they will tell you it means the search for the method of turning lead into gold but, as anyone who has delved onto the mysteries knows, that is just a metaphor. No, the *great quest* is the search for illumination through the perfection of body and spirit."

He traced a finger round the drawing of the serpent.

"Strictly speaking," he said. "This drawing does not represent part of the process at all, rather, this is a symbolic representation of the whole. *Malagma* is Latin, meaning *Amalgamation*. The whole process, the great quest if you like, is to amalgamate the soul, the *microcosm*, with the universe, the *macrocosm*."

"Sorry," I said, trying a smile. "You've lost me old man."

Holmes laughed.

"I thought I might. Alchemical symbolism was obscure even back when it was a relatively common practice among scientists and mystics alike. Let us just say the serpent represents the totality of existence, and the circle inside is the bounds of our mortal life. The goal of alchemy is to break the boundary -- to gain access to the greater circle beyond. For some that is thought to mean eternal life, for others it is a quest for enlightenment and a chance of a glimpse at the inner workings of the universe. In either case," he said, waving the paper at me. "*This* is a clue. I told you this case had hidden depths. We are headed into murky waters, Watson. Very murky indeed."

He handed the page back to me.

"Hold onto this old man. And if you receive any others like it, be sure to tell me in a more timely manner." He smiled to let me know it was not a rebuke, and we lit up smokes. On the way back to Baker Street he pondered aloud about the mystery at hand.

"There is most definitely a pattern of sorts here Watson," he said. "One that we must discern if we are to pierce the veils that hide it from us. We must ask ourselves several questions." He ticked them off on his fingers. "Firstly, why have these men in particular been targeted?

Secondly, why now? And lastly… what is the overall purpose behind these attacks? For, be sure of that one thing if nothing else, there is most definitely a purpose. I will stake my reputation on it."

Once back in the apartment in Baker Street Holmes wasted no time.

"Have Mrs. Hudson fetch some lunch," he said. "I have a book here on the genealogy of the peers of Scotland that I must track down. I have not seen it for some time."

I believe I have mentioned in my notes on previous cases that Holmes' filing methods left something to be desired, being a system peculiar to Holmes himself and one that only he knew the secret of unlocking. To the rest of us it looked less like a system and more like a haphazard jumble of papers, books and journals all piled in stacks of various heights in corners and against the walls of the apartment.

But as usual Holmes was able to find what he was looking for when anyone else would have thrown their hands up in defeat. By the time I returned from making my request to Mrs. Hudson he had a book in his hand.

"My guess has proved right," he said. "All five men did indeed have Scots heritage going back several centuries at least, with numerous shared ancestors; not surprising given the closed nature of the aristocracy in that small country over the centuries. We must find out how long ago any connection might be. The solution to our mystery may indeed lie far back in history."

Holmes started pulling more books from shelves in his small library, and I knew from experience that he now had the bit firmly between his teeth. It looked like the search would take him some time so I sat at the desk in the corner and made some notes while the events of the day were still fresh in my mind.

Not long afterwards Mrs. Hudson arrived with a tray of pies and cold meat sandwiches which she bullied Holmes into eating, but, as ever when a case took hold, food ceased to be a pleasure for him and became little more than fuel to keep him awake and thinking. He shovelled some bread down quickly then went straight back to his hunt. I treated myself to a more leisurely lunch and can report that the pork pies Mrs. Hudson provided were among the best I had ever tasted.

Over the next hour Holmes asked me two questions, both regarding the dates on which Mycroft had indicated the attacks had occurred. Apart from that he seemed lost in study of a series of older leather-bound books. After a while he took himself off to the fireside chair and lit his favourite pipe while scribbling a series of notes on a pad.

It was late afternoon before he spoke again.

"I think I have something Watson, but it may well involve an all night vigil. Are you up for it?"

"You know me old chap, always willing to help."

"Good man. But first I had better explain my thinking. You will remember the five *attacks* on their Lordships? Plotting the time frame was most illuminating. There is a definite pattern, and one I am sure Mycroft has already ascertained. There were sixteen days between the first and second attacks, eight between the second and third, four until the fourth and just two before the very scenes we witnessed today in the Lords. If I am right, and I am sure that I am, the next attack will be sometime in the following twenty hours. And I believe I have narrowed down the possible victims to two men only."

At that he left me alone in the room for a spell, and I heard him dictate a telegram to Mrs. Hudson. I did not catch the full gist of it but it appeared to be instructions for Mycroft to arrange that the intended *victims* be brought together and put under protection until Holmes and I could get there.

"Best got your ablutions done now old chap," he said on his return. "As I have already intimated, we may have a long night ahead of us."

I felt the old excitement rise as I made my toilet. I had realized long ago that one of the reasons I chose to help Holmes in his cases was an urge to feel that same excitement

I had felt in my military service, the quickening of the senses that told me I was fully alive. Holmes was not the only one who needed a case.

After a quick wash and shave I found Holmes already dressed and waiting by the apartment door, eager for our departure and the chance of some action.

"Hurry man," he said. "It would not do for a doctor to be late twice in one day. People might think it to be a habit."

It was only once we were in a carriage and heading for Parliament that he allowed me fully into his thinking.

"You may have noticed my perusal of the genealogy books earlier," he said. "I thought there might be an answer in there, a connection as yet unnoticed. And indeed my reading threw up one most pertinent fact. The five victims so far have all shared a common ancestor in a minor Scottish Earl in the Sixteenth Century. After that initial finding it did not take me too much longer to ascertain that there are only two other members of the House with this same characteristic; Lord Crawford of Cunninghame and Lord Douglas of Dunottar. And as luck would have it both are currently in town. By the time we arrive at our destination Mycroft will have ensured that they will be in Parliament to meet us."

"And then what?" I asked. "I don't know that there is any *medical* solution should one or the other of them be afflicted like the rest, and I cannot for the life of me think of any course of action we might take to prevent it happening."

Holmes pursed his lips.

"We shall see what we shall see. I doubt that we are near the end of the matter, but we may be near the end of the beginning. If I am there when the attack happens I may spot something that has as yet remained hidden. Vigilance Watson. That is what is required now."

On arrival back at Parliament we were immediately shown up a steep flight of steps beside the chamber of the House of Lords; an area of the great building I had never before visited. It was all marble flooring and oak panelling with impressive landscape paintings at regular intervals. Our footsteps echoed sharply as we walked down a long empty corridor. Mycroft was nowhere to be seen but a young policeman showed us to the rooms where the two Lords were waiting for the night's vigil.

"I had them put in separate rooms," Holmes said. "I thought it best to keep them apart. We shall take one Lord each, watch them closely, and see what we shall see. You take Crawford, and I'll take Douglas. I'll be just down the hall, so call out if you need assistance. Keep an eye open for anything that seems untoward, and record all that happens. It may be that there will only be another bout of unconsciousness to deal with, but we must be prepared for any eventuality."

At that Holmes went off along the corridor, leaving me beside a young constable who looked nervous as he opened the door and showed me inside. I was immediately faced with a slightly irate Scottish Lord. He was red in the cheeks and around the nose and at the time I was unsure whether that was due to his temper or his drinking habits.

"This won't do you know?" Crawford said as I entered the room. "It won't do at all. What is so damned important that it will keep me from my bed tonight?"

He turned towards me and looked me up and down.

"Doctor Watson?"

I nodded, walked over to him and shook his hand.

"I don't suppose you have anything you can tell me about this dashed nuisance?" he asked.

"Apart from the fact that there seems to be no immediate danger to you other than falling asleep in the chair, no."

That only irritated him further.

"On top of missing my bed later, I am supposed to be in the chamber this evening, speaking in a debate on reforming the House."

"It wouldn't do to fall asleep there," I said, and got a laugh from him.

"With some of the members it would be hard to tell the

difference."

He laughed again, and finally he seemed to relax somewhat. "Tell me, are you a whisky or a brandy man?" he asked. He moved over to a cabinet against the wall and opened the door to reveal an array of liquor bottles.

"I need to keep my wits about me," I said. "Lest anything happens to you."

"Stuff and nonsense," Crawford said. "Old Menzies told me you made a fuss over him falling asleep this morning. I know, for a fact, the old man has whisky for breakfast, lunch and dinner. 'Tis no wonder he was sleeping in the members' lounge. The wonder is he isn't caught out more often. Now, have a drink with me man. I refuse to drink alone for that way lies ruin." His accent showed more strongly every minute as he fell into a more conversational tone of voice. "Many a good man has been brought low through solitary drinking. But I'll be damned if I will sit here all night waiting for the Lord knows what calumny without a drink in my hand."

I settled for a small Scotch then spent the next hour watching the man consume the larger part of a bottle on his own. I will say this for him; he handled it better than I would have done. He also had some excellent pipe tobacco and we soon had a fug swirling around the fireplace.

I needn't have worried about how we would pass the time as he proved to be an excellent conversationalist. He was at pains to avoid *'shop talk'*, instead choosing mostly to remark on sporting matters. We found a common point of interest in the game of rugger and the university teams in particular. He had strong opinions on the way the game should be played that diverged wildly from current coaching standards. I found myself in agreement with much that he said, and became so engrossed in the discussion that the next hour passed most agreeably before the alcohol started to take its effect on him. I was just relating my tale of a match we had arranged in the palace of the Maharajah when I spotted that his Lordship had fallen asleep, the Scotch having finally taken hold. I almost laughed when I realized that he was already almost exactly in the same state I had been told to be alert for. If it had not been for the fact that his eyes were closed and that he started to snore softly I might not have been able to tell the difference.

So began a long lonely evening. At first I was content to spend my time staring into space and smoking my pipe, but as night came and the old building fell quiet I started to get the jitters and prowled the room looking for something to keep my mind busy. The books on the shelves were little help, being mostly dusty tomes concerning laws and binders of regulations and paperwork, many of them to do with building works currently underway in the city.

His Lordship had a large fine mahogany desk and I thought I might find some less dry reading material there, but the desk was neat, tidy, and bare of anything except an inkstand and a blotter. Just as I was despairing, I found a pack of cards tucked in a corner of one of the bookcases. I was able to pass the time on games of solitaire, all the while accompanied by his Lordship's soft snoring and the tolling of the tower bell to mark the passage of the hours.

At some point after nine o'clock I rose to stretch my legs. I lit a pipe and went to the window but all I could see was my own reflection and beyond that only a handful of lights showing on the south side of the Thames. I turned back to the room.

And that is when it happened. The first indication I had that something was amiss was when his Lordship finally stopped snoring. I thought it might be a sign that he was about to come up out of his whisky-induced stupor, but he was perfectly still. I bent to check on him. He had that same blank stare and regular breathing I had noted in Lord Menzies the morning before. And once again the victim's mouth moved, although no words came. As I had done earlier I made a thorough examination. It seemed that his Lordship had been struck by the same affliction as his countryman Menzies.

I was about to notify Holmes of the situation when Crawford's head came up. The eyes that looked up at me were clear with no sign of any effect of whisky there. He smiled broadly and spoke, in clipped English tones totally at odds with the soft Scots accent he had sported earlier.

"Well, well, if it isn't the faithful dog? If you are here, that must mean Holmes is with the other one?"

I was so taken aback by the change in the man that I did not reply. As quickly as it had started the smile faded. Crawford's head fell forward, he slumped slightly in his seat and several seconds later he started to snore again.

Less than a minute later I heard a loud crash of breaking glass from somewhere close by. I ran out into the corridor and dashed past the young police officer. He seemed startled and unsure as to what to do.

"Holmes?" I called and was mightily relieved when he answered.

"In here Watson."

I entered the office and found Holmes standing alone in the room, white faced, staring out from a broken window to the terrace some thirty feet below. I went over next to him and peered out carefully. A body lay broken on the flagstones with blood, showing black in the gaslight, already pooling around his head. The man was obviously dead. As I looked two policemen approached the body. They looked up to see Holmes and I staring down at them. Holmes pulled me back inside.

"It's a rum do Watson. He jumped and I could do nothing to stop him. We were discussing the situation in the Sudan when he twitched, stood, smiled at me and leapt for the window. It all happened in less than five seconds."

I had no time to ask for more details, for things happened very quickly after that.

"What *have* you done?" a clipped English voice said behind me. I turned to see Lord Crawford standing in the doorway, showing no sign of any malady. The young policeman stood at his shoulder.

"Arrest these men," Crawford said. "They have murdered Lord Douglas."

It took several seconds for me to realize that he meant

Holmes and I, and even then I was of a mind to stand and argue our case, but Holmes had other ideas.

"The trap is sprung Watson, and we are caught. Follow me."

He passed me at a run, knocking Lord Crawford and the young policeman to one side. I hesitated only for a second, just long enough to see Crawford smile as he picked himself up from the floor, then I followed my friend. The sound of a police whistle echoed along the corridor behind us.

So it was that we became fugitives from justice.

My mind was a whirl of images; of Crawford staring at me, bright eyed despite the whisky, of Holmes standing at the smashed and broken window, and of the poor broken body of Lord Douglas, blood seeping on the flagstones. I had no time to try to make sense of it then, being too busy with our attempt to flee.

The first part of the night passed in such a blur that I scarce remember half of it now. I followed behind Holmes as we ran down the long empty corridor, having some difficulty keeping up with his obvious haste. At the far end of the corridor a policeman arrived at the top of the stairs and stood with a hand up, blocking our way.

"Halt!" he shouted.

Holmes kept running and with seemingly no compunction at all, knocked the policeman aside with a blow to the head that sent the man reeling. In other circumstances I may have stopped to check on the prone figure to ensure there was no sign of concussion but Holmes would have none of it.

"Hurry man. I was not joking about the trap being sprung. I have no doubt that preparations had already been made for our apprehension before we even got here. So let there be no dawdling. For tonight at least, forget that you are a doctor."

And with that he sped off down the long staircase. I was still of a mind to stay and explain myself, but I have trusted Holmes' judgement all these years; far too much to go against his will at such a time, even if it might mean complete ruin to follow his lead. I went after him, already limping slightly with the effort but determined to keep up.

Quite how we managed to escape from the Parliament building itself without being apprehended is something of a mystery to me. Holmes said later that he believed Mycroft may have had a hand in ensuring that the policemen on duty were looking elsewhere at the opportune moment, but whatever the case we ran through the main entrance hall without being stopped. With a curt waved good-bye to a startled watchman we were soon out into the night air of Westminster. Almost immediately more police whistles came from all around us but Holmes seemed calmer now that we had escaped from the building itself.

"The battle can now be fought on more equitable terms," he said. "We have wrested away his territorial advantage. Now we must make the most of it."

I was still unsure whom Holmes might be referring to, but he gave me no time to reply. He led me along the north embankment for several hundred yards then, as another shrill whistle and the first heavy footsteps of pursuit sounded behind us took a sharp turn up into the warren of back streets around Charing Cross railway station. More whistles were raised in pursuit but Holmes seemed unconcerned. He took us through the front door of a busy public bar and out again through the kitchen at the rear, oblivious to the complaints of the staff. That brought us out into a tall narrow alleyway that I never even knew existed, but with which Holmes seemed completely familiar.

"Come Watson. We should be clear soon," he said.

Without slowing down we headed north again and quickly emerged into the Strand where we mingled with the theatre crowds before turning up towards Covent Garden. There was now a rising tumult of police activity, but it was all some way away in the distance and by the time we left Long Acre behind there was no sign of any pursuit whatsoever.

It seemed we had indeed got clear away. For the present

at least.

We slowed to a brisk walk and started our way north towards Tottenham Court Road. I turned to look behind us, then again a few yards later when I heard a whistle. Holmes put a hand on my shoulder.

"Gently now Watson," Holmes said. "I think we have drawn quite enough attention to ourselves for one night. Let us pretend we are two gentlemen strolling home from the theatre."

We certainly were not out of place here close to the center; numerous groups of people were out on what was a fine dry night after the earlier rain, and we were able to continue for a while without any notice being taken of us. But once north of the junction with Oxford Street the crowds thinned out somewhat and we needed to be more circumspect.

I thought Holmes intended to make for Baker Street but instead of going to the left we turned right at the top of the road and made for the King's Cross area.

"The Yard will be on our heels again soon enough Watson," he said as he strode, moving faster again, almost at a run. "We cannot give them any easy opportunities to trap us. I will not be tricked twice in one night. We must become invisible before we can proceed."

"How will that be possible Holmes? You are one of the most recognized men in London."

He did not reply, but I soon found out his intention. He led me round the east side of King's Cross station then up and over a rather tall brick wall that required him to give me a hand up before I could clamber over to join him. After checking that we had not been seen he strode across several sets of tracks, past some badly rusted trailer beds and bogeys to what I took to be an empty cargo container. It too was in a state of some disrepair, being badly corroded and weather-beaten, but the main sliding door seemed solid enough. It was held closed by a shiny, almost new, lock. To my amazement Holmes opened it with a key from his fob, slid the door open, and boosted me up inside.

"Welcome to my bolt-hole," he said. He clambered up to join me and pulled the door closed, leaving us in pitch darkness.

"Don't move Watson," he said. "I'll get us some light." I heard the scrape of a match and saw the flare in the dark as Holmes lit a candle. The smoke from the wick wafted in the still air and my gaze followed it up to where it escaped through a small vent in the ceiling. There was now enough light to make out that Holmes' *bolt-hole* was rather well appointed; there were several sturdy armoires filled with clothes, a desk with a large mirror below which the accoutrements of Holmes' various disguises lay scattered, and even a single armchair sitting beside a tall well-stocked bookcase.

Holmes laughed at my obvious confusion.

"I keep this place for those cases when I do not have time to make a return to Baker Street. I got the idea from Neville St. Clair. Remember how he had a secret place where he could change character completely? I have found it useful several times in the past, but surely none more so than tonight. Only a few people know of its presence, and I trust them all to keep that knowledge private."

"I do hope one of the others isn't Lestrade?" I said, and that got me another laugh.

"No Watson, you can have no fears on that score. But it is Inspector Lestrade we must consider now. We need to get out of London, and quickly. Unfortunately Scotland Yard knows my methods and will be watching all of the more obvious escape routes."

"Leave London? But surely we must stay? Stay and clear our names?"

"It is clearing our names that requires us to leave," Holmes said. "We must go to Scotland, and with some haste. Someone has gone to a great deal of trouble to embroil us in this matter. That amount of effort means that the ultimate goal must be a matter of some import. I am worried Watson, worried that we have already been outflanked before we have properly begun."

"But why Scotland?"

"The answer lies in the bloodlines of the men involved, of that I am certain. We must follow that line of enquiry. But we shall have to be cautious; for our adversary will also know that we will be on his trail."

Holmes started to pull clothes from the armoires.

"We must travel incognito Watson. Which would you prefer?" He held up a heavy overcoat in one hand. "A sailor making his way home from the North Atlantic run? Or maybe an itinerant laborer looking for work?"

"You seem to be taking the night's events very calmly old man," I said.

Holmes had already moved over to the mirror and started applying make-up to make his face look darker and more unwashed.

"On the contrary Watson," he replied. "This is a matter of the utmost import. I must contact Mycroft at the earliest opportunity and have him watch Lord Douglas closely -- although I have no doubt that he will already have that matter in hand. But our priority for tonight is to get out of the city unnoticed. And for that, we need a disguise."

I finally relented and spent a most uncomfortable ten minutes allowing Holmes to apply some rather noxious stage make-up to my hands and face. After that he had me choose some clothing for my *disguise* which thankfully proved cleaner and less smelly than it looked to be. Lastly he made me ditch my pipe, my cigarette case and my lighter.

"All would betray us immediately to a trained eye I'm afraid," he said. "But they will be safe here until our return. And fear not, we shall not be short of smoking materials." He handed me a threadbare tobacco pouch and some rather rough papers. "An old soldier like you can surely roll his own given the makings?"

I was immediately hit with a memory of a cold clear night in the hills of Afghanistan, drinking gin and listening to the sound of drums in the wind while smoking a succession of thin cigarettes and waiting for dawn… when the fighting would start. Sitting there in that converted railway carriage, I was a long way from those hills. But the feeling of tense apprehension was almost exactly the same in both cases. I pushed it down. I had learned long ago that what was to come would come in its own sweet time, and worrying about it rarely changed the outcome in the slightest. I concentrated on trying to make my disguise as convincing as possible.

Minutes later we both stood in front of the mirror surveying our new personas. We certainly looked like the pair of itinerant laborers that Holmes intended us to be, and I started to hope that we might succeed in our plan of evading capture. Holmes also showed me the pocket in his belt into which he had sewn a pouch containing five-pound notes and gold guineas. "Just so any fear of us starving on the journey you may have is allayed."

And with that we went once more into the night, our only luggage a battered Gladstone bag containing some fresh clothing and a pair of revolvers hidden in a false bottom.

Our escape was almost foiled before it had properly begun.

"I think the disguises will stand up to scrutiny," Holmes said. "What say we try for a train? It will be risky, but the alternative is to start walking, and it is a long way to Scotland."

I agreed readily enough, for my old wound was already stiff and sore after the walk from Westminster, and the thought of more exertion so soon afterwards did not appeal in the slightest. I was not however completely at ease in disguise, not having either Holmes' aptitude or experience in pretending to be someone other than myself. I felt self-conscious as I walked by his side, taking a long circuitous route around the outskirts of the station to arrive back at the main entrance some thirty minutes later.

I only started to relax somewhat when we split up and independently managed to walk straight past a police cordon without them giving us a second glance.

But our troubles really began on the concourse. Holmes dropped me a wink as we met up again.

"We'll make an actor out of you yet Watson," he said softly. "We're halfway there. Let us stand here for a while and survey the lay of the land for a bit. There may be others in disguise like ourselves, here with the specific purpose of watching for our passing."

He leaned against one of the tall stone pillars while cupping a match to a newly-rolled cigarette. I heard the *pop* an instant before a chip of stone flew less than two inches from Holmes' head, cutting a bloody gouge across his cheek. There was a second *pop* and I felt something *tug* at my sleeve. I had come under fire often enough in my military career to recognize that we were in a dashed sticky situation.

"It seems someone is intent on flushing us out Watson," Holmes said. "Come, it is time we took our leave again."

And without another word he headed off at a weaving run through the crowd. Of course such a thing was always going to attract attention, and the policemen in the entranceway quickly took note. Another *pop* sent a chip of stone flying near my feet, and that was enough to get me moving. I followed Holmes through the crowd.

Another shot *pinged* off the platform at Holmes' feet and I suddenly realized that we were not heading *away* from the source of the shots, but directly towards it. I looked upwards. A dark figure stood on the high walkway that led to the adjoining platforms, a rifle aimed directly at me, too much in shadow for me to make out his features. I ducked and weaved instinctively and when I looked up again it was to see the figure move further into the shadows until he was completely lost from view.

"Damn," Holmes muttered loudly. "Lost him."

Almost immediately several police whistles echoed around the station and a group of officers headed towards us. They were also blocking any chance of us leaving via the entrance.

"This way Watson," Holmes said, and leapt down onto the tracks. I followed, just yards in front of a train pulling in to the station. Seconds later we were heading at pace along the side of the rails, the full length of the goods train now blocking us off from any pursuit as we left the passenger platform behind.

Holmes led me quickly across the tracks and out of the station to the north. I expected him to double back but instead we headed directly into the dark mouth of one of the tunnels that peppered the area. We moved deep into the shadows and Holmes motioned me to quiet.

Framed by the semi-circle of the tunnel entrance the lights of the station seemed very bright at first until my eyes adjusted. I don't know how long we stood there, but it was more than long enough for me to catch my breath and for my heart rate to slow to a more normal level. There were distant shouts and whistles as the police searched for us in vain. No one approached within a hundred yards of our position.

We waited for an hour before slipping quietly out of the tunnel then off the tracks and into the streets to the north of the station. Once at a safe distance we stopped, mainly to allow me to rest my aching leg and share a cigarette with Holmes in the shadow of a tall wall well away from any streetlights.

"We are free, for now," Holmes said, but in truth I felt anything but. I would have given almost anything at that low point of the night to be back in the comfort of Baker Street, sitting at the fireside with my pipe and a large measure of Scotch. Given our current circumstances I surmised that such relaxation might be rather a long way in my future.

Holmes only allowed us that brief rest stop before setting off again into the night.

Our escape from London proved remarkably simple after the near escape at King's Cross, involving as it did a long walk out towards Barnet before dawn then out into the open country beyond as the sun rose. In all that part of the journey we scarcely passed a soul, and those that we did paid us little heed.

By the end of that first long day a series of lifts from farm carts had taken us north of Watford and we finally took accommodation in a small but busy inn several hours after nightfall. Not a single person in the bar gave us a second glance, although I did take quite a turn on seeing our likeness on the front page of every newspaper. "Wanted for murder," was not something I ever thought to see associated with my name; or with Holmes' for that matter.

I mentioned the fact to Holmes when we were out of range of any possible eavesdroppers.

"Yes, I'm afraid we took the bait all too readily," Holmes said. We were sitting in a quiet corner of the bar, supping on some surprisingly pleasant ale, and I was proving to myself that my cigarette rolling skills had not deserted me even after many years of being out of practice. This was the first Holmes had spoken of the events of the night before since we left Kings Cross and I was eager to hear his thinking on the matter now that he had taken some time mulling it over.

"You are certain it was a deliberate trap?" I asked.

"Oh, most certain," Holmes said, keeping his voice low and even, although I knew of old that the fire in his eyes showed just how angry he had been made. "They played to my curiosity and, I'm afraid, my vanity; knowing exactly what would draw me in. And the fact that there was a gunman waiting, just for us, at King's Cross station tells me that whoever they are, they are highly organized – maybe even enough to have people watching at all the stations out of town last night."

"And do you have any thoughts yet on who *they* might be?"

He was so quiet at that I did not think he would answer, but when he did I realized he had indeed given it thought.

"I do not yet know the who, why or how of it Watson," he said. "But we are up against the highest of intellects; an adversary of particular skill and cunning. I know whom I *might* suspect, were he not already dead. But such questions are futile without more facts on which to base our suppositions. As I have said, the answers lie in Scotland; once there we shall see what we shall see."

He refused to be drawn after that, but I knew that his keen mind was always at work during our long journey north in the days following.

The inn proved to be our last chance of relaxation for some time. We had a hard toil through the Midlands, with few chances of help on the way and long days spent trudging along muddy paths in drizzle and fog. I was thoroughly miserable long before we reached Birmingham.

Our fortunes took a turn for the better thereafter when we made passage on an empty coal barge returning along the canal to Manchester. Although the weather did not improve much, my mood certainly did. We were travelling in the right direction, by a path unwatched by the law, and we were able to partially relax while doing so. My only real problem was maintaining the fiction that I was an itinerant worker and I received some strange looks from the barge owner during the journey, although he said nothing to either myself or Holmes, being happy to take the money Holmes had offered for our freight.

There was only one other matter of note before our investigations in Scotland began, and it happened in Crewe. By then Holmes had decided that we were sufficiently far north that we could risk taking a train the rest of the way. He stayed in the crowd on the northbound platform while I went to get tickets for the Glasgow train. And it was there, while standing in the queue, that I felt someone try to pick my pocket. Or so I thought. But when I put my hand down I felt a single piece of paper there.

"Meet me here," a soft Scots voice said. "I know who has done this to you."

I turned towards the voice, already too late, and caught a glimpse of a small figure part running, part limping away. When I went after him I lost him in the station forecourt and could not risk drawing attention to myself by giving chase at speed or by calling out. I went back to the ticket queue, keeping a close eye for anyone that might have noticed the encounter or might be watching me too closely. No one seemed to be interested. There was a policeman sitting on one of the benches by the door but he was obviously off duty, smoking a pipe and lost in a newspaper. I was able to buy our tickets north with no further ado.

On returning to the platform I showed Holmes the page that had been so deftly placed in my pocket. It was another sheet that looked to have been roughly torn from the same book as the one I had received back in Baker Street.

CALX was the heading. An illuminated drawing showed a young man, bound to a burning wheel by hands and feet in a figure X. He was smiling. Holmes studied it for some time before talking. He rubbed the paper between his fingers as he had done with the previous page.

"It certainly *feels* like it has come from the same source," he said. "And it provides us with more alchemical clues. *Calx* is latin for Lime. In this case, it is a metaphor for *calcination*, or the process of purifying by heating. If you burn a body hot enough, it goes black, then, if you burn it even hotter, the ash turns white. Similarly, if you heat limestone, you'll produce a white powder that the Romans called *Calx Vita* or quicklime. This was considered a magical material, for, if you poured water on it, it gave out heat. Effectively, giving warmth back to the giver."

"And now I'm afraid I am lost again," I said.

"This one is relatively simple," Holmes replied. "Look at the picture. Fire purifies. It is also a code that says, in effect, make quicklime. It will give heat back to the giver. And, beyond that, it symbolizes the fact that the adept must purify his soul before continuing."

He tapped at the picture.

"It is from Greek mythology. *Ixion* was punished by Zeus. He tried to seduce *Hera*, and for his presumption was bound to a perpetual wheel of fire. But Ixion had seen the face of the Goddess, and although in eternal pain, was also eternally happy. Everything can be seen from two angles. Everything has at least two meanings."

I told Holmes what the vagrant had said, about knowing who our adversary might be, and Holmes smiled.

"And I believe I know where to go to find him," he

said, but he took some almost childlike delight in refusing to let me in on his latest secret. "You know me, Watson. I must confirm to my own satisfaction that I am right before I share the information."

Our train arrived shortly afterwards and Holmes went quiet. I thought discussion on the matter was finished for the moment, but once we had a carriage to ourselves he continued.

"What we must ascertain is what part these *gifts* you have received play in this matter. I am of the opinion that they are clues, meant to lead us onwards. But are they part of the solution… or part of the problem? That is the question that vexes me now."

This time he did fall quiet and I smoked in silence for the remainder of the journey.

CHAPTER 2

Holmes had already intimated that Glasgow was not to be our final destination, but he did not allow me into his confidence until some time after we disembarked at Central Station. Firstly though we had to endure a walk past a small army of police officers, all intent on studying every disembarking passenger.

"It seems we are expected," Holmes whispered as we approached the ticket barrier. "Keep quiet, follow my lead, and be prepared to run if the need arises. There may be another *sniper* trying to flush us out."

I cursed him inwardly for reminding me of the fact, for all his warning achieved was to make me nervous, and I was sure that was going to be obvious to any of the police officers should they decided to take a closer look at us.

The station itself was a noisy confusion of engine noise, smoke and excited passengers but suddenly Holmes' strident voice carried above them all. It was also the most convincing Scots accent I had heard since my time on the line in Afghanistan with Corporal Black from Maryhill.

"So I said to her, 'Get away wi' ye woman and stop talking such tripe,' but ye ken wit women are like? She only went and skelped me ower the heid wi' a pan. I was fair affronted so I was and…"

Much to my amazement he kept on in that vein for several minutes as we reached the head of the queue and handed over our tickets. We walked through the crowded concourse and out into Union Street. No one stopped us, no one shot at us and there were no police whistles in our wake.

Holmes was obviously well pleased with this latest ruse.

"I say old man," I whispered. "Wasn't that a bit of a risk."

He laughed, and half-dragged me across the busy thoroughfare and down a tall shaded alley I would not have entered of my own free will.

"The bigger risk would have been to stay quiet. People see and hear what they expect to see and hear, and in a city like this, they expect the locals to talk, and loudly at that."

He herded me to a tall wooden door. It was only when he pushed it open that I heard the sound of laughter and smelled the smoke and ale. A sign I hadn't previously noticed above the doorway told me what I had come to guess; we were about to enter a public bar, *The Horseshoe*. Holmes had a quick look round to make sure no one was paying any heed to us and ushered me inside.

It turned out to be a large open barn of a place with much mahogany and some particularly fine large painted mirrors. It was also rather busy, but none of the clientele paid us much attention, intent as they were on their own drinking. Holmes walked up to the bar and, still in character, ordered 'two pints of eighty shilling and two pies.' He leaned over and whispered something to the barman. Several white five-pound notes passed from Holmes across the bar and were so quickly taken out of his hand and spirited away in the barman's pocket that I believe I was the only person in the whole place to notice. We were quickly motioned through to a room at the rear of the building that contained little more than two armchairs, a small table and a fireplace. The barman winked at Holmes.

"I'll see to it that you're not disturbed sirs," he said and left us alone.

Holmes immediately relaxed.

"We're clear Watson, for now at least. George will keep any prying eyes away, and we are safer in here than just about any other place in the country."

"Holmes, you never cease to astonish me. You mean you are known, here in this bar?"

Holmes smiled.

"I have had several cases to solve for the industrialists in this fine city, before your time as my *chronicler* of course, but this old place never changes much. And I have found over the years that this particular spot is an excellent central base of operations."

"But it is a public bar," I replied.

"Where better to hear from the public?" Holmes said

laughing. "I also have arrangements with several other bar owners across the country. My web of information gathering has numerous strands, and this bar is at one of the junctions. Besides, George knows more than anyone about the doings of the criminal fraternity in this area, having been a pawnbroker of some ill repute before seeing the light and turning his hand to inn-keeping."

He took off his overcoat, dropped into one of the chairs and immediately looked as relaxed as if he was back Baker Street. I sat down opposite him and rolled a cigarette for each of us. Minutes later the barman, George I presumed, brought a tray through with the beers and two piping-hot pies. The man left, dropping me another wink as he departed. "I'll be back with some more beer after I've seen to your errands sir," he said to Holmes, and Holmes acknowledged him with a wave.

The pies, although they looked suspiciously gray inside, proved to be delicious and peppery although the meat was unidentifiable, possibly mutton although I could not be sure. Much to my embarrassment I managed to dribble a stream of hot grease down the sleeve of my jacket, which got another laugh from Holmes as I made an unsightly smear while trying to remove it.

"A touch of verisimilitude I had not thought of Watson. I may try it myself."

After eating Holmes took to the ale with relish. To my palate it seemed somewhat heavy on malt and syrup and had too little hop compared to the Fullers' I was used to back in town, but after a while I grew accustomed to the taste and to my surprise polished it off quite rapidly.

"We shall make a Scotsman of you yet Watson," Holmes said and, as if the beer had suddenly loosened his tongue, proceeded to run through his thoughts on the case so far.

"I have been thinking," he said. "And our recent close call at the ticket barrier has firmed up my thoughts. *People see and hear what they expect to see and hear.*' And therein lies the crux of the matter. Our adversary relied on that fact when he set his trap for me."

He took a proffered cigarette, lit it with a taper from the fireside and sucked on it contentedly before continuing.

"He knew of course that I would be making a close study of everything that happened to the stricken Lords… indeed he counted on it. I draw your attention to the mouth movements in particular. That was a work of some genius."

My confusion must have shown, and Holmes smiled.

"I did not think you had noticed, Watson. According to Mycroft, all of the stricken Lords have been mouthing the same thing… a Latin phrase. *Ab ovo usque ad mala.*"

"From eggs to apples. From Horace?"

"Yes, the *Satire*. But it also has been used in several alchemical texts, for the egg is commonly used to symbolize the *macrocosm*, but it also used to denote the beginning of all things, whereas apples represent forbidden knowledge, as in *The Apples of the Hesperides*. But even that is not the most relevant usage in this case. It seems we have a trickster at work against us Watson, for there is yet another place where those same words turn up – in the family motto of the common descendant of the six lords, Angus Seton, Laird of Comrie. I made the connection – I saw what I wanted to see – and thus we were drawn into the trap."

George returned at that moment with two more of the strong beers. I started my second more cautiously, aware that a certain tiredness was setting in to my bones. Starting to relax was potentially dangerous in our current situation, but Holmes seemed to have become settled, at least for now, so I allow myself some laxity and sat back in the chair with a fresh smoke.

"But Holmes," I said. "If it *was* a trap, then surely our opponent will have guessed that we will be searching for an answer here in Scotland?"

Holmes nodded.

"In fact, I am counting on it. Our only hope of clearing our names is to force a confrontation. Even before that, I want to ensure that we are the ones setting any traps from here on. But that is for tomorrow. Tonight, we shall rest up here and let George's contacts do some legwork for us."

What with the ale and the seeping tiredness I was almost asleep when George returned about an hour later.

"You were right Mister Holmes," he said. "I have an address for you. It is an old Medieval Keep up a farm track in Limehouse."

"This Limehouse… it is where I thought it would be?"

George laughed.

"There's not much gets past you sir. Yes… it is a small hamlet just to the east of Comrie."

Once George left I asked Holmes what the significance of the last conversation had been, but he was again lost in thought and I knew better than to interrupt. George also came back soon afterwards with another two beers but I left mine alone; I had further questions before I could allow myself to sleep. But Holmes would say no more, merely referred me back to the latest piece of paper; the one that had been slipped into my pocket in Crewe.

"Lime-house Watson… I told you it was a clue."

I took out the page and studied the image of the crucified youth, smiling as he burned, but for the life of me I could not see how it applied in any shape or form to our current situation. And at that the tiredness finally took me. I fell into a most welcome slumber.

I woke some time later, with a stiff back and a sour taste in my mouth of stale tobacco and beer. That was quickly overcome by the smell of freshly buttered toast and tea. George looked almost embarrassed as he put a tray down on the small table. It had been the slight noise he had made on entering that had woken me. Thin sunlight came in through thick dusty curtains – I had slept all night in the chair. Indeed Holmes had not yet wakened, being still asleep on the opposite side of the now-cold fireplace.

"The missus made me get out the best china," George said. "So for God's sake don't break it or I'll be in the doghouse for months."

The *china* was indeed made of particularly fine porcelain

but I scarce noticed; I realized I was hungry enough to eat almost anything and I took to the toast with gusto. Holmes woke, stretched and reached for the tobacco pouch on the arm of the chair by his right hand.

"Toast Holmes?"

He shook his head. "Not this morning. We have some travelling to do and I fear my constitution will not permit food yet."

"We are travelling?" I asked between more mouthfuls of toast.

He nodded, and looked up at the barman. "That is, if everything is arranged?"

George nodded back.

"I have a carriage that will take you most of the way – up to Aberfoyle then along the side of the lochs. It is not a short trip, and will take all day, but once out of the city there will be little chance of anyone taking notice of you. Just stay hidden in the carriage for the first hour or so and everything will be smooth as silk."

"In that case," Holmes said, removing his rather threadbare waistcoat. "I believe the time for disguise is over. I trust you managed to secure us a change of clothing?"

This was said to the barman. The man tapped his nose and winked. "Some very nice stuff indeed Mr. Holmes if I say so myself. Just don't ask me which gentleman will be looking for his *troosers* this morning." He laughed loudly. It looked like something he did a lot and I couldn't help raising a smile of my own in reply.

"Dashed good of you sir," I said. "But if I can bother you for one more thing? I need a wash and a shave before I'll be fit to share an enclosed space with anyone."

He showed us to a small washroom at the rear.

As I joined Holmes in starting to wash away the make-up and accumulated grime – which was a dashed difficult job in itself – I asked him if he was certain of this course of action.

He smiled thinly.

"Your limping friend found us in Crewe despite all our

attempts at evasion," he said. "And we were spotted easily enough at King's Cross. I don't know about you Watson, but I would rather walk in the light than slink in the darkness. Besides, I am tired of running. It is time we wrested the initiative back in our favor."

I will admit that divesting myself of the guise I had worn these past days did indeed feel liberating, and once washed, shaved and dressed I realized that I felt less like a criminal and more like my old self. The clothes *provided* by the barman certainly helped, being a particularly fine tweed three-piece suit that felt as if it had hardly been worn. Holmes was similarly well dressed, having been given a dark serge suit and matching cape. By the time Holmes handed me a loaded service revolver I was more than ready to make a start on our rehabilitation.

George had a carriage brought right up against the back entrance of the bar and Holmes and I were able to climb aboard without being seen. We were still travelling light, with only our trusty Gladstone bag as company, but once again George proved himself to be a more than gracious host. There was a picnic hamper on the floor of the carriage that on inspection contained several bottles of ale and enough cold pies, bread and cheese to keep us from starving for the day to come.

We did as George had suggested and kept our heads down for more than an hour into the journey, contenting ourselves to smoking in quiet contemplation. My tobacco consumption over recent days was rather higher than I was accustomed to and as a medical man I knew I should be curtailing my use. But I must say I was rather enjoying the old familiarity of rolling my own cigarettes, and was taking some pride in the quality of the final products. Holmes however was lost in one of his reveries and as ever I had no idea what might be occupying his mind. I also knew better than to ask.

After a while Holmes had obviously had enough *confinement* and drew open the curtain from across the door, allowing us access to the view. It was immediately clear that we were already outside the city, being taken through some well-manicured farmland interspersed with the scars of recent mining activity. I leaned out of the window.

"Driver? Could you tell us where we are?"

He didn't even turn round to acknowledge my question. I thought better of asking again, guessing that anyone hired by George would be used to keeping their mouth shut and their mind free of any thoughts as to why they were taking this particular journey. I contented myself with enjoying the view while nibbling on a thick sandwich of bread and cheese.

Holmes chose that moment to enlighten me further as to our destination.

"You asked me why we are headed for Comrie," he started. "The answer lies, as I have already stated, with the common ancestor of the stricken Lords, a certain Angus Seton as I believe I have already said. The old Keep for which we are headed has been the family seat for more than four hundred years, and continues to be so. If there is an answer to be found, I believe it will be there, for the family has a history that points to a study, if not an obsession, with the practice of alchemy."

That gave me a start, but in reality it should not have, for everything we had learned so far had indeed pointed at an *esoteric* background to the case.

Holmes was still talking.

"The Seton family, as far as I could trace, dates itself as far back as the Norman barons of the twelfth century, and seem to have started to rise in favor as trusted servants to minor scions of Scottish royalty around that time. It is also told, although it is probably apocryphal, that the alchemical obsession began early, as a result of an encounter with an Arabian practitioner during the Third Crusade. What is beyond dispute is that the Seton family have been responsible for many of what are now regarded as definitive texts in the Great Quest."

"I will admit," I said. "It is not a matter that I have given much consideration."

Holmes smiled again.

"Yes, and yet no, Watson. For any study of basic chemistry you have undertaken in the course of your medical education was, as you well know, founded in alchemical practices in its earliest history. Robert Boyle himself was known to be a dabbler in the Quest, as was Isaac Newton."

I did indeed know of the history, but as yet I could not see its application to our current predicament, and I told Holmes so in no uncertain terms.

"That is exactly the reason why we are here Watson. Now I suggest you try to get some rest. I fear we have a night of burglary and adventure ahead of us."

And that was that for a number of hours. The carriage stopped at an old stone coach house at what I took to be the driver and the horses' lunchtime. Holmes and I decided discretion was the better part of valor and stayed hidden. We were however well enough served for our own repast, having a bottle of ale and plenty to eat in the provided hamper. We finished off all of the food that George had provided and I was feeling quite heartened as we started off again, having almost forgotten that we were fugitives from justice.

The remainder of the journey only served to further remove me from our predicament as we traveled through some marvelous highland scenery of forest, high hills and tranquil lochs, barely seeing another living soul in the course of a full afternoon. Holmes remained lost in introspection, our only conversation coming from the occasional request for me to roll him a new cigarette.

Dusk was starting to fall when the carriage came to a halt.

"Limehouse, gentlemen." Those were the only words I had heard from the man all day and as we disembarked he added more, almost as terse. "Shall I wait?"

Holmes sent him away.

"We shall make our own way from here, but thank you," he said. "And thank George for all his help."

The driver nodded and without another word left, leaving Holmes and I standing in a quiet country lane at a junction with a long narrow driveway that seemed to lead up into the low hills beyond. Holmes lifted the Gladstone bag and immediately made for the driveway.

"I promised you some burglary Watson. It seems the time is upon us. Tonight we shall start the process of regaining our good name."

Reaching the Keep proved to be a rather strenuous climb of some fifteen minutes, by the end of which I was wishing we had not dismissed the carriage quite so readily. It was also becoming dark and without the benefit of any street lighting I found it difficult to make out the path ahead.

Holmes seemed unperturbed.

"A fine night for our nefarious purposes," he said, and strode on. It was only a minute or so after that we reached the Keep. It seemed to loom up out of nowhere in the gathering gloom so that we were most suddenly confronted with a high stone edifice. It looked to be little more than a tall box, foursquare and solid with only two smallish windows on the side we faced. Walking round to our right brought us in front of a very imposing oak door some eight feet high and firmly locked when I tried it.

"We're not getting in there without an axe," I whispered. "And even then it would take a month of Sundays."

Holmes didn't reply. His attention was already on a small window to the side of the door. He lit a succession of matches while examining the lock and I had to look away from each bright flare to avoid blinding myself. When I looked back after the last match-strike Holmes already had the window open and was clambering inside. When I tried to follow him I found that my frame was too large to squeeze through the narrow gap. I could not see Holmes in the darkness beyond, but I heard him laugh quietly.

"I must have a word with Mrs. Hudson about the size of your breakfasts," he said. "Wait there. I will open the door."

The heavy oak door swung open seconds later. There was an accompanying creak so loud that it disturbed a pair of crows out of the trees, sending them cawing overhead.

"Don't worry about noise old man. It seems we have the run of the place," Holmes said, not bothering to whisper. "The whole Keep is dark and quiet. Cold too - I doubt there has been anyone here in weeks."

He showed me into what felt like a tall hallway judging by the hollow echoes all around us although it was hard to tell exactly, so complete was the darkness. Holmes soon rectified that by finding a tall candle that he took down from a wall sconce. He lit it from a match, and used the light to find several others like it which were ranked at regular intervals along the walls. I saw the light reflecting in the windows at the far end of the hall, and realized that it would be able to be seen from the outside.

"I say Holmes, do you think that is wise? Someone might take note."

"Given our location, I think that unlikely," Holmes said. "Besides, it is a necessary risk if we are to be successful in our efforts. Come, let us see if there is anything here to help us."

I followed him as we made a round of the ground floor of the Keep. As Holmes had already guessed, it was apparent that the place had not been inhabited for some time. Fine dust lay everywhere, spiders had made webbing in most of the corners, and scurrying noises in the dark told of rodents, whether rats or mice I was unable to determine.

The only sign of any human activity at all was in a small library. Holmes lit a pair of oil lamps he found on a console table to show a very well appointed little room. I would have been more than happy to spend my evenings in such a place, with its aged oak paneling, tall bookshelves and wide stone fireplace. Papers lay strewn across a fine mahogany desk, and these became the focus of Holmes' investigation. I perused the volumes on the shelves but their titles were unknown to me. There was obviously an esoteric bent to the content; *The Mysteries of the Wurm, The Twelve Concordances of the Red Serpent* and further titles in Latin, Greek and German that seemed to allude to an alchemical origin. I was about to remark on the fact when I heard Holmes gasp.

I turned to see him have to grasp the edge of the desk to keep from falling. His face was ashen and his eyelids fluttered as if a faint was coming on. I moved over quickly and lent him my shoulder to steady him. When he spoke it was in a whisper.

"Thank you Watson," he said. He waved a sheaf of papers at me. "It was these letters that did it. I fear this matter is more complex than I originally thought. I have been given somewhat of a shock."

"I can see that old man," I said. "Stay here. I'll see if there's any Scotch lying around."

A voice I recognized came from the library doorway.

"I'm afraid your drinking days are over Doctor."

Inspector Lestrade stood in the doorway, with two bulky officers that I did not recognize behind him.

"It seems we will be adding breaking and entering to your charge list," the Inspector said. "Lord Crawford said that this is where we would find you. Your little plot has been foiled, Holmes."

Holmes laughed. He still looked as white as a sheet, but Lestrade's appearance seemed to have taken his mind off whatever had troubled him – for the moment at least.

"And which plot would that be Lestrade?" Holmes said. "Surely you know me better than that? Crawford is the man you need to look at here, not Watson and myself."

Lestrade looked tired and irritable, and was obviously in no mood for any games. It was almost possible to feel some sympathy for the man.

"All I know is that a Lord of the Realm says you threw another Lord of the Realm out of a window in the Houses of Parliament. I cannot find anyone who saw another person in the dead Lord's room, there is no suicide note, and you ran from the scene; both of you. Now come quietly gentlemen. You'll get a fair trial; you know that I am a man of my word on that score. But that is all I can offer you."

Holmes casually shoved the sheaf of letters he held into an inside pocket as if it was the most natural thing in the world and stood straight. I could see the tension rise in him; he was readying himself for action. My hand found the butt of the service revolver in my pocket, but I already knew that I would not be leveling it at the policemen – that would be the step too far. If it came to having to fight with Lestrade in order to escape I decided I would throw myself on the mercy of the law.

"Ask yourself Lestrade," Holmes said. "How did Crawford know to find us here? I myself did not know this would be our destination until early this morning. For you to get here as quickly as you have means that Crawford knew we were coming a long time before we knew it ourselves. How do you think he managed that?"

Lestrade sighed.

"Don't tax me Mr. Holmes. I'm a long way from home and I'm tired. My job is to take you in for questioning. I'll leave it to the legal chaps to sort out the niceties. Now are you coming quietly or not?"

"Not," a Scottish voice said from the hallway beyond. The two officers behind Lestrade shuffled past him into the library, raising their hands above their head. We saw why seconds later when a small man dressed in rags walked into the room; my *friend* from Baker Street and Crewe Railway Station. He carried the largest shotgun I have ever seen – from my close range it looked more like a small cannon. He motioned with it, pointing Lestrade over towards where the two other officers now stood at the fireplace.

"Now Inspector," the man said. "Unless you have a warrant from a Scottish court, I believe it is *you* who are trespassing here. I am probably within my rights as the *Laird* to shoot you first and answer questions later, but I am feeling generous tonight. I believe I will detain you until the law can be brought up here."

"We *are* the law," Lestrade said, and made to move forward. Seton stopped him by pointing the shotgun straight at his chest.

"Doctor Watson," the newcomer said turning to me. "You will find some lengths of rope in the cupboard under the stairs in the hall. Could you fetch them please?"

Holmes laughed.

"It seems my *wee plot* isn't quite ready to roll over and die just yet," he said to Lestrade. "When you have got the time, I suggest you look into a shooting in King's Cross Station on the night of the supposed *murder*. And ask yourself Lestrade, who do we both know that employed a high velocity air gun? If you find the gunman from that scene, I would suggest you will be closer to the actual culprit."

I left them to it.

"You are just making things worse for yourself," Lestrade said. "Any sympathy I might have had for your predicament is rapidly fading. I don't take too kindly to being held at gunpoint."

Seton laughed.

"Maybe you should have thought of that before entering a Scotsman's house without a warrant."

I heard all of this from the hallway before moving to the under-stairs cupboard where I did indeed find several lengths of stout rope among sundry country items including a particularly fine pair of salmon rods and another shotgun. I considered, only for a second, taking that weapon, but there were already too many guns in there, and if I hadn't been prepared to use a pistol I certainly was not about to menace Lestrade with a *cannon*.

When I returned to the library the Scotsman motioned with the gun again towards the trio of policemen.

"Tie them up please Doctor. Nothing too fancy; just enough to give us time to make our escape."

I did as I was bid, although with some trepidation.

"Don't do it," Lestrade said.

"Sorry about this Inspector," I said. "But as Holmes has explained, we are innocent of the charges against us. We just need a chance to prove it."

"You are not doing yourself any favors here Doctor," Lestrade replied as I bound his hands. "We only have you as an accessory at the moment, but aiding and abetting means you are definitely throwing your career away here."

"I'll take my chances with Holmes," I said.

Lestrade was red in the face with anger. He strained at his bonds, but I had tied him quite securely.

"Just make sure he doesn't throw *you* out of a window Doctor. You know how he is when he gets in a mood."

Holmes laughed bitterly.

"I will remind you of that when I present you with the truth of the matter," he said. "But for now, it is we who have the upper hand. I will see you again soon enough Lestrade, and next time it is I who will have the answers, and you who shall have to provide an apology."

I finished tying up the other policemen's hands, then I bound all three together by looping the longest stretch of rope in four tight rings around them. Lestrade continued to struggle.

"I'll have you locked up on bread and water for the rest of your life for this Watson," he said. "You have my promise on that."

The look in his eye convinced me he was telling the truth, but Holmes and I were too far in now for me to back down. Our only hope seemed to lie with the small Scotsman.

Once satisfied the bonds would hold Seton finally put down the weapon.

"Thank you Doctor, it's a heavy beast to have to lug around. I had best leave it here, for we have a bit of travelling ahead of us. Are you ready for a run on the hills?"

Without further explanation he left the room, obviously expecting us to follow. Holmes didn't hesitate. He picked up the Gladstone bag and handed it to me.

"Come Watson. There are answers waiting for us."

The three of us ran out into the night.

We did not go far. Having heard the Scotsman's words

inside I was fully expecting to have to lug the Gladstone bag over hill and moor with Lestrade and his men in pursuit at our heels. Instead he led us quickly round to the rear of the Keep. There was just enough light from the windows to show us a set of steps leading down into the ground.

"A wee present from my ancestors," the Scotsman whispered. "They too liked to hide things from the authorities."

As he turned away I heard him start to mutter to himself, and I remembered our first encounter. The cadence seemed exactly the same, and this time I could make out the words; a form of Gaelic if I wasn't mistaken, the meaning of which entirely eluded me.

We went deep into the ground to what at first looked to be no more than a chamber for grain storage. He led us, almost blind in the dark, to the rear and slid a panel aside. He lit an oil lamp, the light almost blinding until our eyes adjusted and we saw more steps going down beyond. Sliding the panel shut he then led us further into the depths, into what proved to be a warren of tunnels. As we passed entrances I saw barrels of ale and wine, and boxes, obviously imported from the Orient, that looked never to have been opened.

Before I had time for further investigation the passageway opened into a wider chamber. The air felt fresher here and there was the slightest of breezes. The strangest thing of all however was the diagram that had been painted on the floor. A five-pointed star sat inside three concentric circles. Around the outermost ring ran a series of what looked to my untrained eye to be Arabic hieroglyphs, and along the inner track was painted an inscription in Gaelic. As the Scotsman started to mutter again I realized that he was muttering the words that were written on the floor.

"Ri linn dioladh na beatha, Ri linn bruchdadh na falluis, Ri linn iobar na creadha, Ri linn dortadh na fala."

The Scotsman saw me looking and stopped.

"It may seem like a lot of *hocus-pocus* to you Doctor but I assure you it is necessary for my protection," he said. "I will explain soon enough."

Two rough high-backed benches sat either side of the fireplace and the Scotsman bade us sit as he first lit and stoked a fire, then left us as he went to search for something in a side chamber. I realized that Holmes had not spoken since we left the Keep above. He no longer looked like he might faint, but his face was still pale and his brow was etched with what might have been concentration had it not looked so much like worry.

"Are you quite well old chap?" I asked.

"Nothing a smoke will not cure Watson," he said, and managed a weak smile. I did not get a chance to question him further, for our host returned at that moment carrying a whisky bottle and three glasses. He had also had a change of clothes and a wash that quite transformed him. The rags had gone to be replaced by a fine tweed suit, and a pair of clean shoes covered his feet. The mere act of having combed his unruly mop of red hair and tying it back with a bow meant that we could see his face clearly for the first time. He had the brightest blue eyes I have seen, a wide smile and his teeth were straight and white. He acknowledged my obvious consternation with a grin.

"Well met again Doctor. I am right sorry for the subterfuge, and I assure you it was necessary. When we met before you were not the only one in disguise. But if I am to tell my story then we'll need a dram or two, for it might take a wee while."

So it was Holmes and I sat there deep under a Scottish Keep, sipping whisky, smoking my hastily rolled cigarettes and listening to the most outlandish tale that had ever reached our ears.

"First things first," he began. "We have not yet been formally introduced."

He took a cigarette from me when I proffered and he used a long taper lit from the fire to get it going, puffing smoke contentedly before continuing.

"My name is Angus Seton and I am what you might call the master of this fine place. As you are aware by now, my family is regarded as experts in some esoteric fields of research and have been involved in the study of occult practices for many centuries. My own story in so far as it concerns your predicament starts seven years ago, and involves the search for one strand of that knowledge."

He took a long sip from the whisky, which I must admit was remarkable stuff, being peaty, fiery and smooth all at once, and giving one a warm internal glow that lasted long after the liquor had passed the lips. I had to watch what I was doing as it would have been all too easy to take a dive into that particular bottle.

"I received a letter that summer," Seton continued. "It came from Durham, from the University, and showed a great deal of knowledge and erudition. The initial inquiry was regarding the Philosopher's Stone but the writer, over the course of several dozen letters, ranged widely over a variety of topics. It became apparent that he not only knew my family history, but also that he was particularly interested in the areas of research that related to the transmigration of souls.

"Now I myself have always been a practical man, believing that the final goal of the research in the Seton family history was mainly a matter purely of chemistry; that longevity was a goal that could be achieved with the right combination of chemical compounds and experimentation. But the letter writer proposed a more *spiritual* path, one where immortality of the body could be fused with an illuminated mind to produce what he called *the perfect man*. I disagreed with him of course, but his letters were so informed, so erudite, that I could not help but be impressed.

"We went backwards and forwards, corresponding for several years. He was obviously proceeding apace with his own experimentation, and I sensed a growing excitement in his writings; he believed he was close to achieving his goal.

"Then, in the spring of ninety-one, the letters suddenly stopped."

Holmes twitched at that, as if he had been given a fresh shock, but when I looked his way he dismissed me with a wave of the hand, and indicated to Seton that he should continue. The Scotsman took the break in his tale as a chance to refill our glasses, and I for one was not about to turn down more of that fine liquor. I sipped at it, savoring the heat that in some ways was even more comforting than that being given out from the fire. Sitting here in the Highlands on such a night one could well see how the *uisque* came to become so much a part of the local's life. I pulled myself out of the momentary reverie; our host had started up his tale from where he left off.

"There were no more letters after the spring of ninety-one," Seton continued. "But I was to find he was far from finished with me. And here my tale becomes passing strange and I fear it might seem most unusual, if not completely outlandish, but please bear with me. I promise you it is pertinent to your current predicament.

"I had quite forgotten my correspondence with the gentleman beyond occasionally wondering why the letters had stopped coming. I was soon to wish I could forget him completely.

"It started in the summer of ninety-four. I was sitting in my study going over a passage in *The Concordances* when the first attack came. It manifested itself as little more than a bad headache at first, then as a crushing pressure inside my skull such that I felt my head might implode. All at once I felt a presence, an obviously alien *thing* creeping through my mind, and it was only with the full force of my will that I was able to repel it. And somehow I knew the source of the attack; my correspondent had indeed found a means to migrate his soul. The trouble was, he was trying to migrate his essence into my body – and I was still the resident."

I was finding Seton's tale more and more difficult to follow, possibly a result of the Scotch, but more likely because it had slipped into the area of the esoteric with which I was completely unfamiliar and if truth be told more than a tad skeptical of. I was about to voice my feelings when Holmes put a hand on my shoulder.

"Let us hear him out Watson," he said. "I believe we need to."

Seton nodded. "That you do and I shall get to the point soon enough. But first, let me go back to those early attacks on me in ninety-four. As I have said, by some means unknown to me consciously, I knew that the source of the attack was the letter writer in Durham. I did not at first understand why, but since then I have developed a theory that I shall get to in good time. However my family has not studied arcane maters all these centuries for no return, and I was quickly able to mount a defense using a Gaelic chant from deep antiquity. Using that, and utilizing the power of the pentacle that you have already seen on the floor, I was able to keep the attacks at bay."

I believe I let out a disbelieving *harrumph* at that, but Seton did not seem to take offense. He continued after a long sip of his Scotch.

"Doctor Watson here has already spotted that I am prone to muttering the protection spell at inopportune moments, but I assure you it is most necessary, for the attacks are strong and frequent. Back then at the start they came even faster, but when it became apparent that I was not about to succumb, the man in Durham – which is how I always thought of him for I never learned his name – changed tack. Having failed with me, he took to making attempts on people with the same bloodline... my family.

"My first intimation of this came at a wedding. Young John, a nephew barely twenty-three and full of life, was so happy at his betrothal to a sweet lass from Dunfermline. After the vows we all went to the Church Hall for the dancing. John came over, shook my hand and looked me in the eye. The change came on him fast; his mouth went slack, his eyes went dead and he started to mouth soundless words. Then, mere seconds later, he fell, stone dead in my arms."

Seton paused to wipe away a sudden tear before continuing.

"He was only the first of many. Over that first year I lost ten family members, all male, all cut off in the prime of life. And all the same way according to the reports of those present at the deaths. At the same time the attacks on me continued apace and I was sorely weakened through having to constantly defend myself. I decided that I could not wait for everyone I knew and loved to die around me, so I went looking for the source.

"I traveled to Durham in hope, but it ended in despair, for I had scarcely been there an hour when I discovered that the man I sought was dead – perished in May of ninety-one."

I believed I was starting to see where this was going, and I did not like the thought, not one bit. And as ever, Holmes had been ahead of me for some time. He took the sheaf of letters from his pocket.

"I knew it as soon as I saw your letters," Holmes said. "I would know that hand anywhere, despite the lack of a signature."

He handed the papers to me. My eye was immediately drawn to the over elaborate letter inscribed at the bottom of the top one.

A single letter.

M… for Moriarty.

Chapter 3

I was so dumbfounded I was unable to speak for several seconds, and Holmes was lost in thought staring into the fire and chewing on a cigarette. Seton filled the empty space.

"Yes Mr. Holmes. As you have surmised it was indeed Professor Moriarty with whom I was in correspondence, although I did not know it myself until my trip to Durham. And I now believe that you can piece most of the rest of the tale together for yourself. Moriarty's body may have perished at those Falls where you so nearly met your doom, but his spirit lives on. It lives on, and it is looking for a body to inhabit permanently. My body to be precise."

I recognized Holmes' expression.

Something does not ring true.

He gave voice to it before I could.

"And Moriarty, having returned from the Great Beyond, has decided to spend his immortality in having some sport with myself and some distant relatives of yours in the House of Lords while waiting for you to stop fighting him? Is that your story?"

Seton did not reply. He and Holmes appraised each other for long seconds, like two old dogs deciding whether a fight was worth the effort. In the end Holmes' iron will won through, and Seton sighed deeply.

"I should have known better than to try to outfox Sherlock Holmes," he said. "But I have not lied to you – merely been rather economical with the truth. For, you see, I was afraid you might not listen to my tale if I told you Moriarty's real goal."

"Which is?" Holmes asked.

Seton drank almost a full glass of Scotch before replying, and when he did speak it was in the most matter-of-fact manner that made his subsequent statement all the more incredible.

"There is a specific reason why he wants my body in particular. When I said my *family* has been researching in the arcane for many centuries, I was not quite accurate. I really should have said that *I* have been. I was born in the year Fourteen Eighty Three, in Port Seton near Edinburgh, and I know the secret of immortality."

Of course, that kind of thing is a bit of a conversation stopper. Holmes recovered his composure before I did.

"You are right of course; such a statement does raise more questions than answers. But if you ask me to believe that Moriarty's spirit is still *somewhere* in the ether looking for a body, then it is but a small leap of deduction from that to believing the totality of the tale. And I have a feeling that if we are to resolve this matter then we must proceed as if what you say is true, until proven otherwise."

"But alchemy is nothing but gibberish and gobbledygook," I said. "I know, I've tried to read some of the manuscripts, back when I was a student and much more fanciful."

"Gibberish," Seton said, pouring himself yet another whisky. "Even that word has an alchemical history. The word comes from the name of an Eighth Century Islamic alchemist, Jabir ibn Hayyan, the same man who described the making of the stained glass. His name was latinized as *Geber*. He wrote in a mangled verse that was so convoluted and strange that it coined the word. And since him, alchemists have always hidden their secrets in code."

"You mean all that nonsense about pelicans and pheasants actually means something?"

"Well in most texts, the pelican is shown stabbing its breast with its beak and nourishing its young with its own blood. It symbolizes self-sacrifice and the abandonment of worldly things with no thought of consequence. But the pelican is also the name for a piece of apparatus. Double, and even triple, meanings abound. Even after you had deciphered the code, you would still have to struggle through all the possible symbolic meanings to get to the heart of it and find the truth."

"And you are claiming you did?"

Seton nodded in agreement.

"Although there is no way right now for me to prove it to you beyond reciting history that only someone who has lived it would know. Can you just trust me in this Doctor? For tonight at least?"

I owed him *something* for his whisky. I raised a glass in agreement and he continued.

"As soon as I heard of the maladies afflicting the Lords I knew Moriarty was up to some mischief; but the nature of that plot escapes me even now. I do not believe it was done solely for the purpose of having you put under suspicion."

"Agreed," Holmes said. "Although it must suit his purposes to have me out of London for a while."

Holmes turned to me.

"Well, old friend. It seems we are deep in those murky waters I mentioned a while back. What say you? Shall we return to London and clear our names?"

"Certainly," I replied. "Although I don't know how that can be managed."

"Neither do I," Holmes said and laughed. "But with an immortal at our side how can we fail?"

Seton joined in the laughter. For a while we had quite forgotten our predicament, but we were brought back to earth with a bump when Seton motioned us to be quiet. Somewhere above us we heard shouting, as if coming from a far distance.

"Just keep quiet for a minute or two," Seton said. "It seems the Scotland Yard boys have finally slipped their bonds. But they'll never find us here. They think we're off and running in the hills, mark my words."

The sounds soon faded, leaving us sitting in silence. It seemed that Seton had been right in his assessment of the policemen's actions.

"Now gentlemen," Seton said once we were sure everything would stay quiet. "My cards are on the table. I know that I would like to take the attack to the bugger. How about you? Are you serious about returning to London and bearding the lion in his den?"

"Perfectly serious," Holmes replied. "I am tired of

slinking in shadows. I would like to make a triumphant entrance if possible, but with Lord Crawford's testimony hanging over our heads I do not see how it can be done."

Seton smiled.

"That is something I may be able to help with."

Seton left us for several minutes and returned dragging some heavy manacles and chains behind him.

"This old castle hasn't needed these for many years," he said. "But they may prove useful tonight."

He half-carried, half-dragged the chains over to the pentacle on the floor.

"I have been experimenting with a means to take the fight to my attacker," Seton said. "But I have been wary about trying it without someone here to help me in case it goes wrong. Tonight is the perfect opportunity, and might be the only chance we get."

He stepped completely into the pentacle and locked himself into the manacles.

"These chains will wrap twice around my body, if you would be so kind Doctor?"

I did as I was bidden, wrapping him in the chains, the weight of which almost buckled his knees. He sat down hard on the floor and nodded.

"Perfect. Even if he gets control of my body he will be unable to do much about it."

"If who gets control?" I asked, but I already knew the answer to that. Seton ignored me and looked towards Holmes.

"You knew the man. Will you be able to keep him talking for a while? If we can distract him, then I may be able to do some good at the other end in London."

Holmes nodded.

"I see. You plan to give him an opening so to speak – allow him into your body while you switch into Lord Crawford? I must admit to being baffled as to the how of this matter, but I shall take your word that it is possible. If it is Moriarty's spirit that turns up, I am sure we shall find plenty to talk about," Holmes said dryly.

Seton laughed. He seemed to do that more than any other man I have ever met, so much so that I had started to wonder if he wasn't actually quite mad.

"I never said it was possible," the Scotsman said. "I only said that I would try. I do not think the idea that I can emulate his trick has crossed Moriarty's mind, but if it has, he might be prepared for it and all that will happen is that I will sit on this cold floor for a while. We shall see what we shall see. Help yourself to my *uisque* gentlemen. This could prove to take a while as we need to wait until he renews his attack."

With that he fell quiet, sitting inside the pentacle with his eyes closed.

"I say Holmes," I whispered. "You are not taking any of this nonsense seriously are you?"

Holmes took so long to reply I thought he might be ignoring the question, and when he did reply it was in deadly earnest.

"I saw much on my travels in the East that has taught me never to underestimate the power inherent in the human will," he said. "And if anyone had the strength of will to pierce the veil of death, then surely Mortiarty is that man? At this point in proceedings, I am keeping an open mind, and I suggest you do the same Watson."

The absurdity of our situation did not escape me. We were somewhere deep under a Scottish Keep, with Lestrade looking for us overhead, watching a man who claimed to be immortal sitting inside a pentagram, wrapped in chains.

"We are rather far from the fireside in Baker Street," I said to myself.

Holmes chuckled.

"But at least we can still have a smoke."

I rolled us a cigarette each and we smoked in silence, all the while having an occasional glance towards the pentagram. Seton had been so quiet I thought he might be asleep but just as I reached the last puff of my cigarette, the Scotsman's body started to twitch violently as if he was having a seizure. I got off the bench, thinking to go to his aid, but Holmes held me back.

"No Watson. I think it has begun. Let me do any talking that is required."

Seton started to struggle ever more violently, but the chains held and he was unable to move. His head came up slowly and when he saw Holmes he smiled broadly.

"You have come further than I thought," he said. It was the same clipped English voice I had heard Crawford use back in Parliament, and it was quite a shock to the system to hear it again coming from the Scotsman's mouth. "And I see you have made some preparations in the event of my success."

He rattled the chains theatrically.

"What say you Holmes? Is this not my most creative endeavor thus far?"

Holmes made a long slow play of stubbing out his cigarette in the grate before replying.

"It is certainly a very creative act Mister Seton. You must have spent a long time in Moriarty's company to be able to mimic the voice so accurately. I particularly like the way you have captured the slight Northern accent that the man himself struggled so hard to hide. Leeds if I'm not mistaken?"

The chained figure – I cannot bring myself to call him Moriarty – laughed.

"Come Holmes, that is beneath even you. What would Seton have to gain by such deception? And does Seton know that you had a glass of whisky in one hand and a pipe in the other when you allowed a peer of the realm to leap out of a window? What about you Watson -- did I not call you *the faithful dog?* Did you forget that?"

Holmes waved a hand. "Parlor tricks do not impress me. Moriarty was a man of science. He would not stoop to the pretence of the existence of some kind of afterlife."

The sitting figure laughed again.

"If it is proof you want you only have to take your own

life; it is the simplest thing. A touch too much morphine should do it painlessly enough – certainly with less drama than throwing yourself off a waterfall."

He rattled the chains again.

"But come Holmes. Surely you have questions of me? Will you not attempt to uncover my plans? Will there be no dramatic pronouncements of how I will be caught and brought to justice? I think you'll find some difficulty in that area."

"If it is the matter in London of which you speak," Holmes said. "Lestrade is already convinced of our innocence in any wrongdoing. It is a misunderstanding; that is all Mister Seton. If you are seeking to profit from our discomfort I am afraid you will have a long wait."

The man in the pentacle laughed again.

"You mean to keep up this pretence? Very well then, so be it. But remember this night Holmes. There will come a time, and it will be soon, when you may wish you had asked more questions of me."

Holmes raised an eyebrow.

"I have learned all I need to know about you Seton; you are a liar and a charlatan, merely trying to profit from our reduced circumstances."

The sitting man's lips turned up in a snarl.

"Admit it Holmes, this time I have bested you."

It was Holmes' turn to laugh.

"And pray tell me," he said. "Which of us is currently sitting in chains?"

This time the chain rattling was not done for dramatic effect but was a serious attempt to test the strength of the bonds. It did not last long – the iron was old, but it was strong, and it held.

Holmes laughed again.

"Nice try Mister Seton, but I am afraid you have not got the accent quite right. Besides, it has been several years since I killed Moriarty. Why would he return now?"

The sitting figure went still, lifted his head and smiled.

"Why indeed? Now we come to the question you *really*

want to ask. But why should I help you with clues? No Holmes, you have much work to do if you are to stop me this time. I have the upper hand, and you are a fugitive from justice. I will be there to watch you hang," the sitting man said, then, as if a switch had been thrown, his head fell forward and the body slumped. This time when I moved to Seton's aid Holmes did not stop me.

Seton's eyes rolled up in their sockets and he fell in a dead faint, his head hitting the stone floor hard. It took me far too long to get him out of the chains and I had a bad moment or two when I thought he might have died on me, but when we got him over to the fire it became apparent he was still breathing. For how much longer that would be the case I was not entirely sure, for his heart was thudding so fast I thought his chest might burst. He breathed in short sharp gasps, and when he sat up suddenly and screamed I dashed near had a seizure myself.

"Whisky," he whispered. As a medical man I should have said no, but I had a feeling that my medical skills were not actually required. I was proved right seconds later when, after a slug of liquor that might have floored a horse, he was breathing regularly and his heartbeat had slowed to a walking pace. It took him several minutes after that however before he felt able to talk.

"I will not be doing that again in a hurry," he said. "But even if you did not learn anything at this end, I think you will find it was worthwhile when I tell you my tale." With that he stood, shakily at first, then with more confidence. "But I shall have to make haste, for you need to get out of here. Our opponent now knows where you are and, given his position, will surely use the information sooner rather than later. You must be off, and quickly."

Holmes had said nothing since the man's collapse in the pentacle, and he still did not speak, leaving it to me to voice my concerns.

"I cannot leave you man," I said. "You may look as strong as an ox, but I know just how close to death's door you have just come."

Seton smiled.

"I plan on being around a wee while longer Doctor, you may have no fear on that score. But we must split up, for he may attack at any time, and now that he has had access once, it may be easier for him from now on. I cannot chance giving him your location each time."

Holmes finally spoke.

"I can see the logic in that," he said. "And I sense the urgency. So, quickly Seton, tell me what you have learned."

"I do believe I was nearly lost completely," Seton said while filling a pipe from a tobacco box on the mantelpiece. "I drifted somewhere in a black infinity that was almost peaceful. Shadows drifted with me and some even tried to speak, but the voices were faint and indistinct, like shouts heard from a distance through a strong wind. The feeling of kinship, of brotherhood with those shadows was almost overpowering."

He paused, and seemed almost wistful before getting back on subject.

"But that part can wait for more a more conducive time, and after I myself have had time to think on the ramifications of what I experienced there. I shall attempt to stick to the important aspects of my experience. I was in that blackness for a *long* time. After what seemed an eternity I opened my eyes to look into a well-appointed office space. I realized that this must be Lord Crawford's office in the Lords, a room that I believe the good Doctor here is familiar with?"

He went on without waiting for a reply.

"I knew that I might not have much time, and indeed as it turns out I only just managed to complete the tasks. But I did accomplish three things, all of which are pertinent. My first step was to write a letter to Inspector Lestrade, saying that I had recanted my previous statement and that Sherlock Holmes did not in fact kill anyone. It was scrawled rather hastily, and it will not get you off completely of course, but it should sow sufficient confusion to buy you some time.

"I sealed the letter and took it out into the corridor where I made sure the young policeman there knew both what its contents were and to whom it should be delivered. His testimony to our conversation should also lead to further confusion."

Seton had finally got his pipe lit to his satisfaction and was puffing away merrily. He showed no signs that he had been near death just minutes before. I still doubted he was immortal, but he did seem to have a truly remarkable constitution.

"I have saved the last pieces of information for last," he continued. "For I am unsure of their import. As I was acutely aware that my time might be short I returned to the Lord's office and started to go through the items on his desk, in the hope that there might be some indication of his plans.

"I found a note from the Home Secretary asking for recommendations on dealing with '*the current Irish situation*', a large file which contained detailed diagrams and costing for the building of the new Central London underground line, and a railway timetable for the Fenchurch Street to Southend line. Make of that what you will."

"Is there anything else you remember?" Holmes asked.

Seton shook his head.

"I was about to start on the desk drawers when I felt something *tug* at me. The next thing I knew I was back here struggling for breath and in urgent need of *uisque*."

Holmes went quiet again and took on a look that I knew meant a long period of contemplation was looming; one that we scarce had time for. Seton had also spotted Holmes' silence.

"I was serious when I said you must leave... and quickly," Seton reminded us. "I need to stay here, but I will do all I can to help. I may even be able to come to your aid at an opportune moment if the chance arises."

Seton suddenly seemed imbued with a sense of purpose. He led us back up out of the underground tunnels and made us wait in the shadows while he checked that the police were indeed gone. We then made our way quickly back into the small library where we had left Lestrade and the others – there was no sign of them bar some lengths of rope left lying on the floor. The shotgun was still leaning against the wall where Seton had left it earlier.

Seton saw me looking at the weapon.

"Do not even consider taking that with you," he said with a grin. "You'll do yourself a mischief before you get a hundred yards lugging that beast. Let's get you something more useful shall we?"

Twenty minutes later we were on our way down the dark driveway. I carried the Gladstone bag; heavier now, having gained some food and ale to help us on the journey. Before leaving I tried to persuade Seton to reconsider and join us, but he had already retreated back into a muttering reverie and even as we said good-bye at the door of the Keep he was reciting his litany.

I turned and gave one last wave, but he did not acknowledge it and was soon lost from sight in the gloom.

CHAPTER 4

Dawn broke to find us walking along a high moorland road somewhere south of Comrie on a path that Holmes informed me would eventually bring us to the outskirts of Dunblane and thence south to Kincardine where we would finally be able to cross the Forth. I was glad to be with someone with knowledge of the geography for, apart from the salmon runs of the Tweed and the Dee, I had little sense of my way around Scotland outside the cities.

Holmes seemed thoughtful but in good spirits, which is more than could be said for myself. I was finding it hard to come to terms with what I had witnessed in the chamber under the Keep, and daylight brought with it a return to some kind of rational thinking on my part. The more the sun rose, the more the events took on a dream like quality and I began to suspect that we had been hoodwinked completely by a master illusionist.

I explained my misgivings to Holmes, expecting the great rationalist himself to agree with me, but to my astonishment he held to a completely opposite viewpoint.

"No Watson," he said. "I have no doubt at all that it was Moriarty I was speaking to, albeit from Seton's mouth. There were certain nuances in his accent and patterns of speech that immediately identified him to me. He has indeed found a way to pierce the veil of death."

"But surely…"

I was given no time to continue, as Holmes spoke over me, as if to himself.

"Trust me Watson, he has a bigger plan than just ruining you and I. We are merely a diversion, a way to keep Scotland Yard looking elsewhere while he puts his machinations into action."

I asked Holmes to halt for a while and we sat by the side of the track where we had been walking. I rolled fresh cigarettes and we smoked as Holmes continued.

"It is not power he wants, Watson. With Moriarty it was never the power, despite the fact that he could use his position in the Lords to many purposes. No, his criminal tendencies will out, even now. I suspect he has something big in mind, something that his new situation makes him uniquely qualified for. I just have not hit on the heart of the matter yet. But I will Watson… I will."

When we set off again he let me in on the next part of the plan.

"We must return to London," he said. "And begin a surveillance on his Lordship. That is our only recourse now – foil his plan and we may be able to force a confrontation that will unmask the whole affair. We can only hope that Seton's actions while in London last night will work in our favor."

I admit I was still skeptical of the whole affair. I could not bring myself to believe in the transfer of personality in such an esoteric fashion as had supposedly been shown to us. But it seemed that Holmes intended to proceed as if it were fact, and I decided that I must play along, and see the thing through to the conclusion. After all, I did not have many other options, as handing myself in at that point would have served no purpose at all now that we had burned our bridges with Lestrade.

We spent two more days getting as far as Edinburgh thanks to a lot of walking on country pathways and some fortuitous carts of produce driven by farmers that happened to be going in our direction. There was also rather too much dodging through hedgerows and slogging through muddy fields to avoid being seen, so much so that I'm afraid our clothing took rather a beating in the process. By the time we arrived in the capital we were once more threadbare, mud-strewn and bedraggled.

Holmes however had an answer for that, and as he had done in Glasgow, he led me straight to a bar. This one was in the Grassmarket in the shadow of the Castle, and reaching it needed a degree of stealth and the luck of arriving during some heavy rain that kept the streets quiet. I felt somewhat like a drowned rat however when he led me into the bar's doorway. He rapped three times and we were allowed entry into an empty bar.

Holmes was greeted like an old friend by the barkeep. Over a bowl of very welcome hot soup and more ale we discovered that we had become quite a pair of notorious celebrities. News of our escapade in Comrie, and Lestrade's humiliation in being tied up, had reached the press. Holmes suspected Seton's hand in that matter as there was also a tale being told of our escape via a boat to Skye and then heading for France. I supposed that particular tale appealed to Seton's sense of fun, being a mirror of Bonnie Prince Charlie's own flight from the country. There was also news that Lord Crawford had recanted his statement of our guilt, then just as suddenly changed his mind again. My skepticism regarding what had happened in the Keep was slowly being chipped away.

We stayed in that bar for three days, during which Holmes made plans for our return to London and I caught up with some much-needed sleep in a room upstairs. When not abed I drank more ale and smoked more cigarettes than were good for me. My only contact with the greater world outside was through the newspapers. We made the front page of *The Scotsman* which reported our escape from Skye as if it were a fact, complete with an eyewitness report from a local fisherman who had *seen* us getting aboard a boat in the dead of night. There was a quote from Lestrade, who was also in Skye, who said he would be *"pursuing Holmes across the continent if that is what it took to bring him to justice."* An accompanying satirical cartoon showing two rather fine drawings of Lord Crawford arguing with each other about our guilt and innocence. I was starting to wonder just how close to the truth that might be.

I was near to climbing the walls with boredom and frustration by the time Holmes announced he was ready to start the journey south. The announcement came on his return from a trip into the New Town. He did not tell me where he had been, but he waved a sheaf of papers at me.

"Our job is much tougher than we originally thought

Watson." He took a cigarette from me and joined me by the fire before continuing. "I have been researching the Seton family and have found an alarming fact. There exists, in London of all places, a whole scion of the family descended directly from Angus himself. I missed it earlier because I was focusing on Lords and minor dignitaries, but this branch of the family has its roots firmly in the working class. A bastard son of Angus' went to Ireland in the late Sixteenth Century – and it is from him that the line descends. I have found that there are at least twenty men in the East End that can claim direct descent. And if I can find them, then so can Moriarty."

"But why would he?" I asked. "What use would he have of any of them when he could have a Lord of the realm or, if you believe in it, the body of the immortal head of the clan?"

Holmes looked grave.

"It is merely one more thing we have to consider. I have made contact with Mycroft," he said. "It seems that our good Lord Crawford is not a well man and has been confined to his rooms. Mycroft says that the man is not happy at the prospect, whether it is when he is employing a Scottish accent or not. Mycroft also says that there is now more than enough doubt about the so-called murder that, if it ever came to trial, the case would be dismissed immediately."

"Then we are free to return?"

Holmes shook his head.

"Mycroft is as yet unwilling to admit to the possibility that Crawford is, at least some of the time, actually Moriarty. Until I can *prove* that fact to his satisfaction he will not call Scotland Yard off the scent. No, we must return incognito if we are to have any success at all in clearing our names.

"I'm afraid more mummery is called for Watson," he said. "I would have liked to return to town openly, but I'm afraid that there has been too much excitement and noise around the case for that to be possible. What say you? Shall we return to our earlier personas… or would you entertain the thought of something rather more exotic?"

I made the trip to London in the guise of an eighty-year-old Churchman; slightly deaf and mostly cantankerous. It was a role I found remarkably easy to play given my growing dissatisfaction with this case. Holmes did not help my mood by being relentlessly cheerful all the way South, as if delighted to be returning to familiarity.

The only thing that stopped my mood from descending completely into the depths was the fact that the journey went smoothly. No one took much notice of us, and even the few policemen we saw seemed to have lost interest in looking for the escaped murderers. Holmes judged that there was now a common belief that we had fled to the continent and by the time we left York behind I was starting to believe him.

I had expected more policemen to be waiting at Euston on our arrival back in the city but there was only a single officer on the concourse, and he paid us no heed whatsoever. This only seemed to embolden Holmes. He headed straight for Baker Street.

He was not so indiscreet as to enter through the front entrance but went round to the rear and opened the scullery door. He almost received a blow on his head for his trouble, for Mrs. Hudson was in the room and, taking him for an intruder, aimed a skillet at his head. Fortunately he managed to duck in time, but he had to remove his false whiskers before she recognized us and put the pan down.

If she was happy to see us she did not show it at first, berating us, firstly for our stupidity for being caught in the trap and, secondly, for not letting her know that we were safe and not in fact absconded to the continent. Immediately after that she burst into tears and only a cup of strong tea revived her to something like her former efficient self. We were forcibly told to sit at her kitchen table. We told her our tale while she moved around us preparing a meal.

"I'll soon have you back to normal," she said, as if we were somehow starved and wasted. Indeed it seemed she would attempt to do it all at once as she plied us with scones, cream, jam and several cups of her special strong tea. Holmes let me do most of the talking, only interjecting where he thought I had made an error or had mis-remembered something. Mrs. Hudson listened intently, then surprised us.

"I've heard of him," she said. "He was always known as wee auld man Seton. There are plenty of stories told in Scotland about his exploits over the years. My grandmother, God rest her soul, even swore to us that she met him in Edinburgh once back in the '40s. She said he was a prodigious liar, but very charming in his own way."

Having that connection in her own personal history meant that the rest of my tale did not sound outlandish to her in the slightest, and where I had been expecting disbelief I got instead a calm acceptance. I finished with a question as to where we went from here.

"Mister Holmes will find a way," she said with a quiet confidence I did not quite share. And she proved herself quite adept at subterfuge when she installed thick curtains in the main rooms of our apartment. Once these were closed she was confident that no light, and therefore no sign of our presence, would show from the outside.

So it was we were able to achieve some relaxation amid all the comforts of home. But if I had expected to be allowed to enjoy an evening at ease Holmes soon put me right when it came round to nightfall.

"I intend to make a foray to the East End in search of information about the Seton offshoots. We must ascertain whether Moriarty is aware of them or indeed whether they have not already fallen under his malign influence. Are you game?"

"Now?" I said, and Holmes must have heard the reluctance in my voice. He laughed.

"Stay here then old friend, with your warm fire and your pipe and slippers. I shall report on my adventures on my return."

Of course he knew I would rise to the taunting. Ten

minutes later I was at his side as we left the apartment and made for the scullery door.

Our only attempt to hide our appearance was in the wearing of long overcoats and hats with wide brims pulled low over our brows. We scarcely needed to have made the effort, as it was a damp night with the air full of fog and drizzle, and anyone out on the streets was more intent on hurrying home against the weather than in looking too closely at us.

Which was just as well as Holmes' burst of confidence did not stretch far enough to consider taking a carriage. I resigned myself to the prospect of a long, wet, walk. I became rather glad of the overcoat and hat over the next hour as we strode through mostly quiet streets headed for Whitechapel. We took a northerly route to keep away from the busier streets near the city center and the only time we met with any great density of people was when we skirted the Angel Islington before turning south and east.

"What are we hoping to find?" I asked Holmes as we approached the Liverpool Street area. At first I was not sure he would answer. He had been quiet for most of the walk so far, not so much taciturn as lost in contemplation. In anyone else it might be thought rudeness but I had become accustomed to long silences over the years. In fact, on some occasions I have even been known to welcome them. On this particular night, Holmes decided to reply.

"I'm looking for a clue," he said. "A means by which we might start to make some headway against the obstacles Moriarty has so successfully put in our path. I hope to find some of the Seton offshoots, MacAllan as they are now known, and question them, or at least discover whether there have been any recent unusual bouts of *sleeping sickness* in the family."

And at that he went quiet again, walking faster now as we approached our target.

Our first port of call was a pawnbroker's shop on a corner opposite the old East India Company warehouse at

Devonshire Square.

It was a veritable Aladdin's cave, containing more jewelry than I had seen outside Bond Street, row after row of brass and stringed musical instruments and, behind a heavy mahogany counter, a back chamber that seemed to be full of rich furs and overcoats.

Holmes was obviously known to the proprietor, and was greeted warmly.

"Long time no see Mr. Holmes," the small man said. He could have been any age from sixty to ninety years old, stooped and bent so much that he needed the use of a cane to keep him upright. He wheezed when he spoke, like a deflating rugger ball, but his eyes were clear and bright, and I suspected there was not much that got past him.

Holmes spent some time in pleasantries before asking about the whereabouts of any members of the MacAllan family. The old man sucked at his teeth and waved his free hand in a seesaw manner.

"Here and there Mr. Holmes, here and there if you catch my drift?"

Fortunately Holmes understood the man's intent more clearly than I did. Money changed hands and we were given directions to a public bar that I vaguely knew near the Effingham Theatre.

"But beware Mr. Holmes," the pawnbroker said. "They like a drink those lads, and when they're in their cups they also like to fight."

Holmes thanked the man and we went back out into the night. The rain was heavier now, and we hurried along the narrow cobbled streets to the bar, our feet splashing in newly formed puddles.

Holmes stopped outside the bar door. It was apparent that the place was busy, the sound of raucous banter seeping through the thick external door.

"And now we must take a risk Watson," he said. "There will be people inside who know us, and they are not the kind to look the other way if they think the police might pay for their information. We may end up paying dearly for anything we learn. But I believe this is our only course of action. Are you with me?"

"Always old chap," I replied with more bravado than I felt at that moment. "Lead on."

The bar was another huge barn full of mirrors, mahogany and chandeliers, much like the Horseshoe Bar in Glasgow, but on a far grander scale. I had rarely seen a more opulent establishment, even in the palaces of the Raj. It was also full of people seeming intent on getting inebriated as fast as they were able. Street girls worked the room and smartly dressed men from the City mingled with market workers and railwaymen still grimy from their day's labour. Half a dozen bar staff were being kept busy supplying a constant flow of ale and gin, and a space around a card table was the only quiet area in the whole place.

When we entered several people looked our way, but no one looked twice and Holmes seemed satisfied it was safe to stay, at least for a while.

"I'll go and ask some questions Watson, you keep an eye open for anyone paying too much attention to either yourself or to me."

I retired to the bar, ordered a jug of ale, lit a pipe and watched Holmes as he made his way around the patrons; a tap on the shoulder here, a whispered question there. All of his moves were so subtle that no one took offence and no one noticed that he was slowly but surely homing in on a target.

His attentions soon focussed on three men in particular. All three looked skittish, their eyes straying anywhere but on Holmes' face as he sat at their table, even after he had ordered a fresh round of drinks brought to them. Holmes did not give them time to think, bombarding first one then another with questions. It took around an hour during which time I made some inroads into the ale. The barman was on the verge of pouring me a refill when Holmes rose and came back to my side.

"Well," he said. "We have a story, although I am not yet sure what to make of it. But first, let us take our leave. Too many people have seen us already. I feel as if we are *watched* too closely."

We left the bar. The door shut behind us – and at the same moment I heard a *pop* and a chunk of wood flew. We were under fire again.

Without pause Holmes was off and running even as I understood what was happening. As he had at King's Cross he made straight for where he guessed the gunman to be. I held my place, just long enough to hear the next *pop* and see a shadow move in the darkness near the entrance to the Effingham Theatre. I thought of calling out, but I saw that Holmes had also spotted the movement and was headed that way at full tilt. Another shot *pinged* off the cobbles near my left foot then I too was running after Holmes.

He reached the theatre some ten yards ahead of me and by the time I too reached the entrance he had already gone inside. I cursed when I reached for my pocket and remembered that I had left a revolver behind in Baker Street. I padded inside as quietly as I could manage, trying to keep to the shadows and not allow my outline to be silhouetted in the doorway. No one shot me.

The theatre foyer lay in deep darkness and I was forced to stand still for long seconds to let my eyes adjust. The business had gone into liquidation some months before, which would explain the slight smell of mildew and the sound of water dripping from my left. The place was obviously already falling into disrepair. I wondered if any of the light fittings actually worked, but that was a moot point as I was not about to try to find out.

"Holmes?" I said in a stage whisper, then immediately regretted it as a *pop* followed straight away and glass broke in a mirror just behind me. I had enough sense about me to move to one side and keep quiet. Silence descended again.

I was feeling exposed, stuck too far into the open in the foyer. I started to shuffle sideward with my arm outstretched, hoping to reach a wall. Instead my hand found something cold and damp and I almost cried out, thinking it was our attacker, but some more investigation proved it to be a heavy velvet curtain that covered an entrance into the theatre proper. When I carefully pulled it aside I immediately felt a cooler breeze on my cheek, and I heard the sound of footsteps on wooden boards.

There was another unmistakable *pop*, a scuffle of feet and a cry of pain. My heart sank, for I thought for sure that Holmes had been hit. But it was my friend's voice that came next through the dark.

"Get down here quickly Watson. I have him."

I followed the sound of his voice, feeling my way down one of the gangways between the rows of seats. As I got closer to the source of the noises I realized I was starting to make out shapes in the darkness, and after several seconds I could make out the stage ahead of me. Holmes knelt, holding down a prone figure on the floor. The other thing I noticed as I got closer was the sound of sobbing, low and soft like a child who was trying to be brave and hold it in.

"Give me a hand here Watson," Holmes said. "I fear I have broken his arm."

Holmes' *victim* proved to be a youth, barely out of his teens by the look of him and dressed in the cheap woolens and heavy work-boots typical of a local market worker. He had his eyes screwed up in pain and his arm had indeed been broken; white bone showed through a tear in the skin just above the wrist. It was also obvious that this lad was the gunman – the weapon lay on the floor beside him, an air gun, as Holmes had surmised.

"Do you know him?" I asked Holmes.

He shook his head.

"I do not, and he does not resemble anyone who has been mentioned to me tonight. But if he is not a MacAllan then I will eat this hat."

"Jimmy MacAllan, that's me sir," the boy said, grimacing through the pain but suddenly latching onto something familiar in the mention of his name.

"Can you get up lad?" I asked him. "We have to get you to a hospital and get that break seen to."

He tried to shuffle away from us on his backside, banged his arm on the stage and yelped, like a kicked dog.

"Please, don't hurt me again," he whimpered, his obvious East-End roots showing in his speech. Suddenly I felt almost guilty at how we had treated him. I bent to take him by his good arm.

He looked up, fear in his eyes, then suddenly they went out of focus and his mouth went slack – only for a second or so until he smiled broadly.

"That is enough of that," he said, and this time it was in that clipped voice I had first heard back in Lord Crawford's office, and then again under Seton's Keep in Comrie. Three separate bodies, but it was becoming obvious to me that the voice always came from one source, Moriarty himself.

"I only let the boy speak to show you who is in charge here," he said. He looked up at Holmes. "I would advise you to stay away from this side of town," he said, and winked, "It is not safe... as this boy is about to find out."

"No!" Holmes shouted, but his rage was to prove impotent, for there was nothing either he or I could do about what happened next. The boy's eyes went dead again. He started to thrash, feet pounding a rhythm on the wooden boards of the stage. Spittle frothed and flecked from his lips and blood bubbles showed where he had bitten through his tongue. This I *did* know how to deal with – or so I thought.

"Hold him Holmes, he's having a seizure."

But no amount of holding the lad down was going to save him. I was looking in his face when his eyes filled with blood. His neck muscles strained one last time and his mouth gaped. I thought he might scream, but no sound came. He fell back, head hitting the boards of the stage with a sickening soft thud. I checked to make sure but I already knew there would be no pulse. The lad was dead.

"Come Watson," Holmes said softly, taking me by the arm. "We can do no more here."

I shrugged him away.

"We cannot just leave him lying here," I said. "It's not right."

"There is little *right* about this case old friend," Holmes said. "All we can do is ensure that someone who will look after him finds him first. We shall make an anonymous report to the Yard later. But for now we must go. Moriarty knows we are here – there might be more gunmen where this lad came from."

I allowed him to lead me out into the street, and I followed him at a steady pace as we headed back to Baker Street. All the way the lad's dead blood-filled eyes stared at me in my mind's eye.

It was only once we were back in the apartments and settled by the fire with a snifter and a pipe that Holmes talked about the events of the night.

"We are getting somewhere Watson," he said after getting his own pipe lit. "Moriarty would not warn us off unless it were so. And it is indicative of *something* that he has not informed the police that we are back in London, for if he had, I have no doubt Lestrade would be here already to carry out the promises that were made in Comrie. No… we are getting somewhere."

"Did you learn anything of import in the bar?" I asked.

"It was a tortuous process," he started. "But yes, I was eventually able to tease out a thread of narrative from the three men who, in case you had not already surmised, were MacAllans by descent, although rather far removed from the original strain; too far indeed to be under Moriarty's influence directly. But I am getting ahead of myself, in much the same way as the three in the bar tended to. I shall attempt to summarize for you Watson but please, be patient with me, for I had a great deal of information to process, some of it contradictory in nature.

"The MacAllan's tale begins in the early Nineties. Of course it begins much earlier than that, with Seton himself, but we shall skip over that for you already know as much as you need to at the moment about the deeper history. We start in the East End, with a family of itinerant laborers, small time thieves and opportunists. As far as I can gather they are rather a large clan now, but some of them are considered more *influential* than others are, being able to claim direct descent from the *auld country* stock. They are a tight-knit bunch by nature as are many of their type in the East End, and do not take easily to prying questions from strangers. But, sometime in early ninety-one, one such stranger appeared with enough money to loosen tongues. I suspect that man to have been Moriarty himself, these encounters taking place in the months immediately preceding our encounter at the Falls.

"The man was particularly interested in genealogy, and proved able to spend rather large sums of money to be informed of family histories. It was not much later that the family members started to suffer what they call *the sleeping lurgy*. By now you will recognize the symptoms - an unconscious state, the mouthing of words and the memory lapse on awakening. Many of the family were struck in this manner over a period of some weeks.

"But it is what happened next that most concerns us," Holmes said gravely. "In May of that year a number of members of the family walked out of the East End and have not been seen again beyond rumored sightings in the City just these past few months. You see what this means of course?"

And of course I was almost as much in the dark as I had been at the start of his tale before it hit me.

"You think Moriarty is somehow using the bodies of these missing people to travel around town?"

Holmes nodded.

"My fear is that by using them as vehicles he has been able to travel and undertake his nefarious plans, all in complete anonymity. I believe he has been working under my very nose all this time without giving a hint of his presence until now. The mere fact that he chose to set a trap for us at this juncture tells me that his plans must be close to fruition. Coupled with the fact that he made another attempt on us this very night means that we must work fast Watson, for time may be short. Get some sleep tonight, for tomorrow we must seek out the missing MacAllans.''

Finding the missing men proved to be easier said than done. We spent a most frustrating week clad in a variety of disguises, walking the length and breadth of the East End in search of any mention of the MacAllan family. It was only when our search took us towards Wapping that we started to hear stories. Our first intimation came over lunch in *The Prospect of Whitby*. It was a bar that Holmes and I had previously visited several times on cases, and now I worried that our disguises would not pass muster, but we were mostly ignored as we supped some particularly fine ale. We fell into conversation with two fish merchants at the bar.

I sat in silence and watched Holmes work. I continue to be amazed by his ability to blend seamlessly with the character he is portraying and converse at an equal level with any of London's social strata. After spending quarter of an hour relating a completely fictitious but gripping account of a trip across the Channel in a gale he had the men eating out of his hand. During the next hour we got our first hints of the criminal activities of Sad-Eye Joe MacAllan, active in these parts but only having risen to prominence in recent times. The way the man was described; Irish, fiery and quick-witted, but with a strange tendency to drift into lapses of forgetfulness, had me convinced we were indeed on to something with this line of enquiry.

Holmes obviously thought the same. He subtly but firmly quizzed the men and teased out a thread of criminal actions ranging from petty theft to grand larceny, all of which involved Sad-Eye Joe and a small clan of family members. None of the family was ever seen together, and all seemed to suffer sudden bouts of the *sleeping sickness*. The fishermen had not heard whether Joe was plotting anything in particular.

"But it wouldna' surprise me," the elder of the fishermen said. "When somebody suddenly gets ambitious later in life like that who knows what can happen?"

Neither of the fishermen could say exactly where we

might find any of these MacAllans, only that they were usually *around*. But Holmes had a smile on his face when we finally parted company with the men at the bar. We took our ales out onto the small balcony that overlooked the river and lit up smokes. Holmes made sure there was no one in hearing range before speaking.

"My hunch was right Watson. Find this family and we shall have gone a long way towards uncovering Moriarty's plot."

I knew the signs. Holmes now had but a single focus and, like a terrier with a rat would not let go until the job was done.

For the next three days I followed him around some of the most miserable parts of the city I have ever had the misfortune to visit. We listened to tall tales and eyewitness accounts where the *sleeping sickness* was attributed to witchcraft, poison and even the work of old Hob himself. Holmes filed each tale away in its appropriate compartment in that regimented mind of his and moved on. We followed an inward-tending spiral, deep into the heart of the East End, each night hearing more and more about the exploits, mostly criminal in nature, of Sad-Eye Joe. And each morning, as we tried to gain some rest back in Baker Street, Holmes sat in the chair by the fire, smoking his favorite Meerschaum and staring into space, so still that an observer may have thought that he himself was suffering from the very malady we were investigating.

Finally on the fourth evening we made a breakthrough, learning of an address in Shoreditch that three of the MacAllan family members had been seen entering. We arrived in the area at dusk and spent a long hour watching for any sign of activity, none of which was forthcoming. The building itself was a three-story sandstone dwelling, turned black with smoke and soot. It looked like it may at one time have been a warehouse, as there were indeed many such similar buildings in the area, but this one had been converted into a warren of small apartments, cheap housing for poorly paid workers in the local markets. Most of the windows showed no light at all. A single candle flickered on the second floor, but no shadows moved in the room beyond the whole time we were there. Finally Holmes could contain himself any longer.

"Come Watson," he said. "Let us see if tonight is the night we can force him into a confrontation."

I followed him across the street to the doorway. He rapped hard on the door. There was no reply, no sign of movement at all from inside. I made to turn away, but Holmes had other ideas. He turned the handle and put his shoulder to the door. It gave way before him with a loud crack that echoed around the street. I had a quick look round before following Holmes inside; no one seemed to be paying us any attention, and no one shot at me, which I took as a good sign.

Holmes hushed me to be quiet as soon as we entered a long narrow hallway. Unlike the hallway in Seton's Keep in Comrie, this place felt somehow *alive*. The hairs at the nape of my neck rose and I was immediately on the defensive. The atmosphere was stifling; hot and sultry, reminding me strangely of monsoon season in Northern India. Some light found its way in from the street outside, but further inside the dwelling everything was dark and quiet. I was immediately reminded of the events in the Effingham Theatre.

"Is this wise old chap?" I whispered. The sibilant sounds echoed around us, whistling like wind under an ill-fitting door. Holmes hushed me to be silent once more. We padded softly through a series of empty rooms on the ground floor. There was some evidence of recent occupation, but no one had either lit a fire or prepared food there for several days at least. I was starting to think we were on a fool's errand as we climbed the stairs to the first floor.

It was darker here, and the shadows seemed to run around the rooms without any discernable light source to drive them. Or maybe it was just my imagination; this case had certainly awoken a superstitious corner of my mind I had thought left behind in childhood. When we reached a door and heard heavy breathing coming from beyond, the scared boy I had been did not seem very far away at all.

Holmes had no such qualms. He moved quietly into the room and was soon lost from sight in the dark. Several seconds passed, with no change in the timbre or intensity of the breathing. It sounded like a small group of people, all of them asleep. Even before Holmes called me inside with a stage whisper I knew what I was going to encounter.

Chapter 5

It was only a small room, some ten feet square, but somehow twelve people had managed to find space to sleep in swaddled bundles on the floor, so closely packed that I had to carefully pick my way between them.

Of course I say *sleeping*, but these prone figures proved, to a man, to be in the same almost cataleptic state I was coming to recognize, with all of the same symptoms save one. There was no mouth movement apparent, no attempts at forming words. They just lay there, eyes open, staring vacantly into space. The air felt heavier here, stale food mixed with body odor and the rank acrid stench of clothes worn far too long without washing. I had to cover my mouth with a handkerchief when kneeling to inspect the bodies; that is how I thought of them, for any semblance of personality was completely absent. They were all of them male, with ages ranging from the late teens through to forty at a guess, but there was no sign of the one we had heard described as Sad-Eye Joe.

After a few minutes Holmes motioned that we should leave the room. I was glad to agree. We went out onto the upstairs landing where the air was less foul.

"This cannot be, Holmes," I said, keeping my voice low. "Surely even Moriarty can only control one other man at a time?"

Holmes looked grave.

"There is much about this case that goes against sense Watson," he said. "But I fear this is even worse than I imagined. I think that these poor wretches here are completely lost; their essence, their souls if you like, having moved on, or been forced on, leaving only the husks behind for the puppeteer to play with at his whim."

It took me several seconds to come to terms with what Holmes had said, so far was it from my normal frame of reference as a medical practitioner.

"If that is true, then it is monstrous," I said, and I am afraid that, in my anger, I allowed my voice to rise far beyond the whispers we had been conversing in. A loud moan answered me from the dark room.

Holmes took me by the arm and led me further from the doorway.

"We must keep our presence here quiet," he said softly. "If Moriarty knows we have been here then the game is up. But on the other hand, if we can observe, and follow these poor souls about any business he might have them do, then we can crack this case and bring it to resolution."

The very thought appalled me, and I would have told Holmes so in no uncertain manner, but he was already making his way back downstairs and I was loath to spend more time than was necessary standing alone there in the dark. I followed, taking care to tread lightly, listening at every step for any sign that someone might wake. But I reached the front door with no further mishap.

Holmes was on the doorstep waiting.

"We shall need to work in shifts," he said. "I cannot trust this to anyone else outside you and I. We shall find a room overlooking this spot, keep watch for anyone entering, and follow anyone that leaves. Agreed?"

"I am more inclined to call in the authorities," I said. "We could after all be dealing with some disease with which I am not familiar?"

Holmes snorted impatiently.

"Rubbish, Watson, and you know it. You have seen enough already to know exactly who is behind this. Will you help me catch him, or must I do this alone?"

Of course, when he put it like that, I could not refuse him.

That same evening we took a room opposite the building, making sure we got a spot where we could watch the comings and goings without being observed ourselves.

It was to be a longer vigil than either of us had imagined.

By the end of the second day boredom had set in. We took turns sleeping in the saggy bed that dominated one whole side of the room while the other sat by the window and watched for any sign of activity. Between us we got through a prodigious amount of tobacco, and Mrs. Hudson had made three trips already to deliver hampers of food to sustain us. Still, time dragged somewhat, more so when either of us was asleep, or when the black mood took Holmes and he went quiet. As an old soldier I was used to long periods of inactivity between bursts of action, but the tedium of it got to Holmes and eventually he started to fret.

"I may have misjudged the situation, Watson," he said for maybe the fourth time in as many hours. "We should be out looking for Sad-Eye Joe, not cooped up in here watching over the half-dead."

I will admit there had been times over the last few hours where I would have agreed with him wholeheartedly, but in my mind's eye I kept seeing the dead lad on the stage in the Effingham. I was not yet ready to abandon these others to a similar fate if it could be avoided.

It was almost dark again but we had decided not to show any light from our room in case our presence was noted. So it came to be that I was sitting in the dark on the corner of the bed, smoking yet another pipe of tobacco. I looked up when Holmes pulled the thin curtain aside to better see down into the street. I moved to his side and stared down. There was just enough light from the recently lit gas lamps to see what was happening below. Someone had just come out of the house across the road, a stooped figure heavily wrapped in several layers of clothes. A makeshift hood had been pulled over the head, obscuring the face, but from the general build I surmised this to be one of the younger men I had examined in the room. Quite how they survived for so long in that state I was completely unable to comprehend, and I had never expected to see any of them alive again, never mind out on the street and walking around.

"Finally," Holmes said. "Some action. Stay here, Watson. I will follow our man. You must watch in case anything else happens. I will return as quickly as I can."

With that I was left alone in the dark room with only my pipe for company.

The night passed slowly, made even more so by Holmes' absence. I had to open the window and let some fresh air in for the stuffy heat threatened to send me asleep. Even then I was hard pushed to keep my eyes open. As the night wore on and there was no activity forthcoming I found my mind wandering, turning over aspects of the case. I always returned to that single image I could not seem to let go, of the dead lad in the theatre, and the blood-filled eyes staring up at me.

Sometime later I came awake with a start, immediately annoyed that I had let myself down; let Holmes down. And on looking into the street I saw that I had roused myself just in time. A swaddled figure crossed the street from somewhere below me and went into the building opposite. At first I thought it was Holmes himself, for there was something about the bearing that I recognized, but this was a stockier, shorter man than my friend.

I wondered whether it was another member of the MacAllan clan, possibly even one flushed out by whatever Holmes was up to. But this newcomer's intent was much more sinister, and rapidly became clear when, only seconds after he entered the building, one of the upstairs windows smashed sending a tinkle of glass down to the cobbles. Red and yellow flames immediately showed, lapping around the window frame.

Someone intended to burn the unconscious men.

I could not sit idly by and watch mass murder be committed under my nose. I had my revolver in hand as I sped downstairs and across to the building opposite. Flames now rose from three of the windows above and a rising clamor grew in the street as the fire was spotted. I knew it would not be long before action was taken, for a fear of a conflagration in the narrow streets was ever present and something the locals were most vigilant in preventing. But they would not be able to respond fast enough to save the sleeping men. Without a pause for thought I ran into the building.

The hallway beyond was lit in flickering red from the stairwell and I could see immediately that it was going to be almost impossible for me to reach the room where the men slept.

"Fire!" I called at the top of my lungs. There were answering calls from outside, but inside the building there was only the crackle and roar as fire took ever greater hold. I went to the foot of the stairs and was about to head up in an attempt to at least save one man if I could when I was met by a figure coming down. He was no more than a silhouette backed by flame. The upstairs area was now fully aflame, and black smoke billowed overhead, further obscuring my view. I felt smoke tickle in my throat and nasal passages. Time was getting short.

"Thank Heavens, are there any others with you?" I said, before I remembered the man I had seen coming in.

"I doubt that Heaven has anything to do with it," a voice said. It was a soft Scottish accent. The figure turned sideways, his profile suddenly outlined against the fire and smoke. It could only be one man… Lord Crawford. I was so astonished that I neglected to defend myself as he raised a hand, and I saw the stick he wielded too late. A sharp blow to the head sent me down to blackness.

Coming back out of the darkness proved to be hard work, like struggling uphill into a high wind. It felt like a drummer pounded a beat in my ear and my eyes were heavy and tired. I heard the crackle of fire and jerked myself awake.

To my astonishment I came to sitting at the fireside in the apartment in Baker Street. Holmes sat opposite, out of disguise and clad in evening dress. He raised an eyebrow as I sat up and groaned.

"Good to see you are back in the land of the living old friend," he said.

I tasted smoke at my lips and smelled it on my clothes.

"What happened?" I asked.

He laughed, but there was little humor there.

"I was rather hoping you could tell me. Mrs. Hudson found you in the scullery, slouched in a chair. You gave her rather a shock, and you're lucky she held back from using the skillet on you."

It all came back to me in a flash.

"It was Crawford," I said. "The blaggard hit me. Though how I got to be back here I do not know."

Holmes raised an eyebrow again.

"It seems we both have stories to tell of this night's work," he said. "But first, I suggest you get yourself out of that disguise and into some clean clothes. I'll get Mrs. Hudson to bring up an early breakfast and we can swap stories."

I made my way to the bathroom and spent some time recovering my composure. My eyes kept getting drawn to a fresh bruise and lump on my left brow. It was tender to the touch and throbbed constantly, but the pain was bearable, and would soon be made less so with liberal consumption of some brandy.

I rejoined Holmes in the sitting room already feeling somewhat refreshed. He had been as good as his word and there was a plate of poached eggs and toast waiting for me that I took to with some gusto. Then, over brandy and a pipe we brought each other up to date.

In truth it did not take me long to tell my side of the tale, for I remembered nothing I have not already related here, having no memory at all of any journey from Shoreditch to Baker Street. But Holmes listened to it all most intently.

He only asked one question, and that was when I finished.

"It was Crawford, and he spoke with a Scots accent?" Holmes asked.

I nodded.

"It could be no other."

I knew from Holmes' general demeanor that I had just missed something, something important, but slightly befuddled as I was what with a blow to the head and several stiff drinks inside me, I failed to see it for myself. But Holmes' thin smile told me that he was onto something. I poured myself a less generous drink, got a fresh pipe going and sat back to hear his account to the night's adventures.

"I shall start by filling in some of your blank spots Watson," he said, getting a pipe of his own lit. "I arrived back in Shoreditch to find the building completely aflame. I was told that everyone inside had perished, and when I did not find you in the room we had taken I feared the worst. Deducing that, if you were unharmed, you would be making your way back here, I returned with some haste only to find Mrs. Hudson in the scullery trying to wake you. Between her and myself we managed to get you up here by the fire… and the rest you know."

It was still too sketchy and unsatisfying to me. I felt like part of my life had been stolen. And with that thought came another.

"I say Holmes," I said, cold fear suddenly gripping me. "You don't think I fell with that bally *sleeping sickness* do you? Surely Moriarty has not been using *me* as a puppet?"

Holmes shook his head.

"Not unless you have Seton ancestry of which you are completely unaware. Besides, that lump on your head tells me that you were *really* out for the count. No. There is another mystery here, one I think I may now have an answer for. But that is for later. For now, let us go back to when I left you earlier in the evening. The particulars of my story may illuminate some of the blank spots in yours."

He stared into the fire for long seconds collecting his thoughts then started the story proper.

"I arrived outside just as my quarry turned the corner at the end of the street. By the time I reached the corner he was already some way ahead and walking quite rapidly so that I had to hurry to keep him in view. The streets were rather empty so I found I had to stay some way back to prevent being spotted, but after a while I noticed that he seemed to be moving with singular purpose, looking neither to one side or the other. I felt confident enough to move up closer and we went that way for quite some time, with my quarry some fifty yards or so ahead of me.

"After a while I began to get some sense of where we were going. We headed south on the approaches to Liverpool Street Station and down the warren of streets between Moorgate and the Bank. I thought we might be headed for the Bank itself but he took a turn east and we made our way along just north of St. Paul's. He finally reached his destination; a large hole in the ground which denoted the workings for the new Central railway system. You may remember that one of the things Seton found on his Lordship's desk was a ledger detailing its construction?

"My quarry descended into the workings having passed a night guard with no more than a wave of his hand but when I attempted the same I was stopped and asked for identification. I had to part with a five-pound note before I was allowed access and not only did I lose track of my quarry for a while, I fear I also roused the suspicion of the night guard and I do believe he might have recognized me. But I could not spare any worry on that matter, for I needed to catch the man I had followed here. I went down into the new tunnel.

"I was amazed at how far the work has progressed down there. There is a defined tunnel and track system already in place, well-lit at regular intervals with electric lights. By those lights I was able to see my man some a hundred yards further on. I followed as swiftly as I was able but on coming to a bend in the track I found no sight of him ahead. I knew I had not passed him, so there was only one option – he had gone through some kind of concealed entrance.

"I found it seconds later, a cunningly wrought panel that only opened on the correct application of pressure. I slid inside and into another tunnel, one far less well finished than before, and one that was much narrower. It was also obviously still under construction for I heard the distinctive sound of pick on stone from further on inside. It was darker here and I was once again able to close in on the man. And by doing so I was able to witness the most remarkable thing. My quarry was still walking in a very stilted manner, almost as if being led by a set of strings. He walked the length of the corridor to where a much larger man, one I immediately recognized as our long-sought Sad-Eye Joe, toiled hard with a pick-axe to lengthen the tunnel further. When the two men were less than three feet apart the larger man put the pick down and, in a move you would now recognize Watson, fell into the *sleeping* posture. The new man, much less stilted now, lifted up the pick and started to dig.

"I believed I had discovered Moriarty's purpose in using the men; he has been using them to dig, and from the angle and depth of the tunnel itself it was going in a straight line to his goal – the vaults of the Bank of England."

Holmes gave me some time to digest this information before continuing.

"I say I *believed* I had discovered his purpose, but a closer inspection of the work in progress soon disabused me of that notion. There was a rough and ready approach in evidence and the whole effort seemed somewhat lackadaisical and lacking in planning; not something we would normally associate with Moriarty. It was almost as if it was a stage set. And when I saw the small barrels lined against the walls I got a further clue as to what was on the agenda here – the barrels were full of black powder, enough to blow a rather large hole in that part of London."

I stopped Holmes at this point.

"But that is not a plan I would attribute to Moriarty either," I said. "What profit is there in such an act for him?"

Holmes smiled thinly.

"Precisely Watson. But you have failed to see the whole picture. I will come to that anon. Let me return to that rough-hewn chamber and the MacAllans.

"I stayed there for perhaps half an hour while the man made some half-hearted attempts at enlarging the chamber before I realized I had learned all I could at this visit. My choices were to stay, or to return to Shoreditch and rejoin you in the watch.

"I backed out of the chamber silently, and made my way back to the hole by which I had entered and left. This time the guard did not even acknowledge my existence.

"And so here we are, back where I began. But I have several points we have not yet considered. Firstly, there is the matter of your encounter with Lord Crawford. Or rather, someone *using* Lord Crawford. I have been thinking on the timing of events, and I can assure you Watson that the presence we know as Moriarty was most definitely employed with a pickaxe at the time. Whoever you met, it was not Moriarty. And we only know of one other capable of such a thing – it must have been Seton himself. He probably knew that you would want to interfere, which will be why he knocked you out, then looked after you by bringing you here."

I must admit that took me aback somewhat.

"But he murdered all those men. They were his kin."

"I doubt he sees it as murder. I think you'll find that, like me, he believes the men's essence to be long gone. He may well see the act as doing a last service for the poor unfortunates to avoid Moriarty *desecrating* them further."

I still could not agree. As a doctor I had seen people come out of catalepsy none the worse for the experience. If there was a chance of life, the human mind found a way to take it. But yet again I was finding my view of how things were *meant* to work was being challenged, and I had to change my view of things – an occurrence that was becoming all too common these past weeks. I would have pointed that out to Holmes there and then but a knock at the downstairs door interrupted us.

"That will be our carriage," Holmes said, as if he had been expecting it. "I have asked for a meeting with Mycroft. Rather than repeat myself further I will save my conclusions until then. And bring your revolver Watson. We may have need of it before this thing is done."

Minutes later we were once more on our way to the Houses of Parliament. Holmes seemed energized, ready for action, but for myself I went with a degree of trepidation, for our last such visit had not ended well for us at all.

As it transpired I had worried unduly. The carriage took us to the Member's entrance and deposited us as close to the door as he could such that we were able to disembark with no one seeing us. Mycroft himself was waiting and without speaking he led us through a warren of corridors to a small basement room. It was only when we were inside with the door closed behind us that he seemed to relax.

"I did as you asked in the telegram," he said, pouring three glasses of claret and passing them out. "Crawford did indeed manage to get out last night, but he came back of his own accord; slightly confused I must admit. And I have put a watch on the railway workings at Bank. But for pity's sake Holmes, tell me what's going on here."

Holmes sipped at his claret, savoring the moment before starting. He related much the same tale he had told me back in Baker Street before reaching the point where he had stopped previously.

"As I was about to tell Watson earlier," he said. "I believe the whole setup in the railway tunnel to be another trap, an elaborate ruse designed purely to once again throw us off the scent. And, like the earlier trap, it will have a secondary purpose. I have not yet fully determined what that might be yet, but it will have something to do with both the *Irish Problem* and the Fenchurch Street railway line, mark my words."

At that Mycroft went quite pale.

"How did you know about that Holmes? That is a matter of the *utmost* secrecy."

"And this *utmost secret*," Holmes said, somewhat sarcastically. "Did Lord Crawford have access to it?"

If anything Mycroft went even paler.

"We must go, and quick. The Home Secretary needs to hear this. Pray we have time."

"Time for what?" I asked.

It was Holmes who answered.

"I may be wrong, but I do not believe so. The Home Secretary recently put measures in place to deal with suspected acts of terror in the Financial District." He looked at Mycroft, who nodded in confirmation. "And I do believe one of those is the removal of Britain's bullion reserves to a safe place… by means of a special train from Fenchurch Street."

Mycroft did not even bother to reply. We followed him at some haste through more corridors to what was obviously a suite of bedchambers. Mycroft showed no qualms in rapping hard on one of the doors. A somewhat bemused man opened it a few seconds later. The Home Secretary looked much smaller out of his usual rather formal dress and wearing a nightshirt. He looked at the three of us, then addressed Holmes directly.

"Have you come to throw me out of a window too?"

Mycroft looked fit to burst.

"The Fenchurch Street solution. Tell me it has not been implemented."

The man to his credit took it in his stride.

"Why yes. The memo should be on your desk by now. We had a tip off last evening that the Irish were planning an attack and I ordered the bullion moved for safekeeping. It will all be aboard the train by now."

And of course, we were too late. Mycroft marshaled an impressive range of men on the ground but by the time we arrived at Fenchurch Street – after another bone-rattling carriage trip along the embankment – the troops and police were just milling around looking lost.

The train, and Great Britain's bullion reserves with it, had gone.

CHAPTER 6

There was a tremendous tumult of course. Mycroft took charge and sent word ahead down the line to stop all trains going through all eastbound stations, and a thorough search was made of the workings in the railway system under Bank. All that was found there was much gunpowder and two dead men, their eyes filled with blood after suffering some kind of seizure.

But after a few hours it was apparent that Moriarty had won. No trace could be found of the train.

It was Holmes who thought to ask the name of the man put in charge of the transport of bullion. It came as no surprise to him to find that it was a certain John MacAllan, a man who lived a quiet life in Battersea but who on closer inspection was found to have family ties to the MacAllans of the East-End.

As dawn approached, we knew that no further purpose would be served by staying around Fenchurch Street, and Holmes was becoming irritable at Mycroft's demands that we stay hidden in the carriage that had brought us here. When Mycroft finally returned Holmes demanded that we be allowed some freedom.

"Surely you have enough evidence by now that I had nothing to do with the murder?"

Mycroft looked like a man in need of a good night's sleep.

"I'll get word to Lestrade to call the dogs off," he said. "We have more pressing problems at hand. I trust I can count on your help?"

Both Holmes and I were in agreement with that. But Holmes' next request seemed like a strange one to me.

"Would it be possible to have a meeting with Lord Crawford?" he said. "As soon as it can be arranged?"

Mycroft waved a hand in assent. We left Fenchurch Street and the carriage took us back to Parliament.

At first I thought our return trip had been in vain. Lord Crawford had once more fallen into the now familiar unconscious state. The man had been placed sitting up in an armchair in what I took to be a private room where Members could have a moment's peace. There were several armchairs and small tables arranged in a semi-circle around a tall fireplace.

I checked on Crawford. As I got closer I smelled smoke on his clothes. Holmes saw my reaction.

"Yes. There is no doubt it was this man, or rather this body, that you met in Shoreditch."

Mycroft was still having trouble getting to grips with this part of our story. After he arranged some breakfast for us I told him my tale of the happenings of the night before. The breakfast arrived during my telling and I interspersed my story with mouthfuls of toast and some strong sweet tea. Mycroft in the meantime kept looking over at Crawford.

"Sorry," Mycroft said when I finished. "Despite all you have told me, I still cannot bring myself to believe in this mumbo-jumbo."

At that very instant Crawford shook himself like a dog, raised his head and smiled.

"Ah. The Three Musketeers," he said. I immediately recognized the clipped English accent, so different from the soft Scots voice I had heard in Shoreditch. He sat up in the chair, the smile widening.

"Well Holmes, I think you can now admit that on this occasion I have indeed bested you."

Holmes did not reply, and Mycroft looked too dumbfounded to speak.

"I did not however come to gloat," Moriarty said. "I am finished here, with you, and with this body. Killing two birds with one stone so to speak. Good-bye."

The man's eyes went dead, then he started to thrash, feet pounding a rhythm on the carpet. I was up and across to him almost immediately, but I was far too late. His eyes filled with blood and he slumped in the chair. I checked his pulse just to make sure but there was no doubt about it. The man was as dead as anyone I have ever examined.

So you can imagine my surprise when just seconds later the body shook again, the head come up, and a soft Scots voice spoke.

"Good evening gentleman. I'm sorry if I gave you a scare, but I had to wait until the previous occupant departed."

Mycroft almost fell off his chair.

"Crawford? Is that you?"

"I'm afraid not sir. Lord Crawford has taken his leave. Angus Seton, at your service."

He turned and looked at me.

"I'm right sorry to have hit you last night doctor," he said. "But I did not know how much time I had, and you would have had too many questions."

I felt anger rise in me.

"Not only did you hit me – you killed all those men."

He shook his head, and there was sadness in his voice.

"No doctor. They were dead already. Just like this body here, the spirit has fled, leaving only a shell behind. And I would not desecrate this one so if it were not such an urgent matter."

He turned his attention to Holmes.

"I thought I might find you here or at least be able to get a message to you. I managed to find him. I take it you know about the train?"

Holmes nodded and Seton continued.

"I could only make contact for a few seconds," he said. "But that was long enough. He took several diversions to throw you off the scent and is now on the Eastern Counties Railway tracks, making for Colchester and then for Norwich. He intends to transfer the bullion to a boat. That is as much as I could discover."

"It is enough," Mycroft said. He seemed to have got over his reluctance to believe our story, and left the room in a hurry, no doubt to act on the information.

"And where are you Mr. Seton?" Holmes asked.

The man smiled.

"Nowhere near Norwich," he said. "That was for your brother's benefit. We both know that this must be finished between Moriarty and ourselves, not with any official interference?"

"So where is he really?" Holmes asked without confirming Seton's previous point. He did not have to - I saw the agreement in his face.

"He never left London," Seton replied. "He took the train into a disused tunnel. His idea of a little joke I suppose - he is hiding out in Limehouse, beneath the eastbound viaduct, biding his time. In the morning he intends to take the Rotherhithe tunnel south of the river and thence to Dover, where he has a boat waiting. I suggest you get to the train with all haste before he decides to make a run for it."

Holmes stood.

"Thank you sir. Let us hope that together we can bring this to a conclusion."

Seton nodded.

"And now, I must leave this poor man's body, entrusting you with the proper care and attention to his funeral. Good-bye, gentlemen. I shall see you soon."

He dropped his head and went still. When I checked his pulse he was dead. Again.

Holmes and I managed to slip out of Parliament while Mycroft was busy elsewhere. It did however seem that he had been as good as his word, for we passed several policemen none of whom so much as looked at us.

We managed to flag down a carriage and were shortly on our way back to the East End, once again suffering a bone-rattling trot along the Embankment.

"We are approaching a conclusion Watson," Holmes said as the carriage turned off towards Monument. "As yet I am not sure how we shall catch Moriarty, or even if such a thing is possible. But we can at least stop him in this latest crime and recover the bullion."

"That certainly must be a priority," I replied. "The fate of the Empire may rest on it."

Holmes almost laughed.

"I leave the fate of empires to Mycroft. Let us be content with catching a thief; albeit a very good one."

I had my own worries to contend with, and while the carriage took us through the warren of streets beyond Monument on the way to the docks I gave voice to the chief of them.

"I am not entirely sure we can trust Seton," I said. "Not after the affair in Shoreditch."

"I agree in part," Holmes said. "The Scotsman clearly has an agenda of his own. But if he meant us harm he has had ample opportunity before now, both in Comrie and in Shoreditch. And he has provided us with clues when we have needed them. We have taken him at his word thus far, and he has not been proved totally false. If this latest lead is true then he will have gone a long way in gaining some trust with me."

As for myself, I was still ambivalent on the matter; still fretting over those swaddled defenseless bodies burning in silence under Seton's hand. I forced it from my mind, a distraction that could be dealt with later. For now Holmes needed me focused and ready for action. The bruise on my head still hurt like billy-ho but the drumbeat throbbing had eased to a manageable level and the weight of the revolver was a reassuring presence in my pocket.

Half an hour later the carriage dropped us off outside Limehouse station. Holmes had us alight on the side opposite the station entrance and took me, by a series of narrow alleyways and passages, under the station itself. We stopped under the high arch of a brick viaduct.

"Quiet now Watson," Holmes said. "If the train is where Seton said it would be, it is just around this next corner. We do not even know what this John MacAllan looks like, so from now on we should treat everyone as a possible suspect. Agreed?"

"Agreed." I followed him round the corner, revolver in hand.

There was indeed a train in the tunnel ahead of us, and I was somewhat relieved to see that the engine was not up to steam. There was no driver visible, no one stoking the furnace. We sidled along the side of the carriages into the darkness of the tunnel itself. Still there was no sound, no sign of anyone being present.

"I say Holmes, are you sure we have the right train?"

He did not speak but jumped up into the space between two carriages and pulled aside a canvas tarpaulin that had been tied across the top, moving the material aside just enough so that he could look inside. He turned to me.

"We have the right train Watson, there is no doubt of that."

Even before he finished the sentence there was a *pop*. A bullet tore at Holmes' coat and I did not see whether he had been injured as he jumped down beside me and pulled me into the space between the wheels under the carriage.

"I had hoped to investigate a bit further before being seen," he said. "But it cannot be helped. Let us see if we can outflank this gunman. Keep to the walls, and keep low. I'll go left."

And as quick as that he was gone, running along the side of the track deeper into the tunnel. As soon as he left cover there was another *pop* and this time I was able to locate the source better; the gunman was indeed deeper in the tunnel and would be able to see any movement ahead of him silhouetted against the tunnel entrance. I left my spot under the carriage and leapt for the relative safety of the deeper shadows against the wall. I almost didn't make it; the *pop* of the gun and a whine close to my ear telling me I had been lucky not to be shot.

The bulk of the train obscured any view I might have of Holmes but another *pop* told me that he had broken cover. I used that as cover of my own and moved further into the tunnel. I had to stop after only ten yards, wanting to allow my eyes time to adjust but I was not given time as another *pop* told me that Holmes was still under fire. I headed further into the darkness.

"He's ten yards ahead of you, on the carriage roof," I heard Holmes shout. I sent a shot in that direction, the muzzle flare leaving a yellow afterimage behind my eyes that took long seconds to fade. There was no cry of pain but I heard a scuffle from that direction; Holmes had used my shot as an opportunity to press an attack. And now there *was* a cry of pain, although I didn't know whether it came from Holmes or the gunman. The scuffling continued for a few seconds then was followed by a loud *thud* as bodies fell from the train roof to the tunnel floor.

"I have him Watson," Holmes called, and I moved to his aid as my eyes finally adjusted to the dim light. But again, I was too late. Holmes kneeled over another dead body, its eyes filled with blood.

Deeper still in the tunnel someone laughed. When they spoke it was in that clipped English voice I was coming to hate.

"You did not think it would be that easy, did you Holmes? Why not come back here and we can talk about this like civilized men."

At the same time I heard noises from the front of the train; the unmistakable clatter of coal being shoveled into the furnace. Someone was preparing the engine for travelling.

"I mean it Holmes," Moriarty's voice said. "I have someone else here too; a *very* old friend of yours I believe. Come back here and join me and maybe I will let him live."

Holmes started to stand.

"No, Holmes," I said, holding him back. "It is just another trap – don't you see?"

"If it is, it is one I walk into with my eyes open," he said and, pulling away from me, stood. He put out a hand to help me up. "And I would like your company at the end, if you wish to join me?"

"Lay on MacDuff," I said, and let him help me up.

"Just leave the revolver behind, Doctor," Moriarty said from the darkness. "You will not be needing it."

Holmes nodded.

"An end with Moriarty will be between him and I," he said. "Come, bear witness for me."

I left the pistol on the tracks and together we followed Moriarty's voice into the tunnel.

We did not have to go far. We walked past four large goods carriages I guessed were the ill-gotten gains. After the second I started to see dim light at the rear of the train showing us to two opulent Pullman carriages hooked behind the cargo. A man stood at the steps between the two carriages. I did not recognize him, but when he spoke the voice was unmistakable.

"Welcome gentlemen. As you can see, I have arranged for us to travel in style. One of the perks of having Lord Crawford make the arrangements."

He showed us inside the rearmost carriage. The interior lived up to the promise of the outside, being a wonder of mahogany, leather and hand-painted mirrors. In feel it reminded me of nothing less than one of the more exclusive gentlemen's clubs, a feeling reinforced by the six armchairs that dominated the center of the space.

Even more astonishing still was the fact that the Scotsman, Seton was sitting in one of the armchairs, cradling a whisky. He had a rueful grin on his face as we entered.

"Greeting gentlemen," he said. "We meet again. I'm afraid I was too hasty and tried an attempt of my own at heroism and saving the day before you arrived. I'm ashamed to say I am not as young as I once was, and our friend here bested me to the extent that I yielded – for now. His whisky is the good stuff though, so I suggest you get some inside of you before he starts talking. It might make the gloating more bearable."

Moriarty laughed. It was only now we were in stronger light that I was able to see that he inhabited a young man's body. He wore the clothes of a clerk, and not a very well paid one at that, with dried ink on his fingers and thin hair already going prematurely bald on top. What *was* left of the hair was a mousy brown with hints of red, and I guessed this must be the aforementioned John MacAllan.

"What is to stop the three of us rushing you, right here," I said.

Moriarty laughed.

"Go ahead, if that is your pleasure. I shall simply *jump* again and leave you with another dead man on your hands. Would you *really* like that doctor? Are you not tired yet of the trail of dead you are leaving behind you?"

"But at least we would be able to retake the train."

Holmes replied this time.

"No Watson. Given the ease with which he performed the last switch, I suspect there are more *available* bodies nearby. Probably in that other Pullman carriage yonder."

Moriarty said nothing. He did not have to. It was not too great a stretch of the imagination for me to imagine the swaddled bodies, crammed together there in the dark, eyes staring but unseeing, just lying there, breathing softly… waiting. I decided then and there that I would not allow him to desecrate more bodies.

At that moment the train gave a lurch and the sound of the engine starting up rumbled through the carriage.

"Make yourself comfortable gentlemen," Moriarty said. "We have a longish journey ahead of us but, as Mr. Seton has already pointed out, the single malt is particularly fine."

The train started up and, rather than try to keep our balance in the now swaying compartment, we took a chair each while Moriarty served us Scotch. Rarely have I taken part in a more disconcerting tableau, but Holmes seemed to be rather relaxed about the situation so, suspecting he might have a plan he had not yet intimated to me, I decided to play along.

"This time, I believe I will gloat," Moriarty said and laughed. "You have to admit, I have bested you this time, Holmes."

Holmes made him wait, taking his time in filling and lighting a pipe.

"And I suppose you have a cunning plan for our demise?" Holmes finally said.

Moriarty laughed again. He seemed to be enjoying himself immensely.

"Demise? Oh no, Holmes. I have no plans to kill you. I want you to be a witness to the full extent of my victory here today… then I want you to remember it for every hour of every day of what I hope will be a long and miserable life."

The *chug* of the wheels on the rails told me that the train was picking up speed. After several minutes the noise intensified into an echoing roar that made any talk impossible until it abated.

"The Rotherhithe tunnel," Moriarty said to Holmes. "We are now south of the river and on our way to Dover. There we shall transfer the bullion to a boat I have waiting and we shall all make our way to Dieppe. There I shall take my leave of you and Watson. Mister Seton will travel with me, for a while at least. And you will have plenty of time to reflect on this defeat."

Now it was Holmes' turn to laugh.

"I believe it is only a defeat when the game is finally over. This is far from over. Don't you agree Mr. Seton?"

The Scotsman had been sitting quietly all this time but now he seemed to rouse himself.

"Indeed Mister Holmes. We are a ways away from the endgame yet," he said. "Although I have already made a gambit that I believe our adversary has missed." He turned to address Moriarty. "You see, your news that you have spare bodies available to you was not news at all, not to me at least. Before I allowed myself to be *captured*, I spent some time next door. You will never desecrate my kin again; I have seen to that… permanently."

For the first time since our arrival Moriarty's grin slipped a little. Seton's by contrast widened into a smile. Holmes too allowed himself a thin-lipped smile.

"I believe you'll find that Mr. Seton is the winner here," Holmes said. "A fact that I am sure I will be able to live with."

Moriarty produced a small pistol from his jacket pocket.

"You may well have stopped me from using my *spares* as

you called them," he said. "But that is of little matter for this body here suits me just fine, for now. Later, Mr. Seton, I shall be taking residency in yours, but that too can wait. Let us all just sit here like civilized men for a time. I have no desire to hurt any of you."

"And yet," Holmes said. "You may have to. For you see, you have already lost. While you were telling me all about your little plan for the bullion, Mr. Seton here was back in Parliament in Lord Crawford's body, telling my brother every detail. Is that not right Mr. Seton?"

From where I sat I saw the wink that Holmes sent to Seton, but it would have been completely hidden from Moriarty's view. Seton was smart enough to do his part.

"Yes indeed Mr. Holmes. And right glad he was of the information too. He was sending people to Dover even as I left."

Moriarty's smile had gone completely now, to be replaced by something that looked very much like rage. As for myself, I was starting to see some method in Holmes' and Seton's plan of attack, and I was not greatly surprised by Seton's next move. He stood and started to walk, somewhat shakily due to the motion of the carriage, towards Moriarty.

"You have repeatedly assured me that your purpose is to take this body of mine," he said. "So I am now going to strangle you. You have nowhere else to go and to stop me you will have to shoot me. I have lived a *long* time, as you know. But even I do not take bullets kindly. So let us have at it, you and I."

Moriarty's smile came back again.

"No closer, or I'll shoot your friend here," he said. The gun shifted, and was now pointed straight at my midriff. But only for a second, as Holmes stepped forward, placing himself directly in the path of any shot.

"I do not believe you will rob yourself of a lifetime of gloating," Holmes said. "But if you must, go ahead and shoot."

Even as Moriarty's finger tightened on the trigger, Seton had moved close enough to bat the pistol aside. A shot, painfully loud in the confines of the cabin, shattered one of the fine mirrors. Seton reached for Moriarty's throat.

"You have forgotten something sir," Moriarty said as Seton's hands gripped him. "There is always somewhere else to go."

Moriarty's eyes rolled up in their sockets. At the same time his body slumped, but then almost immediately straightened.

"I'm sorry Holmes," Seton's voice said, but from the MacAllan man's body. "That was closer than I intended."

Moriarty's voice, that clipped English with a hint of the North, came from Seton's mouth.

"And yet, you have lost, for I am now in occupancy," Moriarty said.

I myself was in a degree of some confusion. It was apparent that the essence of Moriarty was now inside Seton – and Seton had somehow taken residence in the MacAllan body. But I had no time then to reflect on it.

Moriarty reached for the pistol, attempting to grab it from Seton's hand. All of a sudden his body jerked, as if jolted with a seizure.

"You may have occupancy," Seton said and laughed. "But as I told you, I was busy before I came here. You have recently thrown many of my kinsmen from their *homes* to leave them dancing in the shadows… which is where I found them. As their Laird, it would be remiss of me not to provide them with shelter in their time of need. Under the terms of your new lease you will be taking joint tenancy."

Seton's, or rather Moriarty's, body jerked again.

"Say hello to the clan Seton, and their brothers the MacAllans," Seton said. "I am afraid they are rather a noisy bunch. But they are all most eager to make your acquaintance."

Moriarty opened his mouth, but it was a loud Scots voice that replied.

"Thank you kindly Angus," the voice said. "We shall take good care of him. He won't be getting out anytime soon. We have locked the doors and closed the windows so to speak."

That voice went, to be replaced by another, more Irish sounding this time, uttering vile unrepeatable threats against Moriarty. Then a third, in a Scots dialect so thick I barely understood every second word, but the intent was very clear. Moriarty himself resurfaced for a second – just long enough to scream. The body jerked in multiple spasms, throwing it to the floor. Spittle started to fleck at the mouth. I moved to check on him, but Seton…MacAllan…whoever he was now, held me back. He still had a pistol trained on his former body.

"Just for a few seconds more, Doctor, if you will," he said. "We need to ensure that the family will be able to maintain control; Moriarty's will is strong… but they are many."

And it did seem that he was right. The spasms *were* being brought under some degree of control. The body went still, the only sign of life being the eyeballs frantically moving under closed lids and the mouth working as if holding several simultaneous conversations.

"The boys will keep him busy," Seton said from his new body. "And I will keep him fed and watered. He will not be bothering society again – not for a *long* time."

Suddenly, just like that, I felt angry; enraged by the casual ease with which so many *souls* had been bartered. And I am afraid I took it out on Holmes.

"You knew," I said, rising to face him. "You knew all along that this would be the outcome."

Holmes, to his credit, looked glum.

"I knew there was a high chance of it, yes. As soon as I knew that Seton could duplicate Moriarty's strength of will and *inhabit* another body, then I knew."

"And you allowed it to happen. All those souls, perished."

"Those are on Moriarty's conscience, not ours. It was he who forced those poor unfortunates to break the chain that bound them here, not I, and not Seton."

That made me turn my attention on the other man.

"And you – you are no better than Moriarty. What about the poor man whose body you now have? And him a kinsman of yours too. I…"

Seton's tears stopped me in my tracks.

"John is with his kin," he said, and motioned at the body on the ground. "Moriarty made him leave long before I ever got here. If it makes you feel any better, he has given me his blessing for what I have done."

"Blessing? I doubt there is anything of a *blessing* in any of this business."

Seton's eyes were red and he looked sadder than anyone I have ever seen.

"I agree with you on that point Doctor. But a discussion of the morality of my deeds will have to wait. I believe I will have a long time ahead of me to reflect on them." He turned to Holmes. "I know Lord Crawford is gone from my reach, but is Mycroft also keeping an eye on the one who survived?"

"Old Lord Menzies? Yes. And it would be fitting if his were to be the last actions in this matter, having been the one to bring us in to it in the first place. Tell him to send people to Dover. With luck and speed they should be there waiting for us."

Seton sat in a chair, rolled up his eyes, and was immediately *gone*. The body on the floor had also fallen quiet but on checking I saw that the eye movements were still rapid, and he was still mouthing words.

I looked up at Holmes.

"Maybe it would be for the best if we just shot the both of them?"

"Neither you nor I are capable of such a thing, Watson," he said. "Besides, shooting them would only release Moriarty from the prison where he resides."

"And I promise to keep him there for as long as I possibly can," Seton said, sitting up in the chair. "Mycroft has been informed. They will be waiting for us in Dover."

There is not much left to tell.

We spent a very disconcerting hour or so conversing with Seton in MacAllan's body while Moriarty, in Seton's body, lay mumbling on the floor.

"Having *moved* as it were, are you still immortal?" Holmes asked at one point.

Seton laughed. It seemed his humor had moved with him.

"I know not. I shall have to wait and see. Ask me again in fifty years or so."

When we pulled in to Dover Station there was a large police presence waiting. The train driver and two other accomplices were arrested. Holmes and I made sure the bullion was secure. After that we showed a team of shocked constables to the second Pullman carriage, and left them with the dead who lay there with their eyes filled with blood. When we returned to the rear carriage both Seton and his former body were gone, leaving no trace behind.

PART 2:
THE DREAMING MAN

CHAPTER 1

I have rarely seen my friend Sherlock Holmes so flustered as I found him that morning in September last year.

I myself was not in the best of moods, having suffered a restless sleep plagued by dreams of old battles and old cases — I had seen a hound in the dark, tasted cordite and powder, and heard the screams of the dying. I was more than ready for a hearty breakfast, a large pot of tea and a read of the morning's paper to clear my head of the night.

The first draft of autumn had arrived, and Mrs. Hudson had a fire lit. Despite the chill, Holmes had not yet changed from his bedclothes, although he was wrapped in a rather garish Paisley-patterned dressing gown, and had foregone slippers to warm his toes by the heat of the fire. He sat in his favorite chair, reading *The Thunderer*. Every few minutes he would pause, and, with exquisite dexterity, snip an article from the paper with the scissors he kept for that express purpose, before tearing the rest of the page from the newspaper, crumpling it into a ball and throwing it into the grate for burning. I was not going to get the pleasure of perusing the paper that morning, for there seemed to be only a few pages left and Holmes already had a substantial pile of cuttings on the small table by his right hand.

"More criminality for your files, Holmes? I said.

"Robberies, murders, fraud and blackmail — the rich tableau of the modern city," he replied with no little disgust. "Lestrade clearly needs my help, Watson. Why in the blazes will he not ask for it?"

"This is London," Holmes," I said. "We have the good fortune to live in the greatest city in the world. It is hardly remarkable that there is a certain amount of criminal activity."

He waved me to the chair across the fire from him.

"Don't vex me, Watson. The scale of the villainous enterprises reported these past two weeks is worse than has been seen for several years." Holmes sifted through his pile of clippings, reading out a summary to me at random. "A large bank robbery in the City, two murders in Belgravia, a diamond heist in Hatton Gardens, a prominent peer of the realm in a prostitution scandal, a minor royal swindled out of several works of art, and a ship's captain, gone missing in mysterious circumstances in St. Catherine's Quay. And that is just a small sample — merely those that the papers have chosen to print. My sources tell me that there is more — much more — activity that is not even noticed by authorities nor journalists."

"And yet you wonder why Lestrade has not contacted you? The poor chap must be quite run off his feet."

"All the more reason for him to ask for my help," Holmes replied. He fell quiet as he lit up a fresh pipe, tapping the tobacco in hard as if he could relieve some of his frustration in the process.

"You could always offer the Yard your services," I said, but knew as soon as I said it that I had come close to causing offense. All I got in reply was a raise of an eyebrow and a cold thin smile. I understood immediately — Sherlock Holmes does not look to Scotland Yard for scraps from their table.

But it was obvious to me that Holmes was growing increasingly bored by the recent lack of work. Our last case together had been in the height of summer — the recovery of a gem belonging to a Baroness, thought stolen, but merely lost in a child's toy box. It had hardly begun to give Holmes' mind the exercise he required of it. At least I had my practice and rounds at the hospital to keep me occupied, but Holmes had rarely stepped outside the rooms in almost three weeks.

The intellectual rigors to which he subjected himself almost demanded a constant stimulation otherwise it led to what Holmes himself described as stagnation — and what I, as his doctor, could only diagnose as a form of black depression. That same depression threatened to overcome Holmes on occasion. We were not there yet, indeed might not be for some time — but I could see the warning signs. I resolved to make a hunt for Holmes' stash of cocaine in the near future, before my friend could succumb to its siren call.

Holmes went back to perusing what was left of *The Thunderer* for news, each crime he uncovered bring a fresh sigh of disappointment from my old friend. In an attempt to get a conversation started, I rose, went over to his side and lifted his most recent clippings from the arm of his chair. I merely hoped to spot something we could talk about dispassionately, but a name in one of the columns immediately caught my eye — Lord Jennings.

"I say, Holmes," I said, waving the piece of paper in his face. "I know this chap — or at least, I know his son. I boxed with him in the Army — dashed fine left hook, but a glass chin always let him down. It says here that his father has had a spot of bother and that the Yard is baffled. What say you — shall we pay him a visit? I know the house well, and can provide the introductions. We can be there in an hour."

I expected Holmes to see through my obvious attempt to gee him up, and was waiting for a retort when, much to my surprise, he sprung to his feet and headed for his room.

"In that case, lay on MacDuff," he said, and smiled broadly. "I shall be ready to join you in ten minutes."

Perhaps his stagnation was not quite as far along as I had feared.

We were able to hail a carriage almost immediately and were soon on our way south. Holmes looked pale and tired but the mere thought of a possible case had at least got him out of Baker Street. As for myself, the dreams from the previous night were fading, although I do not think I will ever be rid of the sights and sounds of battle and strife, no matter how much distance and time separates me from it.

I was still lost in reflection when the carriage came to a halt in a quiet street in the southern reaches of Kensington. I knew the area as a place where rich men took up residence when they weren't abroad or running large estates out in the country — a town bolt-hole convenient for theater and society yet far enough from the populace to provide some degree of privacy. Some of the dwellings, like their owners, had clearly seen more affluent days but the Jennings house was one of the better maintained of the properties in the tall crescent of polished sandstone townhouses.

Our carriage dropped us off on a wide pavement at the foot of a sweep of steps leading up to an imposing oak door that would not have looked out of place in a castle. A butler — a stocky cove with the busted nose and cauliflower ears of a bruiser — answered our knock and waved us inside. Holmes paused in the doorway to examine the lock and hinges before following me in.

Jennings had made most of his money in farming in the North — as such he was thought rather common among the exalted company he kept in the House of Lords. A certain degree of social ostracism had never seemed to bother the man, and I had rather liked his son on the occasions we had the chance to meet. It had been several years since I'd been in the father's company, but if I was worried he might not remember me, it was quashed by the warmest of welcomes.

"Captain Watson, as I live and breathe," Jennings said in his Northern brogue, still strong despite his many years spent away from the area. He sat in a high winged leather armchair as close to the fire as possible, a thick tartan blanket over his lap and legs. He looked smaller, more wizened than I remembered. The years had not been too kind to him, and my doctor's eye told me that he did not have too many years left in him, but his handshake was strong enough as he showed us to a pair of chairs opposite him. "To what do I owe the pleasure?"

I introduced Holmes, and the Lord raised an eyebrow.

"Of course, I know of you, sir — your reputation proceeds you. Dashed pleased to meet your acquaintance. But answer me this first of all — are you here at the request of Scotland Yard?"

"I'm afraid not," I started, but was interrupted.

"Good," Jennings said with an almost gleeful grin. "That rabble can't find their arses with both hands. But with Sherlock Holmes on the case, at least I have a hope of seeing my paintings again."

"Tell me what happened," Holmes said, suddenly still and watchful. I knew the signs — a new case had already begun.

There was a short delay while Jennings had his butler fetch us a drink. His whisky was as top notch as I'd expect from a peer of the realm, and I was feeling quite relaxed as I lit up a pipe and listened to the man's tale.

"They could have had anything they wanted," the old man said after taking a swig of Scotch that would have floored a man half his age. "They were in and out so quickly we never even knew they were here. Last Thursday night was a quiet night, with no wind to speak of, and little to no sleep on my part due to the arthritis. But still, they managed it without alerting me to their presence. And they knew exactly what they were after — they only took the two miniatures — Raeburn's, and fine ones at that. They will fetch more than a thousand guineas apiece or I'm a Dutchman. It may even be that they have been stolen at the request of a fellow collector, for, as I said, they are particularly fine examples of the man's work. But that's not why I want — I need — them back. My good wife bought them in Edinburgh, on our honeymoon. That's a memory I can little afford to have stolen."

The old man looked like he might weep, and to hide his embarrassment he tried to light a long cigarillo from a case in his breast pocket, but his trembling hands betrayed him as much as his tears. He thanked me profusely when I went over and lit the smoke for him. He inhaled deeply, and no smoke came back out, as it if it were all infused directly into his tissue. I considered telling him that such a practice would kill him, but by the look of him he knew that well enough already.

Holmes waited until he was sure the old chap was quite recovered before continuing his questioning.

"There were no windows open? If I recall correctly it was a warm night."

"No," Jennings replied. His composure had returned somewhat, although his eyes looked red-rimmed and bleary — I did not think we had much time with him before he would need a lie down and some quiet rest. "My blood grows thin nowadays, and Hector has strict instructions to lock everything down at nights."

"Hector is your butler?" Holmes said. "The man who showed us in?"

"Yes — and don't go thinking he had anything to do with it. That man's been with me for a score of years now, and I could not ask for a more devoted servant — and friend. He was the only one that kept me going when my Janet passed. And he was distraught on Friday morning when he discovered the theft had occurred — he's taking it rather personally."

"Am I to take it there was no sign at all of any forced entry?"

"Not only that — the doors and windows were still all locked, front and back. There was nothing at all out of place — just the empty spots above the mantle where the miniatures have hung since the funeral."

I looked up as he mentioned it — there were indeed two lighter patches on the wallpaper where the small paintings had been hanging. Holmes stood and took a closer look, inspecting the whole area, paying particular attention to the mantle and the area on the floor around the grate, which he inspected on his hands and knees for a good five minutes.

"You are a size eight shoe, and your man is a ten or eleven," Holmes said to Jennings as he rose from the grate. It was not a question. "The burglar took a size seven, and was slight with it. He brought in some dirt — from the gardens opposite unless I'm mistaken — on his soles from outside. There is not a great deal of mess, but the imprint is still quite clear. And he had to stretch to take down the miniatures — there are distinct scuffs on the mantle where his jacket rubbed on the stone. Taking these things into consideration, I am confident that the man we are after is no more than five foot four in height, of small build, and wearing a cheap pair of shoes. The sole of the left is more worn than on the right, suggesting he might have a slight limp, or favors the right leg in some way — tell me, has anyone been seen who matches that description?"

His Lordship merely sat, mouth agape, staring at Holmes with an expression I had seen on many an occasion, too flummoxed to reply. Fortunately at least one of the household had their wits about them. There was a discreet cough from the doorway. The butler — Hector, although I have rarely seen anyone whose name fitted him less — sought Holmes' attention.

"I believe I might be able to help, sir," he said. "Although it was Tuesday when I saw the man you just described, and I had quite forgotten about him until now. I had to move him along from the doorstep — small chap, around five foot four as you said, and with a pronounced limp — I saw that as he scurried away."

"Is there anything else you can remember about him," Holmes asked. "Even the smallest thing might help me."

"I can't rightly recall," the big man said. "I had a busy day as we had just returned from the estate and I had to unpack the master's clothes. I had been down in the washhouse to drop off the most soiled of them, and he was on the doorstep when I came up from the basement. He took no notice of me until I went up to him and asked him to move along, and even then he hardly noted my existence."

"His clothing?" Holmes said, keeping his voice soft, not wishing to break the flow of the butler's memories."

"He wore a long brown overcoat and a soft hat — it was badly out of shape, as if he had spent too long in the rain — and he hadn't shaved for several days. His eyes were blue — I remember that right enough — blue and wild, as if he'd been drinking, although I could not smell it on him. And he said the strangest things — he was muttering to himself, as if holding a conversation with an invisible friend. It was all jumbled up I'm afraid — something about his sore leg, and being sick to the pit of his stomach. And a woman's name; Irene — he kept calling for Irene. Blowed if I can remember anything else, sir, but I thought he was just another passing vagrant, you see? We get a lot of them round here, attracted by the empty properties and the thought of an easy spot of loot."

Holmes was lost in thought for several seconds, then patted the butler on the shoulder.

"You've done more than enough. Thank you."

Holmes returned to his chair and smiled. He addressed Jennings again.

"Well, sir. I believe I will indeed be able to help you. Was there anything remarkable about these miniatures? For instance, did you know the subjects?"

Jennings had now fully recovered his composure after his reaction to seeing Holmes in action — another hefty swig of Scotch had seen to that.

"They were among Raeburn's best work it is said — two fine miniature portraits in plain silver frames. They were both Scotsmen, I can tell you that," he said. "And scientific chaps too — one had a telescope at hand, and the other was reading at a desk. Beyond that, the provenance of each was rather murky, according to the insurers in any case. It was Bartletts, in the Strand — they may be able to shed more light on any other particulars you may require."

"They may indeed," Holmes said softly, but his attention had already moved on.

CHAPTER 2

In the carriage back into town I tried to draw Holmes out in an attempt to get an early feel for his plans, but he was as obdurate as ever.

"We have facts, Watson, but not enough of them as yet. You know my methods well enough by now to understand that I will not indulge in idle speculation. But bear with me — we should have more clarity before the day is done."

I expected us to return directly to Baker Street, but Holmes had other ideas. He had the carriage turn east through the city center, through Oxford Circus, then past Holborn and out towards the banks of the City. Our first port of call was to a jeweler's store in Hatton Gardens.

There are more than a dozen such premises on a short stretch of road, mostly run by European immigrants with links to markets in Holland and Germany. Holmes and I have visited the street several times, but the store Holmes led me to was not one I had been in before. It was large for its kind, with a fine display of gold pocket watches and diamond rings none of which I would be able to afford on my current meager income.

The old man behind the heavily fortified counter had a most enviable white beard that reached halfway down his chest, and he tugged and fretted at it as we entered. His eyebrows were almost as bushy as his beard was, and they went up and down alarmingly as Holmes explained the purpose of our visit. He was loath to talk at first — as if admitting there had even been a robbery would be taken as a sign of weakness and an invitation for a repeat performance. Holmes as is his wont soon got to the heart of the matter.

"I am confident I can recover that which was taken," he said softly. "But in order to do so, you must tell me what happened."

The promise of the return of his goods was enough to loosen the old man's tongue. Indeed, he proved to be a most friendly chap, and rather voluble. He showed us through to a small but very tidy back room that served as both a scullery and a workshop. Over a cup of tea that was far too thin and far too sweet for my taste, and a Russian cigarette that was as black as tar and almost as unpleasant, he told Holmes of a burglary three nights past. None of his many locks seemed to have been tampered with, and no doors or windows were broken. There had been no sign that anyone at all had been present — apart from the fact of the disappearance of a small wooden box of diamonds, as yet uncut. Just as strangely, a king's ransom in cut jewels had been left untouched on the counter.

The old man remembered one other item of note — a strange man had been seen on the doorstep several days before the robbery.

"He was small, I remember that — I had to shoo him away from the door as he was frightening the customers with all that mumbling and fidgeting. He seemed harmless enough though — and I even pitied him, what with all that crying and wailing for his poor wife."

"And do you remember the wife's name?" Holmes said, although I saw in his face that he had surmised the answer already.

"Irene," the old man said. "He kept calling for his Irene."

After our visit to the jeweler we spent the rest of the day talking to the victims of the crimes Holmes had collected in his clippings. Firstly there were people to see in the Egyptian collection of the British Museum and in the City of London. After that we spoke to a witness to a murder in Belgravia and conversed with the ladies of a house of ill repute in Shepherd's Bush. Everywhere we went they all had the same story to tell. The small man was present either at the scene on the day of, or in the days immediately preceding the crime. He was always a figure evoking pity or sympathy rather than fear, and no one ever saw him commit any wrongdoing. But it had definitely been the same man in every case — and everyone remembered him calling for Irene.

Holmes did not discuss the matter until later that evening as we sat by the fireplace back in Baker Street. Mrs. Hudson had provided a fine supper that more than adequately made up for the missed meals earlier, and I was feeling quite comfortable.

"It appears we have a suspect, Watson," Holmes said.

"A most peculiar suspect, it would seem," I replied.

Holmes nodded.

"But it would not be the first time that a good costume and subterfuge served as a mere distraction to divert attention away from the crime itself, so we must not discount the possibility that this man, pitiful as he might appear, is not all that he seems."

"Indeed. And if he has perpetrated all these crimes without being detected, he must be remarkably clever."

"Or remarkably devious — and very possibly both," Holmes replied. "We may learn more when Lestrade gets here."

"You have called for him?"

Holmes laughed.

"I did not have to — we have rattled enough cages today for him to take notice. I am only surprised he is not here already."

Lestrade arrived ten minutes later.

The good Inspector was a regular visitor to Baker Street, having been our man in the Yard for several years — sometimes helping, sometimes hindering our cases. I do believe he had come to respect Holmes' insights, and he often turned to my friend in times of difficulty. But that night, he was in no mood for pleasantries and seemed to be in a state of high dudgeon. His hair was awry, his shirt the worse for wear after a long day on the job, and he was badly in need of a shave. It appeared I had been right in my assessment that the wave of crimes had him working at the end of his tether.

"Now look here, Holmes," he said as he came in. "When I need your help, I'll bally well ask for it."

Holmes feigned ignorance, but it was not an act he

could maintain for any length of time, and when he laughed aloud it only got Lestrade's dander up.

"I could have you locked away for obstruction, you know? Don't think I wouldn't do it."

"But Inspector," Holmes said. "How would you ever solve anything then?"

Lestrade looked fit to burst, and I decided to put a stop to Holmes' teasing before the poor man did himself a mischief. The Inspector was only slightly mollified by the offer of some brandy and a smoke, but at least I got him to sit down and stop blustering.

"All right," he said with no little exasperation after a time when Holmes showed no signs of speaking. "Let's be having it — what have you got?"

Over the next twenty minutes I smoked a pipe and watched Holmes and Lestrade play cat and mouse, each attempting to draw information from the other. As ever, Holmes' victory was assured from the start — on this occasion due to him knowing of the small muttering man — a fact that had so far been completely missed by the Yard's investigations.

"So I'm to look for a small, limping man who misses his wife and talks to invisible companions? He's a dashed peculiar excuse for a suspect, Holmes," Lestrade said as I poured him another brandy. "And if it is him that is doing it, how is he getting into locked houses and shops and getting out again without being seen or heard? My sergeant is adamant that these are all inside jobs, and I'm inclined to believe him."

"What is more probable?" Holmes asked. "That a man, seen at every scene, is responsible — or that scores of strangers have somehow conspired to mastermind a wave of crime the likes of which this city has seldom seen?"

Lestrade eventually came round to Holmes' way of thinking, but he was none too happy about it.

"Dash it, Holmes, I can't have the Yard chasing after mumbling vagrants in brown overcoats — the cells would be full in an hour."

Holmes laughed again. "Then I shall have to see what can be done to narrow the field."

I woke in the morning to the sound of many footsteps clattering up and down the main stairwell, accompanied by Mrs. Hudson's most annoyed shouting. I washed and dressed quickly, eager to discover the cause of this commotion in our otherwise serene accommodation.

I found Holmes holding court in the sitting room. A dozen of the Baker Street irregulars were gathered around him while more continued to cause havoc out on the landing. Mrs. Hudson bellowed at them, long and loud, but even her best Scots insults proved to have little effect on the street urchins, who were used to far stronger fare than that. At least the ones gathered in the sitting room seemed able to maintain a modicum of decorum, although that probably had something to do with Holmes' supply of small denomination coinage.

"Now lads, you know what to do?" Holmes said. "First one to find him gets a florin."

Holmes seemed to have come to the end of explaining what he wanted. The gathered lads departed in a rush of thudding feet, leaving only a smell that I had to open the windows to dispel. Holmes seemed quite satisfied.

"I have deployed our scouts, Watson. Those lads know the streets far better than any of Lestrade's men," he said. "If our quarry surfaces, then they will find him."

I was about to quiz Holmes further on the case, but he preempted me.

"No time for questions now. Get your jacket, Watson — we have been invited out to breakfast — it seems that Lestrade was not the only one who took note of our activities yesterday."

Five minutes later we were in a carriage headed for Mycroft Holmes' club.

The Diogenes Club is the quietest, yet most exclusive, of all the gentlemen's establishments in this great city. It occupies a prime spot in the Strand, and is frequented by many of the great and good, but you would never know it, for they speak not a word to one another. Indeed, they take so much pride in their vow of complete silence that anyone who breaks it is shown the door in short order. Elderly gentlemen sit in voluminous armchairs hiding behind newspapers while sipping the finest port and brandy the world can offer, puffing smoke silently at one another, and reveling in the peace and quiet to be had.

I have, on occasion, felt tempted to burst into song in their lobby, but this time I minded my manners, and allowed the overdressed flunky to show us to Mycroft's back office, where more of the business of state was done than the powers that be would like to admit.

Mycroft stood behind a large mahogany desk and glowered at us when we were shown in.

"Well, brother, what do you have to say for yourself this time?"

Holmes merely smiled. The latest round in this long running bout of sibling rivalry had begun. It was interrupted only as long as it took for two more flunkeys to arrive and set up breakfast on a corner table.

One of the few pleasures I ever got from this club was their provender, and this breakfast was no exception — a thick slice of ham, two poached eggs, and enough buttered toast and strong tea to wash it all down. And at least eating it kept me occupied, for Mycroft was in no mood for idle chatter, eschewing breakfast and preferring instead to remind his younger brother of his failings, and the depth and breadth of Mycroft's own responsibilities. Holmes sat and took it all in silence, though the expression on his face told me that he would far rather be somewhere else.

It was only after the breakfast was cleared away, we retired to the armchairs, and smokes were lit that conversation finally turned to our activities of the day before. Mycroft listened while I talked him through the crime scenes and the people we had conversed with along the way — Sherlock preferred me to take on the explaining duties — it usually meant that the conversation lasted longer before the inevitable argument.

"Tread carefully on this one, Sherlock," Mycroft said when I was done. "Some of these crimes have affected people in high — very high — places, and it is not just Scotland Yard whose toes you would be treading on should you blunder into something untoward."

Holmes raised an eyebrow, but did not reply. Mycroft tried to stare him out, but failed.

"This is not one of our games, Sherlock," he finally said. "You have a suspect, and I know both you and your pet Inspector are looking for him. I must insist that he is turned over to me as soon as he is found."

"You may insist all you like," Holmes replied. "But Lestrade might have something to say about that."

Mycroft smiled thinly.

"Lestrade knows when to do what he is told — unlike some others I could mention."

All that got him was another smile from Holmes. Sherlock took rather too much delight in discomforting his brother, especially when it came to encroaching on matters of state, which Mycroft considered his own special territory. Given Mycroft's reaction that morning, I could only assume that such an encroachment was already underway. It seemed our case had greater depths than I had imagined.

Holmes confirmed that thought for me as we strolled along the Strand after taking our leave.

"Mycroft was right about one thing," he said. "We must tread carefully here, Watson. If my brother is concerned enough to intervene then there are matters afoot of which we have not yet been made aware. I suspect we have only just reached the foothills and have a long climb ahead towards enlightenment."

"If this chap is so bally devious, how in blazes can we catch him?" I asked.

"A serial offender like this almost always has a pattern," Holmes replied, distractedly, as if that great brain was already intent on its task. "We must discern if there is any commonality, whether it be in place, or time or some other variable as yet unnoticed. Let us return to Baker Street. I must think on this."

I spent the rest of that day in my chair, reading *The Thunderer*, drinking tea and smoking more than was good for me while Sherlock sat across from me staring into the empty grate, it not being cold enough yet to light a fire. He only stirred once, to mark out points on the large map of the city above his desk. He stood back, as if considering something he could see that wasn't apparent to me, then went immediately back to his chair without a word.

I saw in the paper that there had been another large robbery overnight — one of the theatres in the Aldwych has lost its takings — but as there was no mention of a limping vagrant, I had no way of telling whether there was any connection to our case. All I could do was wait for Holmes, and hope that he would allow me some explanation when it came to time for action.

As it turned out, the call for action, when it arrived in the early evening was not from Holmes, Lestrade or even Mycroft, but from one of the street ruffians Holmes had sent out earlier in the day.

CHAPTER 3

We heard him before we saw him, his arrival announced by an excited pounding on the front door. Mrs. Hudson showed the red-faced boy upstairs and into the front room, where Holmes had him stand by the fireplace for questioning.

"I done found 'im, Mr. Holmes," the lad said, even before Holmes could start. He was out of breath, and stank of muck and sweat — so much so that Mrs. Hudson made a point of opening all the windows before she retired swiftly to the cleaner air in her domain below us.

If Holmes noticed the stench, he did not show it — the lad had his full attention. He took a florin from his waistcoat pocket and showed it to the boy, who made a grab for it, but was too slow to beat Holmes' reflexes as the coin was made to vanish again.

"The story first," Holmes said.

"After you describe the geezer you was after, George and Ratty and the others went off to Smithfields Market. They thought he might be a stall holder, what with the hat and the overcoat and such, but me and Tom, we decided that we'd have more luck finding a thief where there were plenty of toffs, so we went down to the West End to try our luck. Nearly got pinched by the Rozzers a coupla times too. We had to do a bit of ducking and diving, I can tell you — Tom was getting right fed up, so he was. And right then, right when Tom was ready to jack it all in — that's when I saw 'im — your bloke, Mr. Holmes. Just standing there, mumbling to himself like he were daft, just like you said."

Holmes sighed and waved the florin in front of the lad's nose again.

"Try to keep this as brief as possible, there's a good lad. And where might this have been, young Stevenson?"

"I done told you already, sir — the West End. Outside that big place on Bow Street with the columns and statues and such like."

"The Royal Opera House?"

"That's the one. He were hanging about on the steps, like he were waiting for summat. I left Tom watching 'im, and ran right back here."

Holmes passed the lad the florin.

"Mind to share it with Tom — if you do not, I shall hear of it."

"Will do, sir. I'll head back there now — just to make sure your man's still there."

The boy left at as fast a run as he had come.

Holmes immediately made for his coat and walking stick.

"Bring your revolver, Watson," he said as I rose to join him. "We do not know what is ahead of us this night. Let us prepare for any eventuality."

Young Stevenson must have run like the wind or have known a shortcut unavailable to carriages, for he was already in Bow Street when our driver dropped us off at the corner of Long Acre. He ran up towards us, pretending to ask for money while simultaneously whispering to Holmes. It was a performance worthy of the Opera House itself, and I would have applauded would it not have given the game away.

"He's still there at the foot of the steps, guv'nor," the lad said to Holmes. "Tom said he ain't moved much — the rozzers had a word with him, but didn't ask him to move on. Tom says he's definitely soft in the head though — he keeps talking to someone who ain't there, and when he's not doing that, he's mumbling and shouting for his Irene."

Holmes gave the lad another tuppence; a penny for his trouble and a penny to maintain the pretence that had been so skillfully deployed. Once the lad had trotted off back to his companion, Holmes and I took up a watching brief from a secluded corner by a stall opposite the Opera House entrance.

I finally got a good look at our suspect.

He did not look in the slightest bit suspicious — indeed he seemed rather sad, pitiful almost. He was clearly disturbed, and kept up a constant conversation with some invisible companion. I was too far away to hear any of it, but it seemed alternately quiet and confidential, then angry, almost confrontational. He was as small as Holmes had surmised, unshaven, with a battered hat and a long brown overcoat. I had not yet ascertained that he had a limp, but I was in no doubt of its existence.

"What now, Holmes? Shall we question him?"

Holmes did not move from his position, but calmly lit up a cheroot.

"Now, Watson, we wait. He is here for a purpose — and I want to know exactly what that might be before approaching him."

I joined Holmes in lighting up a smoke, and settled in for a wait, trying to give every appearance of someone content to watch the world go by.

As it grew close to performance time at the Opera House the crowd thickened and swelled. Our man never left his position, although he did keep up his constant stream of chatter, enough to draw concerned glances from many of the well-to-do patrons who had to pass him to go up the steps. I watched him closely, suspecting that he might attempt to pick a pocket or two, but he showed no such inclination. My first instinct seemed to be a sound one — there was more to pity than to fear in the man.

The opera crowd all filtered inside, and the strains of an overture reached us through the still night air — something loud and bombastic — German I think although I am somewhat lacking in a musical education in those rarified realms. And still the small man stood there on the steps, oblivious to everything but the ongoing conversation inside his head. Night fell around us, and the immediate area outside the Opera House grew mostly quiet as the theatres and drinking establishments filled.

Then, just as I was about to light a fresh smoke, the small man moved, going up the steps towards the Opera House, his limp most pronounced, struggling with each step. Holmes moved to follow, and I stepped up to his side, going up into the building a dozen steps behind our quarry. We had him in our sights all the way, until we reached the foyer. He went through the main door — we followed some five seconds behind him.

When we went through the same door, he was nowhere in sight. Three house staff looked askance at Holmes and myself, as if suspecting us of attempting entry without paying. Holmes ignored their pointed stares.

"Quickly now, he cannot have gone too far. You take the left side, I'll take the right," Holmes said softly, and left my side, striding away quickly. I took my cue from him and hurried along the left edge of the foyer, where I was stopped by one of the over officious ticket collectors. He refused to let me pass.

"Not without a ticket, sir," he said. "It's a big night you see. Mahler, introducing Wagner. If we were to let everyone in who wanted to see that, then we'd have half of London at the door, and then where would we be?"

"A damn sight richer, I suspect," I replied, but didn't get a smile in reply.

"Look," I said. "I'm with the Yard. We are chasing a suspect."

"Well, you won't find one here," he replied, and started to manhandle me back the way I had come. "You're the only one to try it on since the curtain went up."

I took that to mean that no small man had been allowed to pass him either.

"There hasn't been a little man in an overcoat and battered hat?" I asked.

"You have to be dressed like a gentleman to get in here," he said, looking down his nose at my rather worn tweeds. I returned to the foyer feeling vaguely insulted, and found Holmes there already, a puzzled expression on his face.

"I have talked to four people who should have had clear sight of our quarry, Watson — and all of them swear that no one entered for several minutes before we did ourselves. It is rather a fine trick — I shall need to discover how it was accomplished. I suspect that, despite not being in the auditorium, we have just witnessed a performance put on solely for our benefit. Someone is taunting me. I intend to find out who."

We remained in the vicinity of the Opera House until the end of the performance, but caught no further sight of the small man. It was only as we were about to leave the scene that we discovered the extent to which the taunting had extended; there was uproar in the ticket office. When we investigated it was to find that the night's takings had gone from the safe — vanished, although the safe seemed to be still locked, and no one had been seen entering the back room where it was kept.

The place had been robbed, under our very noses, and Holmes had been powerless to prevent it.

Chapter 4

Needless to say, Holmes was not in the best of moods on our return to Baker Street. I tried to mollify him with brandy and a smoke, but he was having none of it.

He pushed a new pin into his map with some venom.

"How was it done?" I asked.

"I will not be toyed with, Watson," he replied, and those were the last words I got out of him for quite some time. I sat by the fireplace with a drink and a smoke, but Holmes stood glowering at his map of the crimes, as if attempting to extract its secrets by sheer force of will.

The night drew on, I started to doze off, and he still stood there at the map. He was still there when I dragged myself off to bed.

Holmes banged on my room door just as the first dim sunlight showed through the thick curtains, and came in without being asked.

"I have it, Watson, " he said as I rose, slightly groggy, from bed. While I washed and dressed he explained it to me – or at least he tried to. I was still befuddled and understood barely a half of what he said – something to do with mathematics, Fibonacci and a universal number system. He sighed in loud exasperation as, after finishing my ablutions, I expressed continued bemusement.

"Look," he said, in exactly the same tone he might use to explain something to a five-year old. "It is really very simple when you see it."

He almost dragged me through to stand in front of the map. It had been scrawled all over with straight lines in black pencil, lines drawn between the points where the crimes had all occurred.

"I have seen that already," I said, shaking my head. "I still cannot make head nor tail of it."

"Ah, but you have not seen this," Holmes replied. He took a pencil from his pocket and started to draw freehand in a circular motion, connecting all the dots that made up reports of the crimes. He stood back and waved with a flourish, as if he was a magician at the reveal of a trick.

I looked at the map.

There was now a large spiral marked there, its outermost reach being somewhere in the East End, and with the line converging down to a central spot along the Strand.

"It is a descending Fibonacci series producing a Golden Spiral," Holmes said proudly, as if that explained anything. "And the crimes follow the same descending sequence. I should have seen it sooner."

Half an hour later, after a quick breakfast of tea and toast, he was still trying to explain the *how* of the thing as we boarded a carriage for the spot on the map where the spiral curled in to an end.

"I knew already that there was some kind of pattern," he said as we got our pipes lit. "I just did not see it until I stopped looking too closely. The Fibonacci series is one of the most famous equations in mathematics. It defines a sequence of numbers made by adding together the previous two numbers in the sequence. Starting with zero, we have 0, 1, 1, 2, 3, 5, 8, 13, 21 et-cetera. By making each separate number into squares of increasing size, one atop the other in a spiral, and drawing arcs connecting the opposite corners of the squares, you get the so-called Golden Spiral.

"Fibonacci spirals abound in nature, from the arrangement of leaves and petals on plants to the curve of the shells in snails and other molluscs — and the formation of gemstones. The other place they abound is in classical art — paintings, sculptures — and even in opera. Someone has been trying to tell me something all this time — I have just been too dense to see it until now."

It must have been obvious to Holmes that I was still somewhat confused.

"Look, take my word for it, Watson. These crimes are following one of nature's most primal sequences. And like all mathematical sequences, once you know the formula, you can predict what will happen next — or, in our particular case, *where* it will happen next. And judging by last night's debacle, we are now fast approaching the end game. If I am right, then the next appearance of the small man will be the focus of the last visit — and Lestrade is about to get the surprise of his life."

"Why is that, Holmes?"

Holmes smiled.

"The next stop on the inward spinning spiral is right on top of Scotland Yard."

We had no trouble getting in to see the Inspector — both Holmes and I were well known in the Yard and indeed were given free rein of the place on a regular basis. No one stopped us as we went through the long cold corridors to Lestrade's small, messy office. Case notes, files and ashtrays littered the large desk, with more overflowing on the floor to either side. A tall bookcase contained as many empty teacups as books.

"One of these days, Lestrade," Holmes said. "I shall have to teach you the benefits of a tidy mind."

"Tidiness is all well and good in its place, but I don't have time for it," the Inspector replied. He was painstakingly writing up a file, getting more ink on his fingers than on the paper. He snorted in disgust and tossed the whole thing, paper, pen and ink onto the floor.

"I hope you have something for me," he said. "The Opera House was the last straw for the men upstairs — it was rather too close to their own pockets for comfort."

Holmes laughed.

"It may yet get closer still," he said, and told the Inspector of the spiral, and where the next stop might be.

Lestrade was, to start with at least, completely dismissive of Holmes' new theory.

"It will take more than mathematics from strange foreign chaps to catch this blighter, you mark my words. He's as slippery as an eel, this one. No — he won't be caught until he makes a mistake."

But no sooner had Lestrade finished the sentence than his Sergeant arrived at the door, flushed at the face and breathing heavily,

"He's here, sir — the suspect I mean, a small man with a brown overcoat and battered hat — just standing out in the street talking to himself."

Lestrade looked at Holmes, who merely raised an eyebrow.

"Mathematics, my dear Lestrade. The sign of a tidy mind."

Holmes was smiling to himself as we followed the Inspector out to the street.

The small man was indeed there, seemingly oblivious to the half dozen or so policemen converging on his location. He seemed no different to the last time I had seen him on the steps of the Opera House — slightly more animated if anything.

"Irene," he suddenly shouted. "I'm sorry."

"So, who is this Irene then — do we know?" Lestrade asked, turning to me.

I was loath to reply — I had been wondering the same thing, and the only Irene I could come up with was the one that Holmes refused to call by name. And if that particular lady was indeed involved, then this case might have a way to go yet before any conclusion.

"I think we will find that Irene is his wife," Holmes said softly. "The poor chap seems to be missing her sorely. Let us see if we can help him get back to her, shall we?"

We let Lestrade take the lead and the three of us stepped forward. As we approached the man I heard him more clearly. He seemed to be in discussion with an invisible — to us anyway — companion.

"Please, can I see Irene? You promised that I'd wake up when it was all done…I'd like to wake up now. Haven't I done everything you have asked of me?"

He paused as if listening then continued.

"You told me that the last time, at the Opera House," he whined, like a child denied a treat. Then he fell quiet again as we reached him.

"Don't hurt me," he said as Lestrade took his arm. "I

know what I have to do. I just want to see Irene that's all. She'll be worried, what with me being gone all this time."

"Come on, sir," Lestrade said. "Everything will seem better after a cup of tea and smoke."

The man allowed Lestrade to lead him inside, and several minutes later we were gathered around him as he sat in a chair in Lestrade's office. The Sergeant brought him a cup of strong heavily sugared tea that he took to as if he had not had anything to eat or drink for some time. He also seemed to be a smoker, puffing away happily on one of Lestrade's strong hand-rolled cigarettes like an expert. He kept muttering to himself, more of a mumble now, and mostly indecipherable.

"Well, we got him," Lestrade said as we stood over the man pondering our next move. "But I will be blowed if I know what to do with him. We can't exactly charge him with much — there is no evidence he actually committed any crimes. Everything we have is just circumstantial without any real witnesses or any of the goods."

"I know what I have to do, and I know what you have to do," the man said clearly, before going back to mumbling.

"Well, that is a damned sight more than I know," Lestrade said, and looked to Holmes. "Can you make any head or tail of this, Holmes?"

Holmes considered for a second or two, then nodded.

"I believe I may have an idea — our man seems to be mesmerized, and under the overwhelming influence of another mind. I am not at all sure he can be held responsible for his actions — the crimes must be laid at the door of the one that has him quite so befuddled."

"If what you say is true, and this is not a one time occurrence, then the courts are in for some hard decisions," Lestrade said. "'An invisible bad man made me do it then ran away' is not going to convince many juries."

"Even so," Holmes said. "I believe this man to be innocent. As I said, it is his master we must prosecute."

"And who in the blazes might that be?" Lestrade said, his temper clearly rising.

"Let us see if we can find out, shall we?"

Holmes cleared a pile of old newspapers from a chair that had been almost hidden under them, dragged it onto the middle of the room and sat immediately opposite the small man, such that their knees were almost touching. The man kept mumbling, but his eyes fixed on Holmes, watching him closely, as if wary.

Holmes took his pocket watch from his waistcoat pocket and let it hang from his hand on the length of the fob chain. He twirled the watch, first left, then right, catching the light. He spoke, keeping his voice soft and low, never taking his eyes from the small man.

"Tell me about Irene," he said. "Keep looking at the watch and tell me. She must be worried sick by now with you having been gone so long."

The small man went quiet, his gaze following the soft sway of the watch as Holmes set it swinging, very slowly, from side to side on the length of the chain.

"Irene," the small man whispered. "My Irene."

"Yes," Irene," Holmes replied. "Can you tell me when you last saw her?"

This time when the man responded, his own voice was low, matching that of Holmes in tone and timbre.

"It were three weeks ago now. Three weeks! She's going to be frantic. You promised I'd see her today. You promised!"

Holmes kept swinging his watch.

"Do not worry," he said. "You are calm, all is well. Just keep looking at the watch. See how it sways, see how it catches the light?"

The rising agitation we saw in the small man faded away as quickly as it had come. Holmes let the watch swing for several more seconds before speaking again.

"What was Irene doing when you last saw her, three weeks ago?" he asked.

"Making my supper," the man said. "Pie and mash and a bottle of brown ale. Lovely grub."

A look of sadness, so sudden to be almost comic, passed over the man's face.

"It'll be well cold by now. What a waste."

"And what are you doing while Irene is cooking?"

"Having a kip — or trying to. Bloody dreams keep waking me up. Two nights now, and it's always the same dashed thing."

"What do you see in your dreams?"

"It's not what I see — it's what I hear. A voice in the dark, whispering, every time I close my bloody eyes; a big dog barking and that bloody voice. Just give me peace, will you?"

"What does the voice say?"

"He's telling me to do things — bad things. He says he won't leave me alone until they're done. And he won't bloody stop whispering. What's a man to do?"

"I don't know," Holmes said, almost a whisper. The room had fallen completely quiet, Lestrade and I almost afraid to breathe for fear of breaking the mood. Holmes had the man talking, and it seemed we were getting to the part that was of interest to us.

"What did you do?" Holmes added.

The man started to weep, but his voice did not change timbre or tone as he replied.

"I told Irene I was just popping out for a swift pint — I hate lying to her, but the blasted dream just kept on going and the voice kept on whispering and the next thing I know I'm in a big bleeding house in Hackney stealing a statue."

The sudden leap from domestic issues to a confession of theft took us all by surprise, but Holmes merely kept going in that same soft monotone.

"How did you get to Hackney?"

"How the heck would I know? It's a bloody dream, innit? You can do anything in dreams. One minute I'm going out one door then, bang, I'm going in another miles away."

Holmes kept his voice low.

"Why this particular statue?"

"It was where it was, and where it was, was where I had to be," the man said, as if that explained everything.

"Where did you take this statue?"

"The whispering man took it away. I never saw it go — I asked him to let me wake up then, but he said I had more work to do, more places I needed to be. I dreamed of big houses, and banks, and tiny pictures of Scotsman, and diamonds and all sorts. Can I see Irene now? I need my supper."

"We won't be long now," Holmes said. "Just keep looking at the watch. See how pretty it is?"

The man fell quiet again, his gaze following the swing of the fob chain.

"Who is the whispering man?" Holmes asked.

"I don't know. I ain't never seen him — he's just a shadow in the dark. But he's always there, always whispering. I asked him if he could help me with the gammy leg — it's been giving me trouble all week, what with all this running around and no kip to speak of, but he didn't answer — he just whispers some more. He just keeps whispering, always whispering, there in the dark. Make him stop. Please make him stop."

The man was getting agitated again, and this time no amount of watch swinging seemed to calm him.

"Just one more question," Holmes said. "There's nothing to steal here. Why did you come here?"

"I know what I have to do," the man said. "You know what you have to do too — he told you, didn't he? He told me that you had been shown the way and that you were here because here is where you needed to be. Now, please, I need to see Irene. You promised."

The man's weeping overcame him and he slumped in the chair, moaning piteously. Holmes put out his free hand and stopped the watch swinging. Almost immediately the small man's weeping stopped and he started to mumble to himself again, lost in his interior dialogue.

"What did he mean, Holmes?" I asked' "Why did we need to be here?"

Holmes wasn't given time to reply. Lestrade's sergeant came to the door, motioned the inspector over and whispered urgently in his ear. When Lestrade turned back to us I saw his temper rising in him again.

"Somebody needs to have words — preferably in a dark alley — with that brother of yours."

Two men stood behind the sergeant in the doorway — tall, young athletic types with expensive dark suits and cold eyes.

"You cannot take him," Holmes said. "I need to question him further. He has not yet told us his name."

The newcomers ignored Holmes completely, and when he stood to put himself between them and the sitting man, Lestrade pulled him aside.

"They have the authority," the Inspector said, making his disgust clear. "Your brother has far too much bloody authority."

The men lifted the small man from the chair and half-walked, half-carried him out. The last we saw of him was as he turned in the doorway.

"You promised!" he shouted, then was gone, footsteps echoing away down the corridor.

"There's your answer, Watson," Holmes said. "My brother wants to see the man — and unless I'm very much mistaken, that's exactly what was meant to happen. Hurry — there's not a moment to lose."

We followed the departing men, who were moving at some haste through the corridors of the Yard. Once out on the street I expected them to have a carriage waiting, but they kept walking, turning off towards Whitehall.

"Mycroft is not at the club today, it seems," Holmes said. "They'll take him to his office. Come — I know a swifter route."

Lestrade came with us as we followed Holmes through a warren of streets and alleyways. It seemed a most peculiar shortcut to me, involving as it did much weaving and turning, but we arrived at the rear of Whitehall just in time to see the two young men approach from the south. At that point I expected Holmes to intervene on the small man's behalf, but he waited until they had taken the chap into the building before following on behind them.

We were lucky that we had Lestrade in tow, for although Holmes was indeed known inside these walls, Mycroft would not have allowed us such free access. The inspector's presence, however, ensured us passage, and we were able to hurry along, keeping the three men in sight ahead of us.

We were led deep into the bowels of the building. I have visited Mycroft in his offices in the past — a high, airy chamber with a view over Westminster. Where we were going now seemed more akin to a medieval dungeon. That feeling was reinforced when we followed the men into a low-ceiling chamber of four bare walls and a single heavy chair with manacles in place for hands and feet.

Mycroft was already there, waiting. He was not in the least bit pleased to see us in the doorway.

"I did not send for you," he said to Holmes.

"And yet, here I am, brother. And just in time to stop you torturing this poor soul."

"This poor soul is an enemy of the Empire," Mycroft said.

"Aren't we all?" Holmes replied softly.

Mycroft looked like he might make something further of it, but the small man chose that moment to become animated.

"I know what I have to do," he said and wriggled out of the grasp of the younger men, who might have slackened their vigilance a tad now that they had fulfilled their duty. That gave the man just enough time to throw himself at a clearly startled Mycroft.

"I'm coming home, Irene," the small man shouted. He wrapped his arms around Mycroft's waist, almost a rugger tackle, and the two of them, off balance now, stumbled toward the nearest wall.

I winced, anticipating a bone-crushing collision of flesh

with stone.

No such collision came. The small man, and Mycroft along with him, went through the stone, falling in and through it as if it were no more than smoke and mirrors.

We caught one last glimpse of Mycroft's startled expression, then we were alone in the room.

CHAPTER 5

Holmes was quickest to respond. He strode over to the spot where the men had vanished and wrapped his knuckles on the hard stone. He pushed with his palms, putting his weight into it, then tried with his shoulder, but the wall was resistant to any efforts to pass through.

Holmes turned toward us and pursed his lips.

"There is something going on here I cannot yet fathom," he said. "But I was right about one thing — the crimes were merely a subterfuge, playing to the gallery to draw our attention from one simple fact — Mycroft was the target all along."

He turned to the two young Ministry men.

"What's on the other side of this wall — quickly now — we may not have much time."

The younger of the two regained his composure fastest.

"If I have my bearings right, there's a corridor — it leads directly out into one of the main sewers — it's a quiet way in and out and…"

Holmes cut him off.

"Watson, Lestrade — with me."

I had to break into a run to keep up as he led us out into the warren of corridors. It is just as well there was no one to get in our way, for the look on Holmes' face told me that nothing would stop him in this pursuit. We ran, full pelt, through long empty corridors, and after a while I thought we might be quite lost, but Holmes' innate sense of place and position served him well — he brought us to another long empty passageway, then stopped abruptly. There was a single item on the ground and it was only as we approached I saw what is was — one of Mycroft's expensive leather brogues. The sight of it lying there in the otherwise empty corridor brought home to me more than anything else the fact that the man had been spirited away from right in front of us — and was nowhere to be seen.

Holmes found a sewer entrance seconds later — a plain wooden doorway that opened out into a high, wide vaulted cathedral of brick and shimmering light. The three of us crowded into the opening.

There was no sign of movement but for two rats that scurried away at the sight of us. The small man, and Mycroft along with him, had vanished.

Even then I thought that Holmes might plunge into the sewer in pursuit, but Lestrade held him back.

"It's a maze down there, Holmes — there's no sense in getting yourself lost. I have men that know the tunnels, and I'll get them onto the search. But you can see for yourself that there's no chance of pursuit. However it was accomplished, they've long gone."

Anger momentarily flared in Holmes' eyes, but was quickly quelled as he saw the sense of Lestrade's remarks.

We returned the way we had come — somewhat slower this time. Holmes retrieved Mycroft's discarded shoe from the corridor floor, and studied it long and hard, but if he learned anything from it he did not share the information. Once back in the cell Holmes again spent some time in probing at the stone walls, but quickly gave that up when it was obvious there was no readily apparent answer as to how the trick had been performed. The two young Ministry chaps were still there, standing around as if at quite a loss as to what to do with themselves. Lestrade took charge.

"I'll go with these lads and help them make a report that might make some sense to their superiors," he said to Holmes. "I suggest you two scarper right sharpish — unless you want to be here all night answering questions that none of us can answer yet. I'll check in with you when I can."

We were not stopped on exiting the building and walked up to Trafalgar Square without incident where we hailed a carriage and made our way back to Baker Street in silence. Holmes was lost in thought the whole way. It was only when we were lighting smokes by the fireplace that he spoke.

"I have been tricked, Watson — well and truly. All of the dance — the crimes, the small man, the theatrics at the

Opera House — they were all mere distractions. Somebody knew where my focus would be fixed, and used that against me, misdirecting me from the main purpose — Mycroft's abduction."

"Who would do such a thing?"

"The one who is hidden from us at the moment — the so called whispering man in dreams. Whoever he is, he knows me, Watson, knows my methods well enough to distract me — and he wants me to know that he knows, otherwise he would just have taken Mycroft with none of the theatricality and pomp. We must be more vigilant from here on in — Mycroft's life depends on it."

"So what's our first step?"

"Lestrade will have men searching the sewer tunnels by now. And if there is any kind of ransom note, he will inform us of it. The whispering man's endgame is not yet clear to me — I must think more on it."

But thinking was to be a luxury he was not to be afforded that afternoon. We were still smoking our first cigarettes when young Stevenson arrived at our door again, face flushed, as if he had been running.

"I saw 'im again, Mr. Holmes," he said when Mrs. Hudson showed him in. "I went back to keep watch. I lost your florin, see, had my pocket picked by some scally in Berwick Street — I weren't paying attention like and he had it away out of my pocket sweet as a nut. So I said to Tom…"

Holmes stopped him.

"Just tell me, lad. Where did you see him?"

"Will I get another florin?" the lad said, a look of animal cunning crossing his face.

Holmes sighed and took a coin from his pocket to show to the lad.

"But only if you're quick about it."

The boy's gaze never left the shiny florin as he spoke.

"In the same place in Bow Street — and he had another fella with him — big chap who didn't look well pleased. They were only there for a minute — then a cart went between me and 'im and when it passed he weren't there any more. But I seen 'im, Mr. Holmes, sir. He were there."

Holmes stood and traced his finger on the spiral on the map.

"And I believe you, young Stevenson," he said, tapping on the paper. "We'll be too late in getting to Kensington." He ran his finger along the spiral as it moved out from the central point at Scotland Yard. "Hatton Gardens it is then — and we'll have to be quick about it."

The boy was shifting from one foot to the other.

"What is it lad? Stop fidgetting," Holmes said.

"The florin, sir. You promised."

"So I did,"

Holmes tossed the coin across the room. The lad caught it deftly and secreted it away in his pocket.

"Is there owt else I can do for you, sir?" he said, and Holmes laughed.

"Will it cost me another florin?"

He sent the lad to the house in Kensington.

"Just in case," he said. "I just need a report of anything strange that happens — and yes, there's another florin in it for you if you spot anything and report back in a timely manner."

He was quick all right — the lad was away again even before Holmes and I reached the door.

Mrs. Hudson waited for us at the foot of the stairs. She began to admonish us for missing yet another meal, but we were forced to ignore her in our haste, and she was still shouting her outrage at us as we went out into the street and hailed a carriage.

"Hatton Gardens," Holmes said to the driver. "And quickly, please. It is an urgent matter."

I was glad of the weight of the service pistol in my pocket. Cases have a certain rhythm to them; there are times when I feel that action is imminent, and the old heart starts pumping. This was one of those times — it felt like the case was proceeding apace.

"So why Hatton Gardens, Holmes," I asked.

"It is the next spot on the spiral after Kensington," he replied. "If I am right, they will be returning the way they came, spiraling outward from the Yard — it is part of our adversary's show and tell — another piece of theatricality. I must warn you, Watson — we may be doing exactly what he intends us to do — we may be heading directly into the mouth of a trap."

I patted my service pistol.

"Then this old mouse will do some squeaking."

Holmes smiled thinly, with little good humor in it. I could not tell whether it was concern for Mycroft or merely annoyance at having been so deceived — but it was obvious that the case had taken hold of him. I knew the signs all too well — from now on, he would be at it like a dog with a bone until it was done, one way or the other. All I could do was stand by him and be of any help I could to enable him to see it through.

It was late afternoon by the time we reached Hatton Gardens. The row of jewelers' premises seemed quiet enough. The street was almost empty, it being late in the day with persistent autumnal drizzle setting in for the duration. Holmes had the driver stop at the end of the road, and we sat there for some minutes to see if anyone had taken note of our arrival. Once it was obvious that there was no sign of anything untoward we got out of the carriage and made our way to the jeweler's store we had previously visited.

The old shopkeeper looked up expectantly as we entered. He tugged alarmingly at his beard, and his eyebrows seemed to take on a life of their own, so much so that I had to look away for fear he might think me rude for staring.

"You have found them? My diamonds?" he said, punctuating each word with more beard tugging.

"I'm afraid not. Not yet," Holmes replied. "But we are making progress. I have reason to believe that the perpetrator may return here. If my calculations are right it could happen at any minute. I suggest we make ourselves hidden and see what occurs."

The old man tried to bluster.

"Calculations? Hiding? What kind of policemen are you?"

Holmes laughed.

"We are no kind of policemen at all — for which you should be thankful, for we are the only ones capable of returning your goods to you. Now be a good chap and go into your back room. Watson and I will deal with this."

The old chap left, tugging furiously at his beard, and his eyebrows looked like two gray mice running up and down his forehead as he scurried away to the back room.

I took the dark corner furthest from the door and nestled against a tall cabinet. It is just as well that I am an honest kind of chap, for there were enough gemstones on display to keep me in luxury for life should I have had the inclination to have off with them. As it was, I settled for lighting up a cheroot and making myself comfortable, preparing for a long wait if necessary. Holmes took himself away to the other side of the shop, where I lost him in the shadows as he found his own hiding place between two more of the tall cabinets.

The shop fell quiet. I heard the old chap potter around in the back room making a pot of tea, then he too fell silent. I saw a puff of smoke across the room — Holmes had lit a cheroot — but that was the only movement.

We did not have to wait long — I had just finished my own cheroot when I had the first sign that there was something amiss.

A sound came first, a rushing, as of wind in a tunnel. The air around me seemed to shift and quiver, alternating hot and cold breaths, and everything took on a heightened quality, reminding me of nothing so much as the immediate minutes before battle. I slid my pistol from my pocket — just as the small man walked through the wall to my left. I was so amazed that I dropped the cheroot, and burned my fingers as I grabbed at it to stop it falling to the ground.

The small man paid no attention to me, although he

seemed to look straight at me and must have been aware of my presence. He still had Mycroft in a tight grip, although Holmes' brother was slumped over, a dead weight and clearly out for the count. All of my medical training told me I should step forward to Mycroft's aid, but I waited for Holmes' signal before acting.

It came immediately. Holmes stepped out of the shadows as soon as the small man and Mycroft were clear of the wall. The man didn't even register Holmes' presence. He was talking to himself again.

"One step, two step, three step, four,

"Three little steps and then two more."

He took one more step. Mycroft started to slip, sliding from the man's shoulder. Holmes moved forward quickly, lunging to catch his brother's fall — and met only thin air. His grasping hands passed right through Mycroft's upper chest.

The small man and Mycroft faded, like wispy shadows, and were gone again before Mycroft's head hit the floor, leaving Holmes standing there, looking down in stunned amazement.

The shopkeeper appeared in the doorway to the back room.

"Did you get them? Did you get my diamonds?"

Holmes ignored him, tracing a spiral in the air in front of him with his index finger.

"The docks — it has to be the docks next," he said. "Come on, Watson — the longer this goes on, the further away they are going to get. We need to put a stop to this."

We left the poor shopkeeper with his eyebrows leaping and mouth gaping, and ran out into steady drizzle in search of a carriage.

We were lucky and managed to hail a ride almost immediately at the end of the road. Holmes paid the driver an extra shilling for speed, and we endured a bone shuddering journey, down the streets of the City past Devonshire Square, through the banking district to

Monument then hurtling full-tilt past London Bridge and along the shore to the docks. There was little chance of conversation during the ride as wheels bounced and rattled on the cobbles and we were thrown somewhat roughly from side to side.

Throughout it all Holmes looked grim and full of foreboding, and his mood did not improve in the slightest when we finally alighted at the St. Catherine's docks quayside just as the light was going from the sky. Holmes wasted no time in finding the Harbormaster.

"We need access to *The Chancellor* — there is no time to explain — it is a matter of life or death."

As in most parts of the city, matters of life or death could most quickly be settled with coinage, and half a crown was enough to get us access to number six quay. There we found the slightly faded grandeur of *The Chancellor* — a four-masted barque rigged for whaling, and one that had clearly seen better days.

"Why are we here, Holmes?" I asked as we approached a rather rickety gangway.

"Because the Captain of this vessel disappeared in mysterious circumstances not long before the robbery in Hatton Gardens," Holmes replied. "It may possibly have been a coincidence — but this spot also lies on the golden spiral. I am confident that this is where Mycroft will be brought next — although I will admit I am not sure what good it will do us to be here, given what just recently happened in the jeweler's store."

No more was said as we went up the gangway and into the boat.

At first I thought she was deserted — everything was still and quiet, with only a gentle rocking, almost imperceptible, to show that we were no longer on dry land. It was only as we approached the bow that we heard voices, two or three men in low, almost whispered conversation huddled over a brazier in the center of the deck. They almost jumped out of their skins when Holmes stepped forward and introduced himself.

All three were of a type I knew well — hardy, bearded chaps, barrel chested, with callused hands and wary eyes, but Holmes soon put them at ease. He joined them at the brazier, took tea when offered, and shared his tobacco pouch — it was that act more than any that opened them up to conversation. By the time I was given my tea, Holmes already had them talking. He was questioning them about the night their Captain disappeared.

"It were right here, Mr. Holmes," the youngest of the three said. "But you ain't gonna believe it. We had just tied up and were getting ready to go ashore for some ale and fun. The Cap'n was right where you are — then this chap just popped up out of nowhere. Curious wee fellow, chattering away to himself six to the dozen. We thought he had just wandered up off the dock, and I was going to see him off when he grabbed the Cap'n round the waist, staggered away toward the gunwale — and went over, or so we thought. But when we ran over to see, there was just an empty dock — just as well for the fall would have killed them both anyway. But there was nobody there, and nobody in the water — it were as if they just vanished into thin air."

Holmes quizzed all three men closely, but got exactly the same story.

"Was there anything remarkable about this intruder in your midst?" Holmes asked finally.

"Nothing at all, sir," the youngest seaman said. "A brown overcoat, a floppy hat — and I think he might have carried a slight limp — we see a lot of that at sea — but I cannot be sure."

We settled in to wait again — drinking the sailors' strong sweet tea, smoking Holmes' tobacco and listening to tall tales of whaling in cold northern waters. I was starting to think that we were on a wild goose chase when I felt something I had already felt before that night — a change in the air, a rushing as of a wind getting up. Holmes had noticed it too for he was immediately on his feet and alert. I saw the sailors' eyes widen as I too stood, and got out the service pistol, although Lord knows what I expected to shoot.

It was dashed gloomy now on deck, full night, and no moon to add much illumination. The lights of the city rippled on the water as I looked away to the west, but where I stood up on the deck was all cast in deep dark shadows. The wind rose to a stiff breeze, and it was if I heard voices in it, a far off chanting, like a choir, but in a language I could not place.

Once again I felt the old anticipation, the rush of blood before a battle. I was quite on edge by the time the air rippled, I blinked — and the small man, with Mycroft slumped in his arms, stood right in front of me, no more than two feet away.

"Get him, Watson," Holmes shouted. I moved without thinking, stepping forward and raising the pistol, butt first, aiming to rap the man hard on the head. The choir of voices swelled, a chant echoing and ringing in my head as I brought my arm down — and met only cold air.

My whole arm froze, as if it had been suddenly plunged into ice water. I staggered, almost fell, and tumbled towards the small man. I felt sure that all three of us would take a fall to the deck, but when I hit the wood, rolled and tried to get to my feet, I was once more alone as the sound of the distant choir faded and was lost in the dying wind.

The small man, and Mycroft with him, had once again eluded us.

CHAPTER 6

We had no luck in procuring a carriage when we left the docks. We were both somewhat chastened by our experience, and started to walk in silence westward along the shore toward more populous areas.

"Where next, Holmes?" I asked after a mile or so. My voice seemed to echo in my head, as if I had a cold coming on, and I imagined I still heard that dashed choir, chanting away somewhere in the far distance. Holmes answer distracted me from any concern I might have over it.

"Back to Baker Street, I'm afraid, Watson. The next spot on the spiral is way over the river in the Clerkenwell area — we will never get there — and even if we did, what could we accomplish? And after that, the widening loop takes the stop after that somewhere out past Uxbridge. Beyond that, I will need to make further inspection of the map, but I fear I am currently at a loss as to how to proceed. But one thing is for sure — we will accomplish nothing by chasing phantoms all over the country. So Baker Street it is — maybe a late supper will revive me enough to think clearly."

We finally caught a carriage on the north side of London Bridge near the Monument, and returned to Baker Street, still mostly in silence — Holmes was lost in thought again. As for myself, I still felt a cold tingle in my arm, still heard the ringing of the choir in my head, and I was looking forward to some tucker and a stiff drink.

Mrs. Hudson was only too happy to oblige me, although I had to stand for a good ticking off for having missed our earlier meal. One of her finest meat pies washed down with strong ale did much for my humor, although Holmes barely touched his own supper, and his eyes kept straying to the large map, and the spiral drawn there.

"It all means something, Watson," he said as Mrs. Hudson cleared up around us. "Although dashed if I know what."

I poured myself a stiff brandy and retired to the fire for a smoke, but Holmes went to stand in front of the map again, once more trying to force its secrets to comply with his will. I sat and smoked, sipping at the brandy, and at some point the combination of the liquor and the heat from the fire, coupled with exhaustion from the days exertions, were finally enough to send me down into sleep.

I was carried to slumber with the high choir still ringing their chant in my head.

I dreamed.

I felt a tingling — I cannot really describe it any better than that — as if a mild tremor was flowing over my body. I had a feeling of light-headedness, similar to having drunk too much Scotch, but without any of the associated dizziness. My vision blurred until all I saw was a swirling dance of color. Something took hold of my senses, and my mind roamed elsewhere, but after a time my vision seemed to clear.

I was in a high place, soaring like an eagle above a barren plain under a purple sky. It seemed I spent hours there in the air, drifting slowly toward an unseen destination, but I felt no worry, no fear. It was not like being in a dream at all, I can tell you that much. Everything seemed vibrant and alive. I felt hot wind on my face, heard it rush in my ears, and I could taste the air, acrid and bitter, like cheap tobacco. I was so enamored by the sense of freedom I felt that I failed to notice I was hovering above a vast expanse of dank moorland until I was dragged down toward it, as if I had suddenly lost the ability to soar.

I tried to back away, but a strange compulsion held me, and drew me down ever closer to the ground. At that very moment, far below, something stirred, something that knew I was there, something that was waiting for me.

It was well past time for me to seize some control of the situation, and I would forever berate myself as a coward should I have fled at that moment. I looked down at the moor and willed myself closer. I was almost surprised when it worked and I descended ever more rapidly.

I was still high above the ground but already I saw

things moving below. The dank pools that studded the moorland were full of a viscous green fluid, bubbling and frothing, throwing high spouts upward only for them to fall back with a splash to the festering slime. Thicker globules seemed to swim through the fluid and as I inched closer they gained mass, swelling into familiar shapes. Each had a torso, two legs, two arms, and a head, almost human...apart from the long snouts that gave them an almost dog-like appearance.

Ten of them grew from the slime and stood, stock-still.

As one, they lifted their heads and stared straight at the point where I hung.

They sniffed the air, as if sensing my presence.

I tried to speak, to call out, but if I had a throat and vocal cords in that place, they did not seem to be functioning. I drifted ever lower and the snouts rose in the air, snuffling in almost frantic anticipation.

I might still be there, snuffling alongside them, had the singing not started up, the same high chant that I had heard on the whaler. This time I could discern the words, although their meaning still eluded me, being in a language with which I was completely unfamiliar.

Ri linn dioladh na beatha, Ri linn bruchdadh na falluis, Ri linn iobar na creadha, Ri linn dortadh na fala.

I started to rise up away from the dank moor, slowly at first, then faster and faster, till I was being propelled at dizzying speeds through jet-black space, a snell wind whistling in my ears. Faster and faster I flew, all rational thought being blasted from my mind by the sheer speed of flight and the immensity of the space through which I traveled.

Weeks passed, or so it seemed, and still I flew, through clouds of gas that engulfed whole systems of stars. I traveled through blackness so empty and devoid of anything that it hurt my soul to even consider it, and passed worlds that had once teemed with life but were now as dead and dust-ridden as the most ancient of ruins. My brain could not encompass this journey, could not process it.

Finally, after an age, I seemed to wake with a jolt as if I had been rudely thrust back into my body, and felt at first as if I had been fitted inside a badly tailored meat-suit. I stood in some vast empty space, encased in a swirling vortex of color, blues and greens and gold shifting so fast I felt nauseated and ready to give myself over to a dead faint.

I quickly came back to equilibrium when I heard a noise — a loud snuffle. At first I believed it to be a remnant of that strange vision, but then it came again, louder this time, more insistent.

It sounded like it came from right beside me.

The swirling colors thinned and parted, enough for me to see quite clearly that a shadow shifted near to my right hand.

It snuffled — I screamed...

...and finally woke, sitting bolt upright in the chair by the fire.

I had no idea how long I had been out, but it could not have been much more than minutes — the end of my cheroot in the ashtray was still warm, and Holmes still stood by the map, oblivious to any discomfort on my part. The dregs of my brandy were still in the glass at my right hand, and I tossed it back sharply, the heat as it hit my belly doing much to ground me back in reality.

The memory of the dream was already fading, although I doubt I shall ever really forget that snuffling — and along with the fading memory, the chant finally subsided in my ears, diminished and was gone. But I remembered the effect it had had on circumstances on that blasted heath — how it seemed that the song itself had been instrumental in saving me from some insufferable fate.

I had to fight down a rather annoying tremor in my hands as I lit a smoke.

"I say, Holmes," I said. "You don't think that chanting we heard on the whaler is important do you? The cadence of it or some such?"

"What chanting?" Holmes replied.

It took no little explaining, but I was finally able to give Holmes the complete story, including what scraps I retained in memory from the dream. It took him aback somewhat.

"I heard no such noises," he said. "Not even in the jewelers, when I was as close to them as you were on the whaler. This is something new to add to the equation."

He pointed at the map, tracing the spiral out from a spot in Uxbridge, his finger moving north of the city, east then a tad south.

"Right now they are somewhere in the Romford area — the further out they get, the less precisely I can track them. And after Romford, at some point tomorrow, they will be in Beckenham, or maybe Penge — as I say, it is hard to be sure. Without more facts, we may never find Mycroft — at least not with this method of tracking him."

"Lestrade may yet come up with something," I stated, but Holmes waved me away.

"There has been no ransom note — we would have heard of it by now. And I am sure that Lestrade only knows as much as — if not less than — we know ourselves."

He left the map and sat down heavily in his chair. He lit a smoke and stared into the fire — it seemed conversation was at an end.

I was not in the least bit ready for bed, despite feeling tired and worn — the thought of another dream of that kind kept me awake for quite some time, sipping at the brandy and smoking a succession of cigarettes.

Neither of us spoke. There was nothing to say.

We had been soundly beaten, and we both knew it.

CHAPTER 7

I woke to morning sun coming through the windows. It took me several seconds to disentangle myself from where I was sitting, slumped in the fireside chair. There had, thankfully, been no recurrence of the strange dreams, although I felt far from rested.

Holmes was nowhere to be seen — there was a note on the mantel — 'Gone out, back later.' with no further explanation apparent. Mrs. Hudson had heard him leave in the early hours around dawn but had not noted the time. It did not bother me unduly. Holmes never did keep reliable hours, and I knew I would see him when he wanted to be seen, and probably not before.

I freshened up, had a swift breakfast, and headed out to the Royal Hospital for my rounds. My practice had not provided enough income to maintain me that summer, and the chance of gaining some extra money had been too good to forego — but it did mean a bit of a trek twice a week to Chelsea. It was well worthwhile, however, and a task that personally I was only too happy to fulfill, as my patients were mainly old soldiers like myself, having lately returned from battle with injuries or having been pensioned off to spend their twilight years in the care of the hospital. I spent much of my time in the wards swapping tales of service. Strangely, the work helped with my own nightmares, which somehow seemed less daunting and less severe after talking to others in much worse straits than myself.

Normally I was able to lose myself in the tasks at hand, but I had a sense of anticipation that day — something was coming, as the Bard had it, I felt it, by the pricking of my thumbs. The first sign of anything untoward came as I examined the third patient of the day — a consumptive lad no older than nineteen who was going to need full time care, and whose chances of survival were slim at best. He was by far the happiest invalid I had ever met, full of salt-of-the-earth good humor and the joy of life. It was quite humbling to behold, and made my own fretting over a bad dream feel somewhat ridiculous.

"Just promise me one thing, Doctor," he said as I checked his pulse.

"Anything you need, lad," I replied.

"If it looks like it's getting close to my time, get me a woman — any woman. I want to go happy."

I was smiling as I turned away to make a note on the record when I heard a sound that was becoming familiar — the high off singing I had heard on the whaler. It sounded as if it came from the corridor outside the ward.

"Doctor? Is anything wrong?" the lad said, having seen something in my expression. I left his bedside — the singing got louder. But when I went to investigate the corridor was empty save for a nurse coming toward me. She smiled, but it quickly turned to a frown — like the young lad in the ward she must have seen from my face that something bothered me.

The singing got louder still, and I once again thought I could trace its source — it was now coming from the stairwell on the north side of the building. I followed the sound, but when I got to the door to the stairs themselves the chanting now seemed to be coming from far below me.

A young doctor came through the door behind me, and said something as he headed upstairs, but I couldn't quite catch it.

"Sorry," I replied. "That dashed singing is just too loud."

He looked at me as if I was losing my mind and headed up without speaking again. By now I had to concede the obvious — no one else was hearing the singing but me. I wondered if perhaps I was not losing my mind, but it all seemed too real, too vivid. And more than that — I was pretty dashed sure I was being led somewhere. I started to wonder whether I should have brought my service pistol with me from Baker Street as I followed the chanting down into the bowels of the old building.

It was not difficult to guess where I was headed — there was nothing down this far in the hospital but the chilly depths of the morgue — no one ever came down here willingly. It got steadily colder as I descended to the bottom level, and the chanting rose to a crescendo, as if there was a damned choir gathered all around me. Whatever I was meant to see was close now.

"I get the message, damn you," I muttered, as I pushed through the doorway into the morgue itself, and everything suddenly went quiet.

The place was empty, and as cold as any night I'd spent in the Afghan foothills. Now that the damnable chanting had stopped, I was starting to feel quite abashed. Had I merely allowed my imagination to get the better of me — a combination of a restless night in the fireside chair and the dashed weird dreams?

But when I saw the body on the nearest slab, I knew that any attempt to explain things away was going to be beyond me.

It was a small man, looking even smaller in death, with a mop of disheveled red hair, piercing blue eyes — clouding now that his mind had departed — and what I knew had been an impish grin playing on his lips. When we had last met, his name had been Seton — then it had been something else. Whatever the case, his name no longer mattered to him — he was long past the need for any use of it.

It was obvious that this is what the chanting had brought me to see, and I immediately knew that our case had taken a lurch into unexplored territory. We were suddenly entangled again with Holmes' most brilliant, and most devious rival. This body was — or rather had been the last time I saw it — the vessel, and prison, for Professor Moriarty's immortal soul, trapped there at the climax of a case that almost cost Holmes and myself our freedom, and our lives.

I had quite put that case away to the back of my mind, having considered it concluded to everyone's satisfaction with Moriarty's imprisonment in the red-headed man's body, but now, looking down at the poor dead frame, I knew that conclusion to have been in error. I supposed there was a possibility that Moriarty had gone with the death of the body — but I was not by any means prepared to lose any money betting on it. I already had a bad feeling about Mycroft's abduction — and that had now turned to full blown dread at the thought of who, and what, we were dealing with.

I studied the body closely — it had already been stripped and washed and I could clearly see that there were no signs of foul play, nor of any cuts or bruises indicative of a struggle. He did have a long scar that ran from his left nipple across his belly. He'd been damned near gutted at some point, but that had been many years in the past — the scar was a white line against the rest of the flesh, slightly ridged and raised, but far too old to have been involved in the cause of death.

Nor were there any exterior signs of illness — I checked for jaundice, consumption and rickets — but the man had suffered none of the common ailments of the city. He looked to have been in good health, although he seemed rather pale, as if having been deprived of sunlight for a while. His teeth were good — evidence of a proper diet — and apart from some nicotine stains in his whiskers and faint traces of ink on his fingertips that had survived the washing process there was little else I could ascertain from the corpse.

What I took to be his clothes were piled on a seat in the corner, neatly folded. I went through them quickly, checking the pockets for clues. He had favored a good quality tweed suit — a Harris original if I wasn't mistaken, the jacket being worn somewhat thin at the elbows. A pair of quite expensive leather brogues that hadn't seen hardly any wear and tear whatsoever sat on top of the suit. His waistcoat had once been of some quality, but looked to have been an old favorite, stained at the waist pocket where he kept his tobacco, and worn thin on the other side where his watch would have sat. There was no sign of either smokes or timepiece. There was no wallet, no papers to identify him, and he had been written up in the file as Unknown, both in name and cause of death.

The notes told me something else too — the body had been found on the night the Jennings house had been burgled — no more than half a mile from that property.

Holmes had to be told of this matter — and right away.

My problem was, I had to idea where to find him.

I went back up to the wards, managed to persuade Doctor McPhail to cover the rest of my rounds, and headed at all haste back to Baker Street, hoping against hope that Holmes had returned from wherever he had taken himself. It was drizzling again, and carriages were few and far between, which meant I had to walk a greater part of the way, and I was quite sodden by the time I arrived, and not in the best of moods.

Mrs. Hudson met me in the hallway, and helped me get out of the wet overcoat, giving me another chiding in the process, but I scarcely took notice — my news for Holmes was big in my mind, and I was keen to impart it at the earliest opportunity. I called out his name as I headed up the stairs and entered the apartment.

The rooms were quiet and still. There was no sign of Holmes' presence, nor any that he had been there since last being heard leaving at dawn. I have known Holmes to be absent for days at a time. Normally I would have been content knowing that he was working on the case, but my news was just too important to keep waiting, and I was more than a tad frustrated at not being able to relay it.

I decided to spend the time until his return fruitfully. I headed for the cabinet containing my journals detailing our cases, and quickly found the one I was after. I took it from its place and retired to the fire with a gin and a smoke as I refreshed my memory of the salient points. Our initial investigation had been centered on addled peers in the Lords, but that had quickly turned into a flight from the law on charges of murder, and onward to the revenant of

Moriarty, his soul having survived the Reichenbach fall, and our eventual victory over him. As I read, my memory filled in the gaps, bringing everything back into focus. Some things I remembered as if they were yesterday, and not some two years in the past.

One particular passage caught my eye — reminiscences told by Seton himself — the small red-haired man whose body now lay in the hospital morgue.

"It started in the summer of ninety-four. I was sitting in my study going over a passage in The Concordances when the first attack came. It manifested itself as little more than a bad headache at first, then as a crushing pressure inside my skull such that I felt my head might implode. All at once I felt a presence, an obviously alien thing creeping through my mind, and it was only with the full force of my will that I was able to repel it. And somehow I knew the source of the attack; my correspondent had indeed found a means to migrate his soul. The trouble was, he was trying to migrate his essence into my body – and I was still the resident."

Seton's correspondent had been Moriarty, long before his downfall at the Falls, intent on finding a way to cheat an eventual death. And he had indeed succeeded, in part — his soul — for want of a better word — had continued on in its path of criminality, and Holmes and I were severely tested in our efforts to prevent him taking control of a peer of the realm. We had been helped, in the end, by Seton himself, who even gave up his own body as a prison for our adversary.

I turned pages quickly, reminding myself of that strange climax that brought the case to a close.

Moriarty's voice, that clipped English with a hint of the North, came from Seton's mouth.

"And yet, you have lost, for I am now in occupancy," Moriarty said.

I myself was in a degree of some confusion. It was apparent that the essence of Moriarty was now inside Seton – and Seton had somehow taken residence in the MacAllan body. But I had no time then to reflect on it.

Moriarty reached for the pistol, attempting to grab it from Seton's hand. All of a sudden his body jerked, as if jolted with a seizure.

"You may have occupancy," Seton said and laughed. "But as I told you, I was busy before I came here. You have recently thrown many of my kinsmen from their homes to leave them dancing in the shadows… which is where I found them. As their Laird, it would be remiss of me not to provide them with shelter in their time of need. Under the terms of your new lease you will be taking joint tenancy."

Seton's, or rather Moriarty's, body jerked again.

"Say hello to the clan Seton, and their brothers the MacAllans," Seton said. "I am afraid they are rather a noisy bunch. But they are all most eager to make your acquaintance."

Moriarty opened his mouth, but it was a loud Scots voice that replied.

"Thank you kindly Angus," the voice said. "We shall take good care of him. He won't be getting out anytime soon. We have locked the doors and closed the windows so to speak."

That voice went, to be replaced by another, more Irish sounding this time, uttering vile unrepeatable threats against Moriarty. Then a third, in a Scots dialect so thick I barely understood every second word, but the intent was very clear. Moriarty himself resurfaced for a second — just long enough to scream. The body jerked in multiple spasms, throwing it to the floor. Spittle started to fleck at the mouth. I moved to check on him, but Seton…MacAllan…whoever he was now, held me back. He still had a pistol trained on his former body.

"Just for a few seconds more, Doctor, if you will," he said. "We need to ensure that the family will be able to maintain control; Moriarty's will is strong… but they are many."

And it did seem that he was right. The spasms were being brought under some degree of control. The body went still, the only sign of life being the eyeballs frantically moving under closed lids and the mouth working as if holding several simultaneous conversations.

"The boys will keep him busy," Seton said from his new body. "And I will keep him fed and watered. He will not be bothering society again — not for a long time."

That had been the last I had seen of the little Scotsman until he turned up in the morgue — Seton ended up in a younger man's body, and Moriarty ended up imprisoned in the red haired form, held in check by the souls of all those he had wronged. It had been an ending that displeased Holmes mightily, for there was nothing to be seen, nothing tangible that could be pointed to and said to mark the conclusion. But Seton — MacAllan — had promised us that Moriarty had no means of escape from his new predicament. We took him at his word, and for all intents and purposes the case was closed.

Or so we had thought.

It as now obvious that something had gone wrong. But Seton — or rather MacAllan as he now was, had knowledge that we had never been privy to, knowledge that might yet hold the clue that would allow us to trace Moriarty, and thence Mycroft.

We had to find the man, and fast. I knew it would not be easy, for he was a secretive cove even before that last case, and that might only have served to drive him further from any prying eyes.

But we had a place to start.

CHAPTER 8

For once I had some information that my friend did not, and I had an idea as to how to proceed. But there was nothing I could do with it — at least not until Holmes returned.

In the end I had a bit of a wait — he did not reappear until late that evening. By that time I had fully reacquainted myself with the particulars of the old case, having read the journal all the way through twice, and spent far too much time pondering questions of immortality, afterlife and the schemes of our oldest, strongest, adversary.

I was actually asleep — in the armchair again, but thankfully not dreaming — when Holmes eventually returned. He had been abroad in the city in one of his favorite disguises — the elderly clergyman — and spoke to me from his work desk as he removed the stage makeup and whiskers. If I expected his first words to be of his own adventures of the day, I was to be disappointed.

"So who was it on the slab — Seton or MacAllan?" he asked.

I have long since stopped questioning Holmes' methods. He could have spotted the journal on my lap, smelled the faintest trace of formaldehyde on me, and remembered that I was working in the hospital that morning — or it could have been something else entirely that gave me away — I was rather too tired to give it much thought.

"It was Seton," I replied. "Or rather — it was the red haired body — I have become rather confused over the proper nomenclature in this matter."

Holmes laughed bitterly.

"Well, at least it has been simplified somewhat with this new development."

"How so, Holmes?"

"Well, there's one player in the game off the board now, for good or for ill — although I suspect the latter. Was he murdered?"

I quickly told Holmes all I had seen during my

examination of the body. He pressed me on several points, and seemed almost disappointed that he could not find any fault with my observations.

"His heart gave out then? Is that the prognosis?"

"Perhaps," I replied. "It looked to me like he just decided to stop breathing."

"You might be closer to the truth than you realize," Holmes said.

He finished clearing off his disguise and came over to join me by the fire. We both lit up smokes.

"As for how I knew it must be one or the other of the men," he said. "I too have new developments to report."

He puffed on his cheroot before continuing.

"As you are probably aware, I was up most of last night, pondering the problem. Given our lack of progress, and being outdone at every turn, I decided to take a different tack. First thing this morning I went out to look for our man's wife, his Irene. I went incognito — we have not been having much luck so far travelling openly, I'm sure you'll agree.

"I had spotted something, you see. The small man who took Mycroft told me something — or rather, his coat did — I had got a closer look at him on the whaler than I had previously. His overcoat used to be an expensive one at one time, and after some reflection I believed I recognized its provenance.

"So this morning bright and early I took myself down to Regents Street as a vicar looking for something warm for the winter, having been recommended by a parishioner — Irene as it happens — and began making inquiries.

"As you know, the workers in the retail premises are a fountain of useful gossip if you can stand to spend the time gathering it. My old vicar was just the man for the job, although I admit to becoming rather weary of hearing tales of the latest scandals involving actors and theater folk. But it was all worth it in the end, for eventually I encountered someone who remembered the coat, and Irene, its buyer. I was even fortunate enough to get an address, in Stepney. I considered returning here at that point to include you in the rest of the investigation, but by then you would have already have been on your way to the Royal. Also, I decided to stay in character, for an elderly clergyman is someone a woman is often more comfortable conversing with.

"And that is where I have been these last few hours — talking to the distressed wife of a lost husband. I was happy to assure her that her man — David Finn is his name — was alive. I did not go into the details of just how strange he had become — she was more than happy to know he was not dead, and that was enough for me to get her to tell me their story."

Holmes stopped and tapped off the ash from his cheroot.

"Fetch some brandy, would you, Watson. I have already done a great deal of talking today and my throat is parched — some lubrication is required."

I did as he requested, pouring us both a stiff one, and returned to the fireside chairs to hear the rest of his tale.

"I know you must have had a shock in the morgue, Watson," he said. "Seeing the red haired man again must have brought that case back to you. So you can imagine how I felt when Irene Finn told me that she'd seen the self-same man talking to her husband not an hour before he disappeared out of her life.

"At first I thought it must be coincidence; small, red-headed Scotsmen are, after all, not that rare. But as she described the man she had seen, my own certainty grew, and I made the same connections that you no doubt have now made for yourself.

"I do not know how such an infernal thing has been done — I never really understood Seton's mumbo-jumbo back then anyway — but there can be little doubt of it. Moriarty is back again. And he has Mycroft."

We smoked in silence and sipped our brandy for a time, each lost in our own thoughts.

"There is only one other thing of note," Holmes added eventually. "Just before he disappeared, David Finn told his wife that the red-haired man had invited him to a meeting — a business meeting that would be most advantageous to their circumstances. This meeting was to be held in Colchester — and that is where we must take ourselves first thing tomorrow. This is the only clue we have, and I intend to pursue it, wherever it may take us. We have been reacting to events long enough — it is time to take the lead in this dance."

If Holmes had any further thoughts on Moriarty's intentions, he was not prepared to share them at that time. Besides, I was growing exceedingly tired; recent exertions and having slept in a chair the night before were all well and good, but I'm not the young man I once was. I drained the brandy and dragged my weary body off for a most welcome sleep.

I had given no thought to any dreams — my tiredness had been so extreme that I barely managed to have a quick wash then tumbled into bed. But any hope I had of rest was quickly quashed. It seemed that I had just closed my eyes when the dream came — it was not of the moorland this time, there was no soaring on high above endless vistas. I stood alone in the place of dancing color, encased in a swirling vortex of blues and greens and gold shifting so fast I again felt nauseated and ready to give myself over to a dead faint. As before I knew I was caught in a dream, but was unable to wake myself, or force myself into any course of action other than standing in place and waiting to see what happened next.

The air moved to my right, color shifting, green and red now.

Something snuffled, and I smelled it — the odor of wet dog.

The swirling colors parted, and I saw that someone — something — stood, mere feet away to my right, watching me.

White incisors, as sharp as any razor, caught the dancing auras of light as it raised a damp snout and snuffled. Below the neck the thing looked superficially like a human, although there were rolls of pink fat in places, and taut sinew and muscle in the shoulders and arms — arms that came to an end not in hands, but in coarse paws with black, thorn — like claws. The head was elongated, and covered in wiry stubble of coarse hair, with long, flashy ears. Beady eyes, like black pearls, were sunk in near shadow above a snout with wet, flaring nostrils. It drew too-red lips back and showed me its teeth as it growled. A caustic stench permeated the air, causing me to gag, strong enough to make my eyes water and sting.

I was still struggling to comprehend what I was seeing when the dog-thing pawed at the air, as if distracted by the swirling dance of light. And the color itself seemed to react, pulsing in time to the waving of the thing's arms.

The beast snuffled loudly and stamped its feet. The color pulsed in time.

It raised its head and howled. A swathe of red pulsed strongly and, as if angered, the dog-thing punched at the swirling colors in the air ahead of it. The colors rang, as if struck like a bell.

The beast roared again, bellowing in rage. It threw itself forward against the swirling aura. Blue, green and yellow burst as bright as sunlight, sending the snuffling thing cowering away, arms raised over its head, only a single black eye peeking through the gap, keeping its gaze fixed on me as it snuffled piteously.

The colors softened, sending out a wash of pale yellows and soft oranges, like dusk on an autumnal evening. The singing, ringing chant I was coming to recognize rose up, softly this time, in an almost singsong tone, as a mother would sing a lullaby. The beast's breathing became less rapid, less heavy. It calmed and went still as the color washed over it. The staring eye lost its focus, and slowly closed.

Within minutes the thing was huddled on its haunches, sound asleep.

At the same time I felt the stirrings of waking work

through me.

Just as the dream ended and reality started to fill in around me, I thought I heard a voice speak in my ear, a single word in a Scottish accent.

"Colchester."

Chapter 9

I informed Holmes of the dream early the next morning as we made our way to Liverpool Street Station, intent on taking a train going east.

"I cannot see the relevance, Watson," he replied after some thought. "It may merely have been due to tiredness and confusion after our recent activities. Or it may be that your dreams are trying to tell you something significant to the case — something your daytime mind has forgotten, or chosen to ignore. In either case, we can only hope that all will become clear when we reach our destination."

We traveled light — Holmes decided we did not need to prepare for an overnight visit, so I had only my smokes and my service revolver with me in my overcoat.

"If we get nothing today, there is no time to hang around searching," he said. "I aim to be back here by nightfall. There is still a chance that Lestrade will get a ransom note, and I want to be here for that eventuality."

We breakfasted on the train — a rather nasty concoction of overdone bacon and underdone eggs with tea that tasted of sugar and very little else, and I was glad of a smoke to get the taste of it all out of my system. We had the six-seat carriage to ourselves — most passengers are headed into London, not out at that time of the morning. For once Holmes was in a voluble mood, so I let him talk while I smoked, and tried to rid my mind of the memory of the snuffling beast and the dancing colors from my dream.

"The Moriarty affair has been occupying my mind. I never really rid myself of the thought that we had left that case unfinished," he began. "It was all so outlandish and ultimately unsatisfying. It has however forced me to reevaluate my thinking on the power of the will. It is clear that Moriarty has transcended the mortal form — both he and Seton managed to convince me of the truth of that. But is it merely a matter of will? Or is there some physical or chemical aspect to our bodies that can be transferred from one to another that will enable science, at some future time, to duplicate this phenomenon? What we consider magical or supernatural may merely be a level of science we are not yet equipped to comprehend. At least, that is what I have to tell myself — it allows me to keep firm in my belief that rationality is all. But I confess, Watson, I sometimes wonder. And this case has me wondering even more than ever."

I took advantage of this burst of volubility from Holmes to ask several things that had been bothering me.

"What would Moriarty want with Mycroft?"

"I should think that was obvious, Watson," Holmes replied. "Imagine him doing his trick with Mycroft rather than the man Finn? He would immediately be thrust into a position of great power and authority — and be sitting in the middle of a spider's web of influence — not over crime this time, but over the great affairs of state, all over the world. Imagine what a man such as Moriarty would do with such power. He would indeed have fresh worlds to conquer. We cannot — we will not — allow such a thing to happen."

"And what if it has happened already?" I asked.

Holmes shook his head.

"If he had that power already, he would not have needed all the theatrics in Scotland Yard and The Diogenes Club — he would just have taken it. No — he has been distracting me to gain time for himself. How much time he needs remains to be seen — but I am confident that he has not yet been successful, for surely Mycroft would be back in the world by now, with Moriarty in charge? We have time yet."

Holmes sat back and closed his eyes, but I had one more question for him — I already guessed he was not going to like it. At times like these I was little more than a sounding board for Holmes' thinking out loud — I might as well have been a desk or a bookcase for all the response he expected from me. But one thing had continued to bother me, and I had to voice my concerns, even if in doing so I risked a rebuke.

"This bally walking through walls trick of his — how is it done? It must be some kind of illusion — but I'll be damned if I can make head or tail of it."

"That makes two of us, Watson," he said resignedly. "But before we are done, I will get to the bottom of it — I promise you that much."

I saw doubt in Holmes' eyes, but did not question him further — I saw little point, as the importance of our current mission was amply clear to me. I patted my service revolver to make sure it was still in place in my pocket. I was becoming more and more sure that it would be needed at some point soon.

The train pulled into Colchester in mid-morning dead on time. We had a short uphill walk from the station to the town center, and once we got there Holmes wasted no time in trying to track our quarry.

Armed with detailed descriptions of both David Finn and the small Scotsman we visited every business, retail establishment and inn along the main street. We lunched in an old Drover's inn where Holmes visited every table, after which we talked to the stall owners in the long covered market, and questioned the carriage drivers at the rank in the square. It was there in the late afternoon that we finally got the breakthrough all of our previous legwork deserved.

"I remember him," an elderly driver said. "He passed through a couple of weeks back."

He stopped there, and looked pointedly at Holmes, who knew this particular dance well, taking a shilling from his pocket and showing it to the man.

"There's more where that came from if your information is useful."

The old man's gaze flitted from the shilling to Holmes' pocket, as if gauging how many coins might be there. He sat high above us in the driver's seat, and didn't deign to come down to our level. This meant he had to speak loudly to make himself heard, and everybody within twenty yards heard the ensuing conversation. If Holmes was hoping to stay incognito, this was certainly not the best way to be going about it.

"Peculiar chap, I thought," the cab driver continued, spitting out a rancid wad of tobacco that I had to step back to avoid. "And he was most excited about something. Never got much chance to talk to him, though. It were lashing down with rain that day, and he stayed inside, well under cover the whole way. I got soaked through, and he never gave me a tip neither, so I didn't hang about to wait for him; not that I would, like, not at that house."

Up until that moment Holmes had been content to let the man talk, but he stepped forward then, and handed him the shilling.

"Which house was that? Can you take us there — right now?"

The man sucked his teeth.

"It's east of the river. I don't generally go east of the river."

Holmes sighed and took another shilling from his pocket. The old man took it and smiled.

"It's not a nice spot — no place for a gentleman like you, sir," he said. "And it's a fair way out of town — I'll not be getting any other fares while I'm out there, so it'll cost you extra."

Holmes didn't deign to show the man any more of his money. "I assure you, my good man, I am more than willing to pay." Without waiting for an answer he got up into the carriage, and as I stepped in to sit opposite him the vehicle rattled away across the cobbles.

The journey did indeed take some time — we made our way out of town to the east, crossed the old stone bridge and kept going along a rutted track through dank desolate moorland, a landscape that brought my strange dreams back to the front of my mind.

The light was already going from the sky, the day almost done by the time we turned off into a driveway that was slightly better maintained than the track we left behind. Minutes later the carriage came to a halt.

"End of the line, gents," our driver shouted, and cackled

as if he had just made the best joke ever.

Holmes got out first and paid the man — three more shiny shillings.

"If you want me to wait and take you back with me, it'll be an extra half a crown," the driver said.

"In that case, you may go," Holmes replied after a moment's thought. "I do not know how long we will need to be here. Perhaps you could return in the morning — once the sun is well up?"

I saw relief in the man's eyes — he was not happy at all to be out here in the growing gloom. I wondered just how bad the reputation of our destination must be to affect him so. Then I saw one reason for myself as soon as I descended from the carriage and turned to look at the property.

It was as dismal an outlook as you are likely to see in the country — there were no gardens, no outbuildings, just a squat gray house on two levels with four aged leaded windows around an oak door that was so badly weathered the lock looked scarcely necessary. Ivy had once crawled across the walls but even it had balked at taking a foothold in so bleak a spot, and it was as gray and dead as the stone where it had failed to take root. Clouds slumped across a leaden sky that only allowed us the merest glimpse of an orange sun sinking into the mire to the west. As I looked up to one of the upstairs windows, a shadow seemed to move just inside, as if someone had been caught taking note of our presence and was now attempting to hide. I was about to remark on it to Holmes when our driver let out a yelp of terror, and whipped his horses into action. The carriage was off and away — we could not have stopped him had we wished to.

Holmes and I were left alone on the steps of the old house as the last of the sun went from the sky.

There was no light in any of the windows, no sound save the whistling of the wind in the sedge and the rapidly departing echo of hooves as the carriage made its getaway. I drew my pistol — it seemed appropriate. Holmes raised his stout walking cane and rapped, hard, on the old door.

We got no answer.

Holmes turned to me.

"I did not come all this way to spend the night on the doorstep," he said with a smile. "What say you, Watson? Is a bit of breaking and entering in order?"

I was loath to encourage him in wrongdoing, but the prospect of a night with only the dank moor to look out on did not appeal in the slightest. I motioned towards the door.

"Have at it, Holmes. But try not to do too much damage, there's a good chap."

I need not have worried on that account. The door gave way beneath a single hefty shove of Holmes' left shoulder.

"After you, Doctor Watson," he said with a grin, and ushered me inside with all the mannerisms of an over obsequious butler. I walked past him into a dimly lit hallway. It took several seconds for my sight to adjust to the gloom, but it looked at first glance as if the place had been lying vacant for quite some time. Dusty off-white sheets covered what little furniture there was, the floors were hard wooden boards that had been badly scuffed and scarred over a long period of years, and the sound of a constant drip from somewhere inside probably meant that the roof was in a state of some disrepair.

"It might have been a bad idea to send the carriage away, Holmes," I said. "This is not the most homely of places in which to spend a night."

He clapped me on the shoulder.

"We have endured worse, Watson — indeed, we have slept in far worse," he replied.

"But that still doesn't mean that I have enjoyed the experiences," I answered, but he had already left my side and walked deeper into the dark hallway and was soon out of my sight.

"You take upstairs, Watson, " he said from the darkness. "Shout out if you find anything of interest."

I had my pistol gripped firmly in hand as I went up the staircase, gingerly, testing each step to make sure it would take my weight — given the state of the rest of the house, I was sure that rot must have set in somewhere. After a few steps I stopped hearing Holmes moving below. Silence fell around me, and the darkness got deeper if anything. I struggled to see more than a few feet upstairs ahead of me, and started to regret not having searched for a candle or lantern before ascending. I looked up, but there was only a wall of black shadow at the top of the stairs.

"Blow this for a game of soldiers," I muttered. "There is clearly no one here but Holmes and myself."

I had already started my turn to go back when I heard it — a high singing, the now well recognized chant, coming from a far distance — but also most definitely coming from somewhere up above me.

"Holmes!" I whispered, but he was either too far away to hear, or too preoccupied in his own search to pay me any attention.

The chanting got louder, and something heavy shifted above me — I felt the air move, a slight breeze that brought with it the unmistakable odor of wet dog.

"Holmes!" I said again, as loud as I dared, but there was no answer. I gripped the pistol tighter and held it in front of me. The next step was one of the hardest I have ever taken. But I took it — and three more before I came to a landing.

I took several more steps to ensure I was well clear of the stairs should any attack be forthcoming. There was a certain degree of light here — a high domed skylight up above me let in a pale glow, as of weak moonlight through thick fog. Three doors led off the landing, and the chanting came strongly through the farthest from me. The smell of dog also got stronger as I walked over and put my free hand on the door handle.

The singing rose loud in my ears, as if a full choir stood just on the other side. But even above that another sound was clearly audible, coming from under the door where it met the floor — a loud snuffle, followed by a low growl.

I stepped back, taking my hand from the door handle.

There was no repeat of the snuffling, but the choir got

louder still, more insistent. As before in the morgue, I felt I was being led toward something I needed to see. I stepped forward again and, before I could talk myself out of it, turned the handle and pushed the door open.

The room was empty of all furniture, and dominated by a large double circle painted on the floor in red paint, the inner track of which was daubed, rather crudely, with what I could only take to be occult symbols. A prone figure lay in the center, curled up, clutching his knees to his chest as if in pain.

The figure turned and looked at me as the singing rose to a howling scream. I recognized the man immediately, and saw that he was in clear need of medical help, but before I could go to his aid the chorus of singing cut off, and the man called out.

"Look out, Watson," he shouted.

I turned just in time as something launched itself from the corner of the room behind me. My old soldier's instincts saved me — the pistol came up and fired without any thought in the process. I caught a glimpse of a hairy snout, felt warm, fetid breath in my face, then there was a howl, full of pain and anguish. A blacker shadow fell away from me, gone before it reached the floor, faded into nothingness. I heard another noise to my left, saw shifting light and shadow at the corner of my eye, and turned, gun still raised.

"Please don't shoot me, Watson," Holmes said from the doorway, raising an oil lamp so that I could see his face. "I just came to see what the commotion was all about."

I lowered the gun, and I'm not ashamed to admit that my hand trembled rather severely as I put the weapon away in my pocket and went to the aid of the man on the floor. By instinct I stepped over the paint work on the floor, my feet not touching any of the lines — silly superstition getting the better of me in that instant.

I knelt at the man's side. The last time we had seen him he was going by the name MacAllan — one man inside another's empty shell. He looked like he had been walking a long hard road since then.

He looked up at me from eyes filled with pain.

"You came," he whispered. "I didn't know if you'd understand."

Then he fell silent, unable to talk. He was as fragile as any living man I have ever seen. His eyes were sunk, black pools deep in his skull. His lips were gray, parched and dry and his skin was as thin as the finest paper. I was almost afraid to touch him lest he should fall apart like so much ash in my hands.

"Fetch me some water — or brandy — anything you can find, Holmes," I said. "The poor chap is at death's door."

Holmes ignored me and spoke directly to the man, his voice raised, almost a shout.

"Where is he?" Holmes demanded. "Where is Mycroft?"

"As you can see, he is not here," the man whispered. "This is the beginning — you need to look for the end."

He grabbed my wrist. It would have taken me no effort at all to pull away, but it seemed he had something to ask me.

"The body in the morgue. It is still whole? There was no autopsy?"

It was such a strange question at that moment that my reply was instinctive.

"No — the only scar was the old wound below the nipple."

The man managed a thin smile, although his lips cracked with the effort, and a dribble of clear fluid ran down his chin.

"Ah, but that was a good fight that one. And a close call — like this one." His grip tightened, as if in the clutches of fresh pain. "Break the circle, Watson — quickly. There's no time left. A simple smudge should do the trick."

I looked to Holmes. He looked at his feet, and scuffed a line through both tracks of the circles. The man — MacAllan — looked up at me.

"I will see you soon," he said, and closed his eyes.

His hand fell away from my arm, and when I checked his pulse it was to find what I already knew.

The man was quite dead.

CHAPTER 10

As I stood there looking down at the body I truly believed we had come all this way only to endure yet another failure.

"We were too late, Holmes," I said. "There's nothing here for us."

"Perhaps not, Watson," he replied. "There is something downstairs you should see."

We left the body on the floor — he was not going anywhere, and neither were we, until the morning at least. Holmes led the way with the lamp as we went back down stairs and into a large, well-appointed sitting room cum library. Where the rest of the house had seemed in a state of some disrepair, this room looked like it had been lived in until recently. Someone had been using a Chesterfield sofa as a bed, and books were piled high on either side of the high winged armchairs by a fireplace that had a large pile of fresh firewood in front of the grate. The library itself was a well-appointed one, the shelves full on all sides of aged leather bound tomes in which I could gladly have lost myself for weeks.

The thing Holmes had brought me to see was immediately obvious as he moved over to stand beside it — the left hand wall of the room was dominated by a large map of London and the South-East, produced to a much larger scale than the one above Holmes' own workbench. Despite the difference in degree of scale, the similarities were immediately obvious when Holmes raised the lamp closer. A large spiral had been marked on the map, connecting a series of pins centered in the Westminster area and spiraling outward — with the last pin right at the spot where we now stood — on the remote moor to the north and east of Colchester.

"I believe this was MacAllan's residence," Holmes said. "And he was intent on following the same pattern as we have been — the difference being that he already knew the starting point."

"The start of what?" I said. "I am still somewhat at a

loss as to the bally point of all this, Holmes."

Holmes smiled thinly.

"Perhaps this will make things clearer."

He led me through the length of the library to the back. There was a stout oak door at this end of the room — in rather better condition than that at the front of the house. The door had once been locked from the library side by a series of hefty bolts, but it now lay open, revealing another room beyond.

As I stepped inside I saw that I had been wrong — this was not a room. It was a cell, and it was obvious that someone had been imprisoned here for some time. The bed was little more than a straw mattress and thin pillow, there was a single hard chair, a short shelf of books — mathematical principles and astronomical theory mainly — and a table containing a chamber pot and tall water beaker for ablutions. Beyond that it was a dismal place, as bad as any police cell anywhere.

"Do you see?" Holmes said, but I am afraid I had been somewhat befuddled by the whole experience since our arrival at the house — and I had no desire to stay in that cell a second longer than was necessary. I retreated post-haste to the library, where I helped myself to a glass of Scotch from a decanter on the mantle of the huge fireplace. The liquor was just what I needed — more fiery and peat-filled than I was used to, but none the less welcome for it. I felt its heat spread through me, restoring my equilibrium, and by the time I lit a smoke I was feeling more like myself.

Holmes came through and showed me something he held between his thumb and forefinger — three hairs, human, and clearly ginger. He tossed them into the grate and joined me in a smoke

We both stood in front of the large map, as he traced his finger along the spiral.

"He had Moriarty in there, Watson," he said, inclining his head toward the back room. "Or rather the body containing Moriarty's essence — soul — consciousness — whatever you choose to call it. And it looks like he kept him there for some time — possibly months. Then something happened — my guess is that Moriarty found a way to get the Finn chap here, and that precipitated a whole series of events."

"Events? You mean the crimes in London?"

"Yes, Watson. Events that were all part of some elaborate scheme to distract me from his real purpose." He ran his finger inward along the spiral. "Events that lead all the way to Whitehall."

As his finger landed on the pin that marked where Mycroft had been taken from us, we both spotted something else, something the smaller scale of Holmes' own map had not allowed us to pinpoint — there was another pin in this map, inside the last, in Central London.

Holmes took the lamp closer and peered at the map, then had me lean in to take a look. The pin was stuck in The Strand — right over the top of the building containing the Diogenes Club.

I remembered the dying man's words in the room upstairs.

"This is the beginning — you need to look for the end."

"We have been distracted again, Watson," Holmes said, and I heard the anger in his voice. "The sightings after Mycroft's abduction were just more diversions to lead us off the scent — he was never going to be brought out here — Moriarty's plans are too tied to the seats of power for him to stray this far out. But by finding this place, we may just have put ourselves ahead of his game. We have to get back to London."

I looked around us. Beyond the circle of light afforded by the lamp, everything in the house seemed to sit in total darkness.

"That will be easier said than done, old man. We sent the carriage away."

Holmes laughed bitterly.

"That I did. And I regret it now." He stepped and thought for a few seconds. "Well, I shall waste no time in worrying — the walk back to Colchester would take us all night in any case, stumbling around on a moor where we do not know the path. We shall stay here in the dry and relative warmth, and then make all haste in the morning when the carriage returns."

I was about to remark on my uncertainty that the frightened driver who had taken off so readily would ever, in fact, return, but I kept quiet — the night was going to feel long enough with adding any worries we could not in any way influence.

We did our best to get a fire lit in the grate, shared some stale biscuits we found in a pantry in a rear scullery, and helped ourselves to more of the admittedly fine Scotch as we resigned ourselves to a night in the fireside chairs. As we settled, Holmes showed me a book he had lifted from the top of a pile beside his chair.

"I believe this is a journal of sorts, Watson — MacAllan's journal. We may find something of use in here."

Holmes sat the lamp on top of the pile of books beside him to enable him to read the journal, so all I could do was watch the fire, have a smoke, and listen to my friend as he related snippets from the Scotsman's writings.

"The first entry is dated January the twenty first, of this year," Holmes started, and read — he put a slight Scottish accent into his reading, which did much to bring it to life for me.

"'It is just as well that they have come. They have been in Scotland this past year at the ancestral home, and for a time they had control, keeping him way down below the surface of their thoughts. But M is far too strong for them to contain. He has been seeping into their dreams — he must have a truly prodigious mind, the like of which I have never encountered before in all my long years. But he is not strong enough to escape completely from his cage — not yet. He is forced to remain in my old form, and will stay there for as long as I can keep him here. I have to make preparations, for it might turn out to be a long stay — for both of us.'"

Holmes looked up.

"So now we know what happened after the incidents in that blasted train — some time after, I will admit, but I feel better in knowing that they were both hidden away here, these past months. At least Moriarty's ambitions have been contained. Until now."

He went back to reading, and didn't speak for so long that I thought he had no more snippets of interest for me. Just as I lit another smoke, and was considering fetching more Scotch, he started to read again.

"From an entry dated the tenth of February.

"'I have been left alone with him. My clansmen can take the dreams no longer, and have departed the vessel, drifted away to whatever part of limbo they choose to inhabit. There is only M now, and I find I cannot look at him — to see the body I inhabited as a mere container for another now that my kin have moved on is too much for me to bear. I have put bars on the window of the back bedroom, and heavy bolts on the door. I shall keep him in there. He will not speak, and I am not sure if he can — he has not learned how to control the body — his time with my brothers seems to have weakened his connection to the physical, which may yet prove to be the only saving grace in this whole affair.'"

Holmes paused and looked up.

"This may indeed be good news, Watson — it may be that there is little more to Moriarty's plans than some curious mental gymnastics — and that is something I can deal with."

He flipped pages, then read again.

"This is dated the fourth of April.

"'I can hear him in my dreams. He has taken the persona of a great black dog, snuffling and growling — all huff and puff that will avail him nothing, for the protection chant is more than sufficient to keep him at bay. Let him howl.'"

Holmes paused to get a fresh smoke lit. I took the opportunity to make a visit to the decanter for more Scotch for both of us, and filled the glasses with stiff measures. I had a feeling it was going to be a long night.

"The chant is written out here in Gaelic, Watson — it looks like it is the same one you have been hearing. This grows more curious by the minute — I an starting to wonder who is the more insane of the two men who lived here, the captive or the captor?"

He read and I smoked. The house lay dark and quiet around us, and I was all too aware that there was a dead man somewhere in the rooms above us. There was also the black dog to consider — it may only have been some kind of mental projection according to Holmes — but I had smelled it well enough, and felt the heat of its breath. I ensured that my service pistol was still close to hand, and resolved that this would be my last glass of Scotch. If I was destined to meet that hound again, I intended to do it sober.

Holmes spoke up again.

"He has reached June now — and now he does not sound nearly so sure of himself."

"'I believed that my chant was enough to keep M out of my head, but it seems I have underestimated both the strength of his will and his cunning. He has grown mightily strong these past weeks, and although he still does not speak I now suspect it is because he has no desire to do so, rather than from some innate inability. The black dog still haunts my dreams — but it is now manifesting itself in the shadows in the corners in my waking hours, becoming ever more solid with each passing day.

"'I can scarcely believe it possible, but he has mastered the art of the transmutation of matter, molding it to his will. This is a great magic I have not seen performed in many a year — only those with access to the oldest books and the deepest knowledge have managed it in the past. As far as I knew, the only one who knows the manner in which it can be accomplished is myself, locked away in the depths in the dark places of my memory. Yet M has been there, that much is obvious now — he has rifled through my secrets and used them for his own devices. And I am worried what else he has learned. He may not be able to take another body — not yet — but he can certainly influence one, and if anyone other than myself comes to his attention or comes close enough to fall under his influence, I fear for their safety.

"'Perhaps I should just put an end to him, here and now. My kin have long fled, so there is only M there, locked in the body. But it was my body, all those long years — I still find that I cannot harm it. However, if M gets much stronger over the next weeks, I may have to.'"

Holmes looked up again.

"We are seeing a pattern here, Watson. Moriarty is getting stronger, and MacAllan — Seton — whatever we call him, is getting weaker. We have almost got the whole tale now."

"But we are still no nearer to finding Mycroft."

"I wouldn't be so sure about that," Holmes said.

He turned several more pages, then let out a gasp of astonishment. I thought he might throw the book away from him before he stilled, regaining his composure.

"I'm sorry, Watson — I have just had a bit of a shock. This last entry is in a different hand entirely. And it is addressed to me personally."

"'My dear Sherlock,

"'I hope this missive finds you well. If you are reading this, I am long since gone and my plan has already come to fruition. All of your intellect, your will and your fury have availed you naught, for you see, just as you are still here, as am I. We are both survivors of a great fall, but only one of us can be the Lightbringer and lead the world out of darkness.

"'I will admit it has not been the easiest of journeys to this point. I have done my penance in the wilderness, in the dark. My time is at hand, and I am glad you shall be here to see it.

"'Seton almost had me. But he was too certain of his own strength — a fatal flaw in any man, I am sure you will agree. All I had to do to best him was find another, more appropriate, vessel for my will.

"'I found the Finn man with ease — he has the most malleable mind of anyone in London, and is the perfect tool for me to use for this next stage of the journey. I fetched him here, and had him overpower and cage the MacAllan body, the way I myself was caged. It is only fitting. You will find him upstairs, if you have not already done so.

"'I can only manage short bouts of control, as evidenced in the writing of this letter. However it is only a matter of time before I can leave Seton's old body behind completely and move into Finn for a while. His mind does not have the necessary rigor and structure for me to do much more than move him around like a chess piece.

"'I believe, however, that I have the perfect answer to this little difficulty, one that will ensure that my rise shall be a swift one indeed.

"'The next time we meet, you will look me in the eye and call me brother.

"'Until then,'"

Holmes looked over at me again.

"It is signed, simply, 'M.'"

Holmes tossed the journal over to me.

"There is more to the journal than that of course — a lot of mumbo-jumbo ritual and magical rites that I do not care to peruse. I believe we have the gist of it. Moriarty has taken complete control of the situation. He and Finn left that poor chap upstairs, then discarded Seton's body in London during the night of the Jenning's burglary. He is now in Finn's body, which is a mere way station in his quest to take over Mycroft — I suspect for the power it will bring him as much as for any great need for my brother's mind. So we have learned the how and why of it at least. And we have a single clue — the last pin on the inward spiral. The morning cannot come quickly enough for me, Watson. And there is still much I do not understand. Could you fetch me another Scotch please? Maybe that and another smoke will help."

We sat in silence for the longest time after that. I had the journal in my lap but could not read a word of it for Holmes still had the lamp at his side, and there was insufficient light reaching to where I sat. I contented myself as before, with smoking and staring into the flickering flames of the fire.

I was thinking of the black dog again, unable to get the snuffling and growling out of my mind. I was also thinking of a cold night in the Afghan foothills, and a group of squaddies gathered around a fakir, a local mystic intent on both giving us a show and relieving us of smokes and liquor. He had a trick where he had Sergeant Emery believing that there was a snake down his pants, and I was wondering if this black dog was not something similar in the way of overwrought suggestion.

I had almost convinced myself when I heard it.

Something sniffed, loudly, in a far dark corner of the library.

CHAPTER 11

Holmes looked up.

"You are not going mad, Watson, I heard it too this time," he replied, keeping his voice low and steady, and never taking his eyes from the dark corner that had been the source of the sound. "You have your pistol?"

"Yes," I replied, hardly more than a whisper.

"Keep it ready — but don't shoot unless you absolutely have to."

Holmes stood, lifting his stout walking cane from where it had been leaning at the side of his chair. The thing in the corner sniffed again, then growled, a low rumble that sounded like it came from deep in its chest.

The shadows grew thicker, and I smelled it — wet dog — a slightly rancid odor, as if it had been rolling in the bog waters outside. It growled again; closer now, and I made out its shape as it came forward into the dim light cast by the oil lamp. It was a huge hound, almost wolf-like but squatter, less hairy and with red eyes burning with an inner fire, eyes that were fixed firmly on Holmes.

Holmes moved forward and raised his stick. The beast kept coming. It had a strange, almost translucent quality to its aspect, and glowed with faint green phosphorescence. And it was then that I realized — we'd seen this very beast, or something very like it — on the Baskerville case.

"Holmes, I whispered. "It is that blasted hound. I see it — but I do not believe it."

"That's the ticket, Watson," Holmes said, still not taking his eyes from the beast. "Believing in it will only give it more substance, if I am right about this."

He stepped closer to the beast, which sat back on its haunches, ready to pounce. We were close enough to hear it breathe — hot and wheezy, smelling of bad meat. It pulled back its lips and snarled — almost a smile I thought, as if it were taunting us.

And then Holmes did the strangest thing — he started to sing, the same chant I had heard in my dreams, the words sounding slightly different, slightly off, the cadence not quite as fluid as the unseen choir had managed. But it seemed to do the trick — the beast seemed confused, and its growls turned to pitiful whimpering before it went completely quiet. It was fading now too, losing cohesion as Holmes grew more confident and advanced on it.

His singing rose to almost a shout and he raised his cane to strike — but when he brought the stick down there was nothing for him to hit but wisps of light and shadow that fell apart and were gone even before Holmes turned to me in astonishment.

The room fell quiet again.

"Tell me, Holmes," I said, heading for the decanter of Scotch, all thought of a quiet night gone, trying to keep a tremor from my voice. "Is that just another parlor trick — or is it perhaps something more sinister?"

Holmes had turned away again, and stood staring into the dark corner.

"It is something of both, unless I am very much mistaken," he finally replied. "It seems that Moriarty left a sentry, of sorts, on duty when he vacated the premises."

I swallowed a most welcome shot of the Scotch, the stiffener doing its job immediately.

"I'm blowed if I understand any of this," I said. Holmes smiled grimly in reply, and made for the chair by the fire. He sat with the cane across his lap, and calmly lit up a smoke, as at ease as if we were back in the comforts of Baker Street.

"The mind is a stronger tool than it is given credit for," he said softly. "You know that, Watson — I have explained often enough how I have honed mine into a weapon against criminality. I suspect that others have honed theirs in other directions. Seton, for example, seems to have been a remarkable trove of occult lore and a certain kind of mesmerism that allowed his mind independence from the body, along with some degree of mental control of the physical realm. The adepts in Tibet have a word for such thought forms — they call them *Tulpa*, and I believe they are sometimes so strong and vivid that they can prove difficult to dispel if they are too fully realized. It is something I had not considered possible, something I had consigned to tall tales and legends in my mind, but it is certainly something I will have to consider, now that we have seen the evidence for ourselves."

"And the hound? It was one of these — what did you call them — *Tulpa*?"

"As I said, Watson, it was a guard dog — a defensive mechanism left by Moriarty to scare off the unwary. It is as well that we are neither unwary, nor easily scared."

"Speak for yourself, old chap," I said, and had another gulp of Scotch. "And it is the Baskerville hound. I cannot be mistaken about that, for it too has haunted my dreams. How could that be?"

"You said it yourself. The image, the dream if you like, was plucked out of your own mind, I suspect," Holmes replied. "A nightmare given form as a combination of our own fears, Seton's knowledge, and Moriarty's will. But despite our foe's best efforts we prevailed, Watson. As Seton's journal says, music has charms to soothe the savage beast — and even the most trite of aphorisms must hold a kernel of truth."

"I must say, you are taking all of this remarkably calmly, Holmes," I said.

"What choice do we have?" Holmes replied.

I saw his point. Short of venturing out onto the night moor, we had little option but to endure whatever Moriarty might have planned to throw at us.

The night wore on. Holmes sat perfectly still. His eyes were closed, but I am sure he was quite awake, merely lost in deep mental contemplation. As for myself, I struggled to stay awake, for I knew with rigid certainty that the black dog would be waiting for me, should I descend into dreamland. At least I managed to forego any more Scotch, but I did smoke more than was good for me.

Every hour or so I got up and stoked the fire with some

new logs from the pile at the side of the grate. I was feeling pangs of hunger by this time, but nothing would persuade me to go alone through to the darkness of the scullery. I jumped at the least small creak or groan from the old house, and all things considered it was one of the longest nights of my life. But at least the hound stayed at bay.

I was quite stiff from sitting in the old chair by the time I spotted that dawn light had started to seep in through the windows. I was about to remark on it to Holmes when I heard it again — a snuffling in the dark corner — but even as I turned in that direction a thin burst of morning sun pierced the clouds and lit up the whole room. There was nothing in the corner but bare floorboards and dust.

We had made it through the night.

Much to my surprise, the coachman was as good as his word. Scarcely had Holmes roused himself from his chair than we heard the welcome sounds of hooves and wheels on gravel from the driveway outside. The old man must have done the first part of his journey in darkness, and have been more eager for Holmes' coinage than I anticipated. However he had managed it, I was most grateful to see him when I checked from the window. He saw me looking, and waved me on, suggesting rather forcibly that we should depart with some haste, so perhaps the fight within him between shillings and his fear was not quite won yet. I decided to hurry, in case the wrong side lost the battle.

I stowed Seton's journal in my coat alongside my pistol as I left — we might still have need of it. On the way out the door Holmes cautioned me to silence concerning the body in the upstairs room.

"If we mention it at this juncture, we will only have to explain things to the local police and we will never got out of Colchester. It is best to keep silent for the time being — we will let Lestrade handle it from London after we are safely returned."

It went against the grain to leave the poor man upstairs in such circumstances, but I could see the sense in Holmes' request, so I kept quiet when the coachman asked if everything was as it should be.

Holmes offered the man a crown if he made all haste for the railway station, and we flew away at quite a gallop. I was not at all displeased to see the last of that old house on the moorland. My last sight of it was from a mile away across the moor, looking back to where it sat, square and squat, like the black head of a great hound, peering after a fleeing prey.

To cut the details of a long and tedious journey short, we made our way back to London via the carriage ride, then a train journey that stopped at every small station en-route. It was not even a catered service, so we could not break our fast apart from a cup of insipid tea. Following that trial we took a carriage from Liverpool Street that got caught in traffic in Holborn. I eventually managed to grab a bite to eat — two of Mrs. Hudson's sweetest fancies — during an all too brief stop in Baker Street for a change of clothes and another scolding from our landlady. All of these matters contrived to slow us down to such an extent that mid-afternoon had come around before we were able to present ourselves once again to Lestrade in his office in Scotland Yard.

The Inspector was not in the least bit happy to see us.

"Where in blazes have you been?" he almost shouted. "The brass are up in arms. There is still no sign of your brother, all of those crimes are still unsolved — and to cap it all we've lost a red headed man from the morgue at the Royal Hospital — I hear you saw the body, Watson? Well, your dead man got up and walked away yesterday evening. I don't suppose you two can shed any light on that subject?"

Strangely, to me at least, Holmes did not seem at all surprised by this latest development.

"The body in the morgue is of no consequence at the moment," he said, addressing Lestrade. "I believe I know where Mycroft is being held — if we find him, all the other matters will tend to themselves — but I will need your help."

"Anything you need," Lestrade replied. "As long as it gets them upstairs off my back."

"I need you to find us an excuse to get us into the Diogenes Club. I know they will not allow me entry — not without Mycroft's say so. I am seen as something of a disruptive influence."

Lestrade grinned.

"I think I can come up with something disruptive of my own, Holmes. It might even be a bit of fun."

Five minutes later we were in a police carriage, at the head of a small convoy of three of the vehicles, headed for the Club.

An over officious flunky tried to stop us at the main door.

"I am afraid this is an establishment for members only."

Lestrade pushed through the man, none too gently.

"And I am afraid that I do not give a damn. We have had reports of lewd behavior, gambling, illicit use of opiates and solicitation on these premises. I would be remiss in my duties if I did not investigate. We are the Yard, son, and we're coming in, whether you like it or not."

The Inspector did indeed seem to be enjoying himself. And I had to suppress a grin of my own at the shocked expressions on the faces of the regulars as a squad of London's finest marched through their inner sanctum.

Holmes and I made straight for Mycroft's rooms at the rear where he did his private business. But the office lay empty, and the ashes in the grate felt stone cold to the touch.

"He ain't here," Lestrade said as he joined us, stating the obvious as ever.

Holmes was undeterred. He went around the room, rapping his knuckles on the wall and checking all edges of the old oak paneling and cabinets.

"My brother always likes to have a way to come and go as he pleases away from prying eyes," he said. "There is a passageway here somewhere, I can guarantee you that much."

Right on cue his fingers found a hidden switch to the side of a bookcase. The whole shelving unit swung aside on small oiled wheels to reveal a passageway and a set of stone steps leading down into darkness. Two oil lanterns sat on a shelf just inside — Holmes quickly lit one, and stepped down away from us without any hesitation. Lestrade looked at me, shrugged, and motioned me forward.

"It seems Holmes is right, again."

I took out my pistol, Lestrade lit the second lantern, and we followed Holmes down into the dark.

CHAPTER 12

It was immediately obvious that the tunnel in which we descended was of some great age — far older than the proud building occupied by the Diogenes Club above us — older even than most of the old city. To my untrained eye this passageway could be Roman — or even older still, stretching back into dim and distant antiquity. The passageway was marked in places with carved writing and even had some statuary in recessed cavities in the walls, but there was no time for scholarly study, for Holmes was descending quickly ahead of us, and we had to scurry along to keep up.

At first we could still hear the far off rumble of carriage traffic in the Strand, then even that faded. I lost all sense of how far down we had descended, but I had a feeling we were already some way below the level of the sewer system. I was trying to bring to mind the layout of the underground railway system to calculate whether we might emerge into any of its tunnels when we almost walked into Holmes, who had stopped in a rough-hewn passageway where the steps leveled off.

"There is light ahead," he said softly, barely raising his voice more than a whisper. "Quietly now."

Lestrade and I followed him, moving as slowly and carefully as we could manage.

The light Holmes had seen came through a barred opening at eye level in a heavy door set at the end of the corridor. An odor of stale sweat pervaded the area immediately around the door, and I did not want to consider the stench that might await us on entry.

Holmes sidled forward first, and chanced a glance inside, then motioned us forward. He pushed the door, which proved to be unlocked — it swung open, revealing an ancient cell beyond. It looked to have been crudely hewn out of the rough stone bedrock. Four sets of manacles hung on the wall — only one of them was occupied. Mycroft Holmes was suspended on tiptoe, naked above the waist, hanging from thick chains. His head hung low on his chest, but he seemed to be breathing, if a tad too shallowly for my liking. I pushed past Holmes, my medical instincts overriding any thought of personal safety.

It was only when I got fully into the room that I saw there was another occupant. The small confused man, David Finn, still wearing his hat and overcoat, sat in a plain kitchen chair inside a ritual circle drawn in red chalk on the floor, staring blankly into space at a bare patch of wall to Mycroft's left. He did not seem to be in any distress, so I headed without any further pause for Holmes' brother. I was stopped by a shout from Holmes himself.

"Careful, Watson," he said. "Things may not be what they seem."

Mycroft lifted his head and looked at me. He seemed drawn and fatigued, but his voice was strong when he spoke.

"For pity's sake man, get me out of these chains," he said.

Once again I moved forward until I was within touching distance, and once again Holmes stopped me.

"No, Watson. Not yet."

"Let Watson do his job, Holmes" Lestrade said. "That's your brother hanging there."

"Is it?" Holmes said quietly. "Are you sure?"

Mycroft ignored Holmes and looked at me.

"You know me, Watson. Get me down from here."

I stood there in two minds, caught between my duty as a doctor and my loyalty to Holmes. In the end, it was a whisper from Finn that got my attention first.

"Irene? Are you there?"

Mycroft looked over to the man.

"He has been confused for some time, poor chap," he said. "If you are going to leave me here, perhaps you should see to him, Watson."

He dropped his head again, and fell silent as I turned to check on the man in the chair.

"Don't smudge the chalk," Holmes said. "I know it is probably all mumbo-jumbo — but these chaps believe it, and that is what is important about it."

I stepped gingerly over the lines and approached the man.

He did not register my presence as I took his wrist and felt his pulse — it was strong, but rather too rapid for my liking. His pupils were dilated and he was having great difficulty in focusing. But he seemed healthy enough otherwise.

I turned back to Holmes — Lestrade was off somewhere on the far side of the cell inspecting a long table and some sacks that had been thrown there, seemingly willy-nilly.

"How is he?" Holmes asked.

"He'll live," I replied. "But if you're asking me if he still has Moriarty's essence or soul inside him — I have no answer for that. How could I tell?"

"How indeed?" Holmes said, as if pondering the question to himself.

Lestrade called out from across the cell.

"The swag's all here — money, jewelry, diamonds, portraits — it looks like everything that we know was stolen, and then some more."

Holmes bent beside me, looked the Finn man in the eye, then stepped carefully out of the circle and went over to stand in front of Mycroft.

He spoke, quoting a line he had read out from the journal back in the house on the moor.

"The next time we meet, you will look me in the eye and call me brother," Holmes said, and smiled. "Hello, brother."

Mycroft — or Moriarty — smiled back.

"Sherlock, unchain me. Please?"

"If you are indeed my brother, you will know that it is not as simple as that. The fate of the Empire is at stake, right now, in this small room. What would you have me do to ensure its safety?"

"Just get me down from here," the chained man said. "If there are matters of state to be dealt with, I need to get to it right away."

Holmes smiled grimly.

"You see, that is completely the wrong answer. My brother, when asked that question, would have had no hesitation in asking that I put a bullet in his head."

Holmes put his hands on either side of the man's face and looked deep into his eyes.

"Fight him, Mycroft. Fight him as you would fight me. And damn'd be him that first cries, 'Hold, enough!'"

The chained man's face seemed to melt and reform, showing us a snarling, grimacing figure in some pain, one that was quickly pushed to the background as the smiling face took control.

"Now, now, Sherlock — just let me down, there's a good chap. Or do I have to get my young men in the black suits to come and show you how things really work in this country?"

Holmes smiled, and held the face tighter.

"At least I know Mycroft is still there. If you can hear me, brother, do something about it — take control of your mind, man — it is yours after all. Give it work to do — work that will keep Moriarty too busy to escape from you or control you — give me a list. You do remember the lists? A long list — you recited one all day back in the garden when we were boys, just to prove you could best me." Holmes voice rose to almost a shout. "Well look. I'm better than you are now. What are you going to do about that?"

The smile faded on the chained man's face, turning to a look of some consternation that quickly turned into a grimace of pain and hurt. He started to speak.

"Kingdom Animalia, Phylum Arthropoda, Subphylum Hexapoda, Class Insecta, Order Hymenoptera, Superfamily Xyeloidea, Family Xyelidae, Genus Macroxyela."

"What the blazes is he on about now?" Lestrade said.

Holmes turned and smiled.

"It's one of Mycroft's mind exercises — this one is the taxonomy of the Hymenoptera."

Lestrade still looked puzzled.

"It's the Latin names for ants, bees, wasps and sawflies,"

I added, trying to be helpful.

"Well, it all makes perfect sense now," Lestrade said sarcastically, as the chained man's voice dropped to a mumble, still reciting Latin nomenclature.

"Superfamily Tenthredinoidea, Family Argidae, Genus Arginae, Species Arge."

Holmes had a long look into the man's eyes, then turned back to us. He looked grim and determined.

"My brother has control back — for now. Moriarty's scheme to make things look like a simple rescue has been thwarted. And there will be no more of his escaping by walking through the wall nonsense for the time being at least. But I must find a way to bring Mycroft back to himself and remove Moriarty's malign influence."

Lestrade looked around the room, motioning to Finn, who still sat, almost catatonic, staring into space, and to the piles of stolen valuables on the table against the wall.

"And what about him — and the rest of the mess?" he said.

Holmes smiled thinly.

"This poor chap has no defense in the case against him — at least none that will stand up in court — but at the same time, he is innocent of all crimes. I have a proposition for you, Lestrade. You have the loot — and I can give you a body — a dead man that can easily be 'fitted up' as you say, for the crimes; after all, he has a map on his wall detailing all the scenes. Just go to Colchester and ask any carriage driver to take you to the old house on the moor — he's there waiting for you."

Lestrade scarcely thought about it before nodding in agreement.

"And this one?" Lestrade said, pointing at Finn.

"His name is David Finn, he lives in Stepney, and his wife Irene is waiting for him — please make sure he gets home safely."

"And what will you be doing?" Lestrade asked.

Holmes went quickly through Finn's pockets and came up with a key for the manacles.

"I'm taking my brother home," he said.

"Superfamily Formicoidea, Family Formicidae," Mycroft replied.

CHAPTER 13

Mycroft proved able to walk and climb the steps out of the tunnel on his own, mumbling Latin names all the way. We drew some pointed stares from the members as we escorted him from the Diogenes Club, but they held to their no speaking rule, at least long enough for us to get out and into a carriage, headed for Baker Street.

Mycroft continued to mumble the whole way there.

"Superfamily Apoidea, Family Apidae, Genus Apis,"

"The honey bees," Holmes said softly. "Always our mother's favorites. Did you know, Watson, that honey bees traditionally signify immortality and resurrection in several heraldic systems, and were the royal emblems of the Merovingians? Which in turn brings us around to our little red haired Scottish friend. Wheels within wheels."

He refused to elaborate on the statement, and as I had not a dashed clue as to his meaning, I kept quiet. After that we sat in silence, smoking cheroots as the carriage wove through traffic on our way north.

"How do you propose we return him to his normal self?" I asked Holmes as we got Mycroft out onto the pavement outside the Baker Street apartments.

"I am not quite sure yet," Holmes replied as Mrs. Hudson came to the door to let us inside. "I fear it might be a three pipe problem."

On seeing us manhandle Mycroft upstairs, and the way he was so listless and in truth rather pitiful in our grasp, Mrs. Hudson became a paragon of efficiency, fetching strong tea and more of her sweet fancies before we had hardly got ourselves settled in the front room.

We sat Mycroft down near the fire in Holmes' favorite chair — his brother did not so much as register the small kindness, merely continued with his Latin muttering. I was coming to believe that the sound might become rather wearing after some hours of it.

"Superfamily Platygastroidea, Family Platygastridae."

After some most welcome ballast in the form of tea and cake, Holmes and I had a smoke. I tried to light one for Mycroft, but he had one puff, put it down then either forgot about it or could not afford to give it any of his attention, focussed fully as he was on his list.

"This is a rum do indeed, Holmes," I said after listening to another prolonged bout of the muttering. "He cannot go on indefinitely — he is already very tired, and sleep will surely take him at some point, whether he wants it or not."

"I am only too aware of the urgency of the matter at hand, Watson. But we are in uncharted waters here, and must proceed carefully. One false move, and we might lose all that remains of Mycroft forever."

Holmes stubbed out his smoke, rose and took his pocket watch from his waistcoat.

"This proved effective with Finn in Lestrade's office — let us see if it works on a stronger mind."

I was of a mind to point out that this too was a course of action that was not without its own risk, but I knew that Holmes would have already included that into his thinking. I held my peace as he pulled over a stool and sat on it, knee to knee with Mycroft.

He started the pocket watch swinging on the end of the fob chain. "Watch this, brother. Keep going with your list, but watch this closely."

He had already lowered his voice to match the tone and intonation of Mycroft's mumbling.

"Superfamily Xiphydrioidea, Family Xiphydriidae."

I was just close enough to see that Mycroft's gaze moved from side to side, matching the watch's swing.

"Keep watching, brother. See how the light catches father's watch?"

Mycroft's whole attention was now on the watch, and Holmes' quiet voice.

"I need you to step aside for a moment, Mycroft," Holmes said. "Keep on reciting your list, but quietly now — I need the other one there to come forward."

The fear in Mycroft's face grew large, but Holmes did

not change his tone.

"There is nothing to worry about, brother. I am here, and no harm will come to you while I have any breath left in me. Remember the list and just step aside for a minute. I will tell you when it is safe to come forward again. I need to talk to the other one — it is the only way I will find out how to rid you of him."

"Superfamily Orussoidea, Family Orussidae, Genus Chalinus," Mycroft replied, much softer this time.

Holmes matched the lowering of his brother's tone.

"Come on out, Moriarty. It is time we settled this."

Mycroft's head came up, he smiled, and he spoke in a normal, almost conversational voice.

"Oh, this is far from settled, my good chap," he said. Moriarty — for I presumed this was now the personality at the fore, grinned widely. "It will only be settled when you share the fate that befell me at Reichenbach — and I intend to be here to watch the great Sherlock Holmes take that fall. Your brother cannot persist with holding me at bay forever — and when I emerge fully, I shall merely stand and walk away from you, as I did in the Opera House, as I did in Whitehall. There is nothing your rationality can do to stop me — I am far beyond that now."

"But not yet beyond your over-reaching egotism, I see," Holmes said, smiling. "Here, you have me in front of you — but you are as powerless as you ever were. I could destroy you utterly, right here and now, and you could do nothing about it."

Moriarty smiled back.

"And kill your own brother? I think not."

"You overestimate the extent of my filial bonds," Holmes replied, but that only got him a smile in reply.

"Go ahead then — do your worst," Moriarty said. "I have made my peace with my destiny. How do you think your brother feels about his?"

Holmes looked into his eyes, then sat back.

"Mycroft, come forward," he said, and stopped swinging the pocket watch.

The smile vanished from the sitting man's face, to be replaced with a straining grimace of rapt concentration.

"Superfamily Vespoidea: Family, Vespidae," he said.

We sat there though the course of a long evening as the city went quiet outside, Mycroft mumbled and Holmes was lost in thought, wreathed in pipe smoke for the most part. Mrs. Hudson made some of her hearty mutton and potato soup and much to my surprise Holmes got Mycroft to eat some, spooning it into him like a parent feeding a child. After Holmes and I took a more solid supper — some fine pork pie, mash and ale to wash it all down — I spotted that Mycroft's mumbling had changed. He had now moved away from the taxonomy of insects.

"Dot ball, dot ball, four, one, dot ball, leg bye, dot ball."

"It seems we are on to cricket now, Holmes," I remarked.

"Yes. And trust me, Watson — my brother can keep this topic going for as long as he needs to. I know from all too bitter experience."

"Wicket, dot ball, three, two, dot ball, dot ball,"

"I wonder what match he is replaying?" I said.

"I don't," Holmes said, and retired to his chair and his pipe.

Holmes did not show the slightest inclination to retire to bed, and despite our exertions over the previous days — and nights — I myself was too tightly wound to sleep. I too returned to my chair, armed with my smokes and a snifter of brandy. It was only then I noted the heft and weight of Seton's journal, which still nestled in my jacket pocket alongside my pistol.

"I say, Holmes," I said, taking out the book and placing it on my lap. "There may yet be something in here that can help us."

Holmes grunted. He did not speak, but I saw from his look that he gave little credence to my idea. But Mycroft was looking increasingly tired, and Holmes seemed bereft of any idea of how to proceed, or at least unwilling to share them with me, so I stuck my nose in the book, looking for a clue. I picked a page at random and started reading.

Without the Sun and its shadow, the Moon, we can have no change in the quicksilver, and he is foolish who attempts to accomplish our Magistery in their absence. On the other hand he who knows how to tinge quicksilver with the Sun and Moon is in possession of the basest part of our arcanum which may become red sulphur, and at first is called white sulphur. Gold is the father, and silver the mother of the proximate substance of our Stone, for out of these bodies, prepared with their sulphur or arsenic, is our medicine elicited.

Holmes must have seen the confused expression on my face, for he laughed softly as I read on.

Ye must expect to have it exceeding Black, within 40 days after you have put your Composition into the Glass over the Fire; if it be not Black, proceed no further, for it is unrecoverable: it must be as Black as the Ravens Head, and must continue a long time, and not utterly to lose it during five months.

If it be Orange color, or half Red, within some small time after you have begun your Work, without doubt your Fire is too hot; for these are tokens that you have burnt the Radical humor and vivacity of the Stone.

"I told you, Watson," Holmes said as I put the book down, "It is just mumbo-jumbo and loose thinking. We will get nowhere with that alchemical nonsense. If there is any chemical reality described there, I could not see it, only code, hidden clues and hints at a bigger picture that is never explained. It is the work of a charlatan intent on extorting time, or money, or both from lesser thinkers, and I will have nothing more to do with it."

"One, two, three, dot ball, dot ball, wicket." Mycroft said in punctuation.

Evening turned into night. I heard Mrs. Hudson retire downstairs, and the sound from out on the street lessened to the occasional rumble of a passing carriage. And still Mycroft mumbled his way through the cricket innings.

"One, two, dot ball, four, four, six."

At least that sounded like an entertaining over, but it was just about the only entertainment to be had from the interminable mumbling. Whatever Mycroft was doing seemed to be enough to keep the other personality at bay, but Holmes' brother was clearly starting to flag. His eyelids grew heavy, and he slumped alarmingly in his chair as sleep suddenly overwhelmed him. Holmes rose quickly to stand before him and slapped him open-palmed, hard on the left cheek. Mycroft's head rocked and he looked up at Holmes, smiling.

"You enjoyed that rather too much, brother," he said, before the smile turned to a grimace of pain and Mycroft, awake again, once more took control.

"I will not have any weakness," Holmes said. "Do you hear me, Mycroft? Are you really going to allow me to see you fail?"

Mycroft sat up straight at that, and his voice rang out strong for a while.

"Wicket, wicket, dot ball, dot ball, four, one."

But all too soon his voice started to fade again. I saw the tension in his shoulders as he tried to maintain a stiff sitting position, but sleep was dragging hard at him, and it seemed only a matter of time before he succumbed fully to its charms.

"Is there anything you can give him, Watson?" Holmes asked me. "Something to fend off sleep for a time?"

I shook my head.

"Given his current state his heart might give out."

"There might not be an alternative course of action," Holmes replied.

"And yet the risk is too great," I said. "I wish it were otherwise, Holmes, I really do."

Holmes took matters into his own hands the next time Mycroft's eyelids started to droop. He fetched a long needle from his work desk and, without any warning, thrust it, hard, into the back of Mycroft's hand. The older brother sat up with a jolt as if struck.

At the same instant, I smelled the odor I will never

forget — wet dog, slightly rancid, as if it had rolled in a bog. Holmes threw me a look — he had spotted the same thing.

"To me, Watson," he said.

Shadows thickened by the windows, as if black smoke curled through from the city outside, the darkness swallowing the light from our lamps. The odor got stronger, and something snuffled, searching for us.

Holmes started to sing softly, the same Gaelic chant as before.

The blackness took shape, thickening and coalescing in dark clumps that merged and swelled until once again the great black hound stood before us fully formed. It raised its head. Red eyes blazed as its gaze found us.

Holmes raised his voice. Mycroft continued to mumble, but seemed to match his rhythm to Holmes' chanting.

"One, dot ball, one, two, four, dot ball."

Holmes didn't stop, but motioned with a hand gesture that I should join in. My singing isn't up to much at the best of times, but I added what I could. The beast growled and paced under the window, but did not advance. Instead it was Holmes that took the initiative, stepping forward and raising his voice to a shout.

The beast did not back away. It roared back at Holmes with a high howl that set the light fittings swinging, reverberating through the whole house — I would not be surprised if it did not wake half of London. I heard a door slam, then footsteps on the stairs — Mrs. Hudson in a panic I presumed — but I dared not take my eyes from that blasted hound.

It growled deep in its throat, and rocked back on its haunches, ready to leap into an attack.

Holmes shouted, I bellowed and stamped, and Mycroft recited his cricket scoring, but our efforts were not rewarded. The beast grew firmer, more solid than ever. Ropy strings of drool fell from slavering jaws and a too long, too red tongue lolled as it drew back its lips and smiled at us. The back legs sprung in attack and I braced myself to meet it.

The door flew open and a small figure burst in — it was clearly not Mrs. Hudson, and at first I did not know who it might be. A new voice joined our chorus, a different set of words but in the same cadence and rhythm, the call ringing around the room, echoing and growing in volume until it sounded like a mighty throng shouted alongside us.

"Ri linn cothrom na meidhe, Ri linn sgathadh na h-anal.
"Ri linn tabhar na breithe Biodh a shith air do theannal fein.
"Dhumna Ort!"

At that last cry the black beast fell apart, mere inches from throwing its full weight against us, wisps of black shadow and smoke dissipating as if taken by a wind until there was nothing in the room but we three, and the latest intruder.

The Scotsman, Seton, looked over at me and grinned.

"Well met, again, Doctor Watson," he said.

The only sound in the room was Mycroft's mumbling.

"Dot ball, dot ball, dot ball, dot ball, dot ball, wicket."

CHAPTER 14

"But you were dead," I said, not knowing how else to respond. "I saw your body on the slab."

"Technically, I suppose I was," the small Scotsman replied, smiling. "Twice, for I died again when I left you in the house on the moor. But there is death, and there is death — a tale that would take far too long in the telling without a bottle or two of something from the Highlands to wash it down. Explanations will have to wait — we have work to do here."

For a dead man he seemed remarkably jaunty. He pushed past me and headed for Mycroft, leaning over the sitting man and looking into his eyes.

"We don't have much time," he said. He looked over at Holmes. "Are you open to an extreme measure? It is risky and may not work, but it may be our only chance."

Holmes needed no time to come to a decision. He nodded immediately.

"I yield to your obvious experience in these matters. I am prepared to do whatever it takes to get Mycroft whole, and Moriarty gone."

"It may not be as simple as one or the other," Seton replied. "But we must make the attempt — and it must be now."

Then he turned to me.

"I shall need you too, Doctor Watson — and I am afraid you are not going to like it."

Seton had me fetch a tub of salt from the kitchen — Mrs. Hudson was not at all pleased at having been roused from her sleep.

"He has a dog up there now, has he?" she said. "And don't try to deny it — I heard the blasted thing howling — I nearly fell out of bed."

She was clearly in no mood for any further disturbance, but was mollified slightly when I told her that what we were doing so late into the night concerned Mycroft's wellbeing.

"Well why didn't you say so straight away?" she said,

thrusting the salt into my hands. "Get away with you and see to it, before the poor man suffers any further."

By the time I got back upstairs with the salt Seton and Holmes had cleared a large space in the center of the floor, lifting the rugs to reveal the floorboards below. The Scotsman took the salt from me, and started to mark out occult circles, similar to the ones we had already seen in the house on the moor and the crypt under the Diogenes Club.

"Is this mumbo-jumbo really necessary?" Holmes asked.

Seton continued to draw his circles as he replied.

"It is merely a means of focussing the mental faculties on the task at hand," he said. "It is a most necessary part of the process, for purity of thought and purpose is the main requirement if this is to work."

"You are saying that it is a mesmeric trick, like Holmes' use of the pocket watch?" I replied, trying to make sense of what we were being told.

Seton laughed.

"It is somewhat the same, but also completely different. These circles allow us to access something we have forgotten — the undeniable fact that we all share the same microcosm, and macrocosm. At heart, we are one — all of creation is one, and in the right circumstances, our experiences, our memories, and our reality can all be shared — or fought over."

"I'm not following you," I replied.

"But Holmes is," Seton said, finishing the outer track of two concentric circles and starting to fill in the space between with occult symbols. "Aren't you, Holmes?"

"I think so," Holmes replied. "You intend to enter Mycroft's mind — or at least this 'shared reality' part of it that you speak of. There you will find Moriarty and somehow drive him out."

"You have understood it," Seton said, finishing the circles with a last flourish. "But it is not I who will descend into the dream world. You must go. This is your fight, Holmes. He is your brother, not mine."

Holmes seemed momentarily startled at the very

thought.

"I am not even sure that I believe such a thing is possible."

Seton pointed at Mycroft.

"Do you believe that Moriarty is in there, trying to take over his mind even as we speak?"

Holmes nodded.

"All evidence points to that being true," he said.

"And how did Moriarty get there? How has his essence survived all this time since his apparent death? I'll tell you how — he inhabits that place you called the dream world — he learned how to project his personality there, and used it to cheat the final oblivion."

"There is no cheating death," Holmes said softly.

"And yet, there he is," Seton said, and then thumped his chest with his right fist. "And here I am, all evidence to the contrary. But we have no time for philosophy — Mycroft is losing. You need to do this now, or not at all."

Holmes looked at the sitting figure, then back at Seton.

"Very well. What needs to be done?"

Seton looked over to me.

"This is the part you will not like, Watson. We need some cocaine."

"I have none on the premises," I replied. "I will need to send to the hospital — and that will have to wait for morning."

Holmes looked sheepish as he spoke up.

"Would a seven per cent solution suffice? You will find some in the top drawer of the work desk."

I did not have time to admonish Holmes as I would have wished, for Seton impressed the urgency of the situation on us at every turn. He had me fetch the cocaine while he and Holmes got Mycroft, still seated, into the center of the salt circles.

"Would you do the honors, Watson," Holmes said. "And don't look at me like that — the bottle is full. It has been there for months now. Just knowing it is there is enough — I have not actually had to use it."

"Until now," I replied, and he nodded.

I turned back to Seton.

"I am loath to administer this to him — I know only too well the effects it has on his stability."

Seton spoke softly.

"Yet it must be done, Doctor. It is the only way I can get him into Mycroft's shared consciousness. Anything else would require months — years — of rigid mental training."

The Scotsman handed me the bottle of cocaine solution and a syringe. I took it, and looked over to Holmes. I could not let my friend do this alone. I turned back to Seton.

"Will it work for both of us — can two share this dream world?"

"Aye. Two, three, it makes no never mind. It is the ritual, and the focus it brings that is the thing."

I stepped into the circle alongside Holmes and Mycroft.

"Then let us have at it, before I change my mind."

I did Holmes first, a syringe of the solution at the joint of his left elbow, His pupils dilated immediately, and he sagged, almost fell until steadying himself against the back of the chair. Seton started to chant as I refilled the syringe and pushed the needle into my own vein. The last thing I heard before I was plunged into swirling darkness was Seton's singing, and Mycroft, still mumbling a cricket score.

"No ball, one, dot ball, dot ball, dot ball, dot ball, dot ball."

Chapter 15

I was lost, in a dark sea of nothingness, content to swim in warm shadows, all worldly cares forgotten, too far off to remember, too insignificant to need worry. I might be drifting there yet in the dark had not I heard Mycroft somewhere ahead of me, the cricket scoring acting like a beacon, leading me forward.

"Four, two, four, one, dot ball, one."

I tried to take a step, unsure of my bearings, but as soon as I decided on a course of action, the swirling darkness shifted, and I immediately knew where I was standing.

We were back in the crypt under the Diogenes Club.

Holmes stood at Mycroft's side — his brother was once more hanging in manacles on the wall, head down, still mumbling the details of the cricket innings. As I walked forward toward them I saw that a figure sat on the chair inside the occult circles drawn in red on the floor. On this occasion, it was not David Finn.

The sitting man had the air and manner of a Professor, slightly round shouldered, with thick graying whiskers at his cheeks and piercing blue eyes under hooded brows. He looked like some malignant crab, slumped as he was inside a huge black overcoat several sizes too large for his frame. Moriarty laughed when he saw me notice him.

"Splendid. We are all here, I see," he said. "Welcome to my humble abode. It is not much to boast about, but it is home."

The whole scene had a strange, otherworldly quality, as if the walls melted and ran in a fever dream. I struggled to maintain my tenuous grip on the situation — I felt other ideas strive for prominence in my mind, other places my dreaming mind would prefer to wander, not the least of which was that warm sea of shifting shadow in which I had recently felt so at peace. It had a seductive siren call that was most alluring, and it was all I could do to keep it at bay. I fixed my attention on Holmes as he stepped forward.

I saw that he meant to advance directly on Moriarty, but

he was stopped when he reached the edge of the painted circles, as if he had hit a wall. Effort showed in his whole body as he strained and pushed, but even Holmes' will power could not get him past that barrier. Although there was nothing to be seen, it appeared to be a solid obstruction in his path.

Moriarty laughed again. He seemed to be enjoying Holmes' failure to reach him.

"It seems we have come to an impasse. You cannot get in here — and I cannot get out. In the meantime, your brother grows ever closer to succumbing to my will. What do you propose to do about it, Sherlock?"

"I propose to drive you out of here like a whipped dog," Holmes replied, to which Moriarty laughed again.

"If it is dogs that you desire, I am happy to oblige."

Dark shadows gathered in all corners of the chamber — I knew only too well what came next. And so did Holmes. He immediately started to sing; his voice raised in the same soft Gaelic chant that had previously dispelled the hound. I joined in, stamping my feet and clapping my hands in time, and Mycroft's mumbling fell into the right cadence to enhance our efforts.

"Two, two, one, leg bye, stumped, dot ball."

Our efforts seemed ineffectual. The shadows gathered ever thicker. I smelled wet dog again, the odor was almost enough to make me gag. Snuffling came from all directions, and a howling rose up, from a chorus of canine throats, as if a large pack of excited dogs had just spotted their prey. Red eyes — six pairs of them, peered from out of the shadows, and I steeled myself for the assault that was surely coming.

Holmes seemed calm and unperturbed. He stepped forward toward the nearest mass of shadow, crouched down on his haunches, and, still singing softly, began to rub the shadowy beast behind the ears. When he stood, a black dog walked to heel beside him.

He went to stand in front of Moriarty and laughed in the sitting man's face.

"My dreams are no less vivid than yours," he said. "And I remember our old dog, Sam, too well to let him be turned into a figure of menace."

The blackness in the corners of the room swirled, and went still, drifting apart into nothingness. The black dog at Holmes' heel wagged its tail. Holmes patted its head.

"Off you go then, Sam," he said.

The dog licked at Holmes' hand, then it too fell apart into smoke and mist and was gone.

Moriarty applauded. "You have always been a quick learner — I will give you that much," he said. If he was at all perturbed by the lack of menace provided by his dogs' failed attack, he did not show it. "But I still have the upper hand, for you still have not shown that you can breach these defenses of mine. Tell me, Holmes. What do you propose to do now?"

Holmes looked around the chamber.

"Dreams can tell a lot about a man's state of mind, don't you think?" Holmes said. "The fact that you choose to spend yours sitting in an occult circle, locked in a cell with a chained man, tells me more than you know about how to approach this problem."

Holmes ignored the sitting man and turned to me in conversation, as if we were sitting by the fireside in Baker Street.

"Have you a smoke on you, Watson?" he said. "I think I need to get the smell of wet dog out of my system."

At first I thought the cocaine had addled his mind, then he spoke again.

"Remember, this is your dream as much as it is mine, Watson. And in our dreams, all things are possible."

By instinct I checked my pockets. I found my service pistol in one — and cigarettes and a lighter in the other. I got Holmes and I lit up and we stood there puffing at each other as if we were just out for a morning stroll and not locked inside some grim nightmare.

"You see, Watson," Holmes said. "This is not so bad after all. And this is not only our dream — it is also

Mycroft's dream — indeed, I believe this is mostly Mycrofts' dream."

He turned to his chained brother. "What do you say, brother, shall we take the fight away from him? Shall we adjourn to our own playing field?"

Mycroft raised his head, and smiled grimly.

"Dot ball, wicket, dot ball, six, six, six."

The walls of the crypt swam and melted, Moriarty's smug grin fading at the same time.

We went elsewhere.

I still had the half-smoked cigarette in my fingers, but we now stood in a totally different room. As it solidified around us I knew exactly where we were. Mycroft still had thick manacles on his wrists, attached to chains that snaked away behind him to attachments on a oak paneled wall. But now he wore his best tweed suit, and sat in a high chair at the huge mahogany desk that marked his territory in his office in Whitehall. Moriarty sat in the center of the room inside red circles crudely painted onto the carpet, still in his voluminous black overcoat, but looking somehow smaller now, less intimidating than before.

Holmes walked across the carpet and stood next to the painted circles.

"What do you think, Professor?" he said. "Might there be some give in this boundary, now that we have you away from your domain?"

He reached out — his hands passed through the circles' protective barrier, as if pushing through some thick fluid, although it was clear that the effort caused Holmes some discomfort. He had, however, succeeded in wiping the smug grin completely from Moriarty's face.

"I do believe we are getting somewhere," Holmes said, turning back to his brother. "What do you think, Mycroft?"

Mycroft smiled, his eyes cold as ice.

"Three, four, one, three, four, one."

The office door opened. There seemed to be a throng of smartly dressed black-suited, athletic chaps in the corridor beyond. Moriarty turned to look, and for the first time I saw doubt cross his features as the new arrivals started to crowd into the room.

"You have your black dogs, and Mycroft has his," Holmes said, as the room filled and the crowd started to press in on Moriarty's defenses. The space above the circles sparked with blue flashes of static, the air suddenly filled with a burnt taste and smell like the aftermath of a big thunderstorm. Moriarty stood from his seat, and we saw now, for the first time, that he was hunched and strangely misshapen inside the voluminous overcoat, as if he had been broken and put back together wrongly. He grinned, looking more like some demented creature from a fairy tale than a professor, and addressed Holmes through the throng.

"You cannot best me, not here. I am too strong."

"We shall soon see about that," Holmes replied.

The blue flashes grew stronger and more frequent and the whole room hummed and buzzed. My skin tingled, my hair stood on end then there was a thunderclap to end all thunderclaps.

I blinked, and when I opened my eyes we were somewhere else entirely again.

I did not know the place — a country garden as well tended and pretty as any I have seen — apart from the crude red painted circles on the lawn and the huge husk of a burned out tree to my left to which Mycroft was thoroughly shackled. I turned to Holmes — he was looking over his shoulder at a neat detached cottage at our back.

Mycroft muttered, the sound carrying loud in the still air, sounding more like a child's rhyme that a cricket score.

"One, two, three, four, four, four,"

Holmes turned his attention back to Moriarty, who stood inside the painted circles The smug grin was back, although the simple act of standing seemed to be causing the man some pain.

"Home is the sailor, home from the sea, And the hunter home from the hill," Moriarty said.

"And yet it is not your home, is it? This is another of Mycroft's places," Holmes said. He wasn't smiling now — it had turned into a serious matter, one I believed was now only going to end in death in this strange place where I could not seem to stand still long enough to keep my bearings.

I still had the cigarette in hand, and I smoked it down to the last of it while Holmes and Moriarty stalked each other in the next round of their verbal spat.

"We should end it here, Sherlock," Moriarty said. "Is this not where it all began?"

The old tree creaked and moaned, its branches twisting and distorting, dragging the manacles wide and threatening to pull Mycroft's arms from their sockets.

"You forget, Moriarty" Holmes said in reply. "I know this place as well as my brother. I know every inch of it — every blade of grass."

He bent and stroked the grass of the lawn. It immediately started to grow, an inch, two inches then faster still until it was at my knees and heading for my waist. Moriarty was in similar straits inside his circle. Tangled stems wove and spun around his legs, threatening to pull him to the ground. He raised himself up to his full height, trying to stare Holmes down, but Holmes stepped forward, up to the edge of the circle and, with another step, stepped over the lines of paint and strode inside to join Moriarty there.

The Professor threw a punch, which Holmes did well to dodge, then another that caught Holmes full on the chin and sent him reeling. To my trained eye it was obvious that even despite his broken body, Moriarty was something of a pugilist — this fight might not go all Holmes' way.

I was about to step through the grass to my friend's aid when the scene changed for the last time.

This time I knew exactly where we had been brought — although I was unsure which of the two struggling men had made the decision to come here of all places. We stood on the lip of a dizzying cascade of roaring water, with towering cliffs rising all around. The noise was as deafening as it had been the last time I had seen this view — the Reichenbach Falls are just as impressive in the dream world as they are in reality.

And as before, Holmes was in a fight for his life, one that had ended in disaster the last time. The difference was that on this occasion, I might be able to go to Holmes' aid.

The pair stood locked in a dance of grips and wrestling holds, each struggling with all their might to throw the other down and away into oblivion. Neither seemed to have the upper hand as I moved to step forward on the narrow cliff path.

Something snuffled.

I looked down just in time to see a black dog thicken into existence, blocking my route. I saw Moriarty get Holmes in a stranglehold and inch him towards the edge of the falls but could not get there; the black beast advanced on me, growling and slavering, red eyes fixed on mine.

I had no dog like Holmes' old Sam in my family past to fall back on, no memories of placating such a creature — our family dogs were working animals, trained for hunting foxes and rounding up sheep and cattle. But I did remember Holmes' words to me.

"Remember, this is your dream as much as it is mine, Watson. And in our dreams, all things are possible."

I put my hand in my pocket and slowly took out my service pistol. The beast snuffled, as it trying to smell its purpose, then growled alarmingly. I had no time to check whether the blasted thing was loaded as the hound sprung and I fired, twice.

The hound's weight hit me hard, almost tumbling me off the cliff, but when I rolled away and raised the weapon again the hound stayed where it lay, bleeding profusely from two gaping wounds in its chest and whimpering, like a kicked pup.

I stepped over the body and headed to Holmes' aid.

The two old adversaries were still locked in place, with Moriarty having the upper hand, a chokehold effectively holding Holmes immobile over the deadly drop, although Holmes had a firm foothold and his strength, and force of will, were preventing either of them from taking the fall.

Moriarty saw me coming along the path.

"That is far enough, Doctor Watson. One more step and he goes over. And this time there will be no coming back. You know the old wives tale that if you die in dreams you stay dead? Would you like to test its veracity?"

I raised the pistol and aimed for his face.

"Would you?" I said.

Moriarty laughed at me.

"Your weapon might work on a projection like the dog, but, you see, I know this is just a dream. Are you seriously trying to shoot me with a tobacco pipe?"

I looked down to my hand — I was clutching my old hardwood briar, tight enough for my knuckles to show white and bloodless. I suddenly felt rather foolish and let my hand drop.

Moriarty tightened his grip on Holmes. And that was when I spotted that my old friend had a smile on his face. He was looking at a spot over my shoulder.

"Here we are again, Watson," he said, his speech slightly wheezy due to the chokehold. "And I see you brought the old dog. Come on, Sam, come here."

Even above the roar of the falls I heard the noise behind me. It took me a second to identify it, then I had it — it was the sound of a wet tail thumping happily on the ground. Holmes grinned and shouted.

"Come on, boy."

I had to press against the cliff face as a bundle of excited dog leapt past me. Moriarty had barely time for a single yelp of surprise before the dog hit him and Holmes side on and sent them off balance, tumbling toward the precipice.

I too leapt forward. The dog had Moriarty at the throat, worrying at him as if he were a feisty rat. All three of them started to fall away out of view, but Holmes just looked up at me, smiled and thrust his hand into mine at the same instant as Moriarty and the dog fell away, screaming.

I looked over Holmes' shoulder as I dragged him back up onto the ledge, in time to see two distinct black shapes be torn apart into wisps of shadow and smoke that were quickly dispersed by the spray from the falls.

Somewhere in the distance, a Scotsman started to sing.

CHAPTER 16

The scene around us faded to gray, then to black. Clouds swirled and parted, and I felt faint, feverish almost.

"It's all right, Watson," a well-known voice said. "It is over. We have prevailed once again."

I opened my eyes to see morning sun streaming in through the windows in Baker Street. Mycroft was sitting upright in the chair, fully awake and trying to dislodge the needle from the back of his hand.

Holmes took my hand and shook it warmly.

"I would never have come back without your help, old friend," he said.

"I'm just glad I made it in time on this occasion," I replied gruffly, returning his handshake.

I headed for the Scotch. It was only then I noticed. The salt circles on the floor had been smudged away, as if by the scuff of feet, and there was no sign of the small Scotsman, or of his journal.

Mycroft joined me as I poured the Scotch, and he knocked back three stiff fingers before turning back to Holmes.

"It is really done? He won't be back?"

"You tell me, brother. How does your head feel?"

Mycroft managed a weak smile in reply.

"Empty."

The proper conclusion to the case came almost a week later. Lestrade squared away the thefts with his superiors, and there was a report in *The Thunderer* of his excellent work in finding the perpetrator, who 'died resisting arrest.' Mycroft, seemingly none the worse for wear, returned to his duties in Whitehall, although I assume he had some explaining to do at the Diogenes Club. The Scotsman, Seton seemed to have gone to ground completely, and Holmes was in no hurry to find him.

"This case has taxed the limits of my credulity," he said over a smoke by the fire on the Saturday morning following all the excitement. "You may document it in your journal if you must, but I intend not to think of it again for rather some time to come."

Our peaceful morning was interrupted by a knock on the door and Mrs. Hudson announced the arrival of visitors. She showed in a married couple — I did not recognize the woman, but the man was the one we had chased all over London — David Finn. He seemed none the worse for his ordeal.

"I just came to thank you, sirs, for getting me back to my Irene." They stood there, linked arm in arm, as if never intending to be parted again. "I do not remember much of the time I was gone at all — it all seems little more than a nightmare."

"You are, perhaps, more right than you know," Holmes replied, and sat for the rest of the day in quiet contemplation, staring into the fire, as if lost in a dream.

The End

ABOUT THE AUTHOR

William Meikle is a Scottish writer with more than twelve novels published in the genre press and over 200 short story credits in thirteen countries.

He is the author of the ongoing Midnight Eye series among others, and his work appears in a number of professional anthologies. His ebook THE INVASION has been as high as #2 in the Kindle SF and Kindle Horror charts.

He lives in a remote corner of Newfoundland with icebergs, whales and bald eagles for company. In the winters he gets warm vicariously through the lives of others in cyberspace, so check him out at www.williammeikle.com.

CPSIA information can be obtained
at www.ICGtesting.com
Printed in the USA
LVHW091611121118
596835LV00001B/116/P